Praise for Bryan Hall's
Containment Room 7

"Hey Hollywood, listen up! You have got to make a movie out of this book. [It] is one of the scariest zombie tales I've ever read. In fact, I think I would rather eat broken glass than fight the kind of nightmares Bryan Hall puts down on the page.
This guy is scary good."
–Joe McKinney, author of *Apocalypse of the Dead* and *Flesh Eaters*

"Dark, fast and fun…a compelling read."
–Nate Kenyon, award-winning author of *Sparrow Rock*
and *Starcraft Ghost: Spectres*

"A brutal genre-bending debut, Bryan Hall gives us a gripping sci-fi/zombie story permeated with a horror master's sense of scene and scares."
–Jonathan Moon, author of *Heinous*

Containment Room 7

Bryan Hall

A

GRINNING SKULL PRESS

Publication

PO Box 67, Bridgewater, MA 02324

DEDICATION

For my kids, Levin and Destiny. They're the best of me.

PART 1

Chapter 1

The retrieval room was electric with anticipation. Wilson could feel it as soon as he stepped through the door. It was divided in the center by a massive glass wall; a few control panels and computer screens were mounted on the side he was on. A dozen scientists and engineers bustled about the room, tweaking dials and huddling around the screens.

In the center of the room stood chief science officer Gruber and Captain Carlson, conferring with one another.

On the opposite side of the glass divide was a large room, the center of which held a series of control stations, some for manipulating the loading arms and entrance bays, others with various scanning tools. At the far end was another glass wall, this one looking out into space. Millions of stars and swirling gas pockets were visible in the distance, but directly in front of them was a blackness so profound that it seemed to dim the stars nearest to it: a black hole—the main objective of this particular DARC mission. Time travel, an energy source, faster space travel, even a weapon of mass destruction were things the physicists on the ship were hoping to develop from the research done on the dead star. Instead, they'd apparently discovered something else entirely.

Wilson joined the captain at the glass. "Captain."

"Big day, Wilson."

"That's what I've heard."

"What have you heard, exactly?"

"Just that we found something."

Gruber spoke up. "Something that shouldn't be here."

Wilson glanced at the scientist. "What do you mean?"

"We're orbiting around a black hole, four hundred miles from its gravitational pull."

"I know that, Gruber. We have been for six months, last I checked."

"And you know the strength of that gravitational pull?"

"It was in the security briefing before we left. If we get too close, we'll get trapped. It'll suck us into it."

"Exactly. Nothing can resist such a massive force. The only reason we're as close as we are is because our research on the hole requires it."

"And?"

"Two hours ago, our scanners picked up an object moving out of the black hole and settling into an orbit about six miles closer to it than we are."

Wilson blinked. "What kind of object?"

"That's what we're going to find out," Carlson said with a smile.

"It's small," Gruber added. "Ten feet or so in diameter."

"It just came out of the black hole?"

"That's how it appeared," Gruber said. "It showed up on our scanners about two hundred miles from the hole's event horizon, moving opposite its pull. Our preliminary scans suggest it's organic in nature, but it's too soon to be sure. Hell, it doesn't even show up on half of our equipment."

"So it could be—"

"That's why we called you up here, Wilson," the captain said. "Protocol. Any chance of encountering alien life or objects requires Head of Security to be here."

Wilson nodded. "So, what exactly do you expect me to do?"

"Just watch," Gruber said. "It seems to be inanimate, so it's probably not a danger."

Wilson turned his attention to the front of the room, where a trio of engineers had entered in full protective suits, one of them wheeling a transport cart. It was a walk-behind forklift with a large, hermetically sealed box mounted atop it.

"Who've we got working in there?" Wilson asked.

"Roger Han, Jim Sutter, Lorenzo Hill," Gruber answered. "They're the three most experienced engineers we've got on board."

Wilson knew all three men—Jim Sutter more than the others. He was, in Wilson's opinion, one of the luckiest men on board DARC12. Most of the crew were single men and women; the long jaunts into deep space were enough to scare off companions. Finding a partner who could be assigned to the same DARC as you was the only way Wilson could see to build any kind of meaningful relationship. And Sutter had managed to do just that: find someone to love who was just as skilled at her job as he was at his. Someone who could join him on board the ship for years at a time and still keep each other happy in that close proximity. The way Wilson saw it, Jim Sutter was lucky to have found his wife, Elle. A trickle of envy crept into Wilson every time he talked with the engineer.

"Six minutes to encounter," a scientist seated at a nearby computer called out.

Gruber joined the man at the computer screen, staring over his shoulder with wide eyes.

"We've been on the ship for two years now, and I don't think I've ever seen him this happy," Wilson said.

"Of course, he's happy," Carlson said. "The first organic material ever found in space? Alien life? Earth's been waiting centuries for it, and we may be about to load it onto this ship. He'll be famous back on Earth. Hell, we all will."

"And if it's not organic? If it's just a rock?"

"Then Doctor Gruber's going to be really disappointed."

"Three minutes," Gruber shouted. The other men in the room grew quiet, a few murmurs rippling through them as they stared into the loading room.

Roger Han situated himself behind the arm controls, manipulating the levers with experience. Outside, the massive hydraulic arm swung into place, its four fingers widening in preparation.

Sutter and Han stood at adjacent terminals, their attention focused on the screens in front of them.

"Two minutes," Gruber said.

The room had fallen silent.

A moment passed, and Gruber broke the silence. "There it is. Prepare to adjust the ship's thrusters. We have to match its trajectory."

"Sixty seconds to encounter." Gruber glanced to another computer terminal. "Jenkins, do you have the speed locked down?"

"Decrease starboard thrust two hundred sixteen percent in thirty-eight seconds," Jenkins said.

To the right of the room, through the massive glass, Wilson saw it approaching. It was a tiny dot, growing larger by the second.

"Twenty seconds. Fire thrusters."

There was a nearly imperceptible shift in the ship, so slight that if Wilson hadn't known it was coming, he wouldn't have noticed it. The research ship's massive size and sophisticated stabilizers made it feel as though they weren't even moving.

"Five."

Outside, it looked as though the thing would slam into the side of the DARC.

"Four."

It whizzed past the front of the ship, passing in front of the glass window a hundred yards in front of them.

"Three."

The object seemed to slow as DARC12's speed matched its own.

"Two."

Now it appeared to hover in front of the ship, nearly centered in the window.

"One."

To Wilson, it looked like a tiny asteroid, nothing special. He glanced to Gruber, who stood unblinking, his mouth slightly agape. He looked like a man who'd just fallen in love.

Roger Han began to work the arm, swinging it outward and extending its length until the hand reached the object. He closed the steel fingers around it with finesse and began to haul it toward the ship, plucking it from space like an apple from a tree. Within minutes, he'd placed the thing onto an elevated platform inside the loading bay. It was a room with a door on either end, one leading into space, the other into the main area.

The outer door closed, and Sutter began to punch commands into his computer terminal. Inside the loading bay, a series of lights flashed as the object was scanned.

Gruber read aloud from the screen in front of him. "Organic composition. Unknown genetic makeup."

"So that thing's supposed to be an alien?" Wilson asked.

"Just because it's not the little green man you were expecting doesn't mean it isn't alive," Gruber snapped. "The scans just mean that there's some organic matter in it. It could just be microbial life on the surface of the thing."

Sutter and Lorenzo steered the transport cart into the loading chamber, bringing it to a stop underneath the platform the thing was sitting on. They stood on opposite sides of the glass box and pulled two levers, opening the cart completely. With it in place, they moved away and pressed a switch. The platform lowered until the alien thing was seated on the cart, and then slid backward.

The two techs moved to close the containment box around the thing and stopped, heads cocked to one side as they gazed at it like dumbfounded puppies examining some new, wondrous discovery.

"What the hell are they doing?" Wilson asked.

They each reached out a hand and laid it on the thing, circling it and looking it up and down.

Gruber pressed the intercom switch and leaned into the microphone. "Don't touch it, goddamn it! Just do your job."

The techs jerked, as if snapping out of a daze, and moved back to the cart, working the switches so that the hermetic case sealed itself around the thing.

They backed the cart out of the loading chamber and into the main room, bringing it close to the dividing glass where Wilson was standing. Wilson's stomach knotted as it approached him, and his heart began to quicken. The thing looked benign enough—a brownish-green, lumpy sphere about four or five feet in diameter. To one side of it, a thin, gray tube protruded, hanging lifeless off of the thing. It looked like an intestine.

Despite the innocuous appearance, it terrified Wilson. It filled him with dread for no reason he could think of.

Finally, Sutter and Lorenzo moved the thing toward the room's exit.

"Take it to Bio-lab Five," Gruber said into the intercom. "Do it quickly. I'll meet you there."

He turned to Carlson and Wilson and grinned. "Smile, Wilson. You're a part of history."

Chapter 2

The doors to the lab slid open, startling Lisa Michaels. She stared as the engineers brought the discovery inside. She'd spent the past hour readying the workstations for the various tests and scans Gruber had planned and had scarcely taken the time to consider just what it was they would be working with.

The call from Gruber had her excited.

As a genetic biologist, the research she was on board to do had nothing to do with the black hole they were orbiting, and their proximity to it made her nervous. One miscalculation on the pilots' part and the ship could be sucked into the collapsing star.

But Gruber had stressed since leaving Earth just how important their discoveries could be. He'd even mentioned an odd radiation signature that suggested to some it could be a "white hole," something that most thought impossible outside of mathematical equations.

Lisa doubted they'd find anything useful. She'd heard some of the lead physicists discussing it, and harnessing or controlling such a thing sounded far beyond the capabilities of mankind. To think that anything, especially a human, could dictate the laws of time and space seemed arrogant and misguided to her. That was the realm of gods that had been dying slowly since the discovery of science.

Then again, she wasn't a physicist. For all she knew, they could just fly into the damn thing while clicking their heels together, think about where they wanted to go, and be there a few seconds later.

The research ships were mostly filled with physicists, astronomers, and other scientists who were primarily concerned with finding and studying black holes, outlying solar systems, and finding other planets possible for mining.

In addition to the astrophysicists, a few chemists and biologists were along for the ride, conducting various experiments that were banned on Earth. Cloning, genetic manipulation, hastening and altering the evolutionary process, reanimating dead tissue, and other things too controversial (and illegal) for the planet were fair game once they exited the orbital jurisdiction of Earth.

These projects were far more profitable for the company than the antimatter and black hole research Earth's general public believed were the primary purpose of the DARCs.

Aside from their normal responsibilities, every scientist, no matter what their field, was given a quick briefing on the possibility of encountering alien life. Biologists were given first priority for examining any creature they might encounter, even if said encounter was unlikely.

The farther into space technology allowed humans to go, the more excited people grew over the possibility that alien life would be found. Lisa had even dreamed she would be lucky enough to be on a ship that found this life. After working her ass off and managing to get out of a Philadelphia ghetto, with no help from anyone but her aunt, she felt entitled to a stroke of good luck.

So, after all the dreams, hopes, and wishes of mankind encountering some other form of life, here it was.

Now, face to face with the thing, she was somewhat disappointed.

A big lump of space shit. That's what it looked like to her. As a biologist, she'd been hoping for something more…lifelike—not a miniature asteroid.

"Containment Room Seven," she said to the engineer, gesturing to the large glass-walled room in the center of the lab.

They wheeled the thing by her, and as it passed, her breath caught in her chest. The tube, hidden from view when they'd brought it in, was visible. Her disappointment abated, and she crossed the deck for a closer look.

The tube pulsated. Once—just a faint murmur, like a heart beating its last time. She froze as a wave of excitement churned through her body.

Life.

As they situated the thing in the containment room, Gruber entered the lab, accompanied by the chief biology scientist, Dr. Coulet.

The two men walked straight to the room and watched as the engineers sealed the door, standing so close that their noses nearly touched the glass.

"Thank you," Gruber said to the engineers. "Jim, tell Elle I said hello, all right?"

There was no response. The two suited men were rooted in place just outside the containment room door, staring at the object they'd just delivered.

"Jim?" Gruber said, louder this time. "Lorenzo?"

Finally, one of the men nodded. "We'll leave you with it, then."

They backed away from the room, eyes fixed on its contents, until they reached the lab door. They paused for another moment, then opened the door and left.

Without turning his attention from the thing, Gruber said, "What do you think, Lisa?"

She joined him and Coulet. "It isn't what I was expecting."

"It never is. What do you make of the tube on the side of it?"

"Nutrient intake, maybe. It could even be a cocoon, the tube bringing in air to whatever's inside. At any rate, it moved as they were bringing it in."

Gruber turned to her. "What moved?"

"The tube."

"Moved how?" Coulet asked.

"It flexed, just once. Like a heartbeat, almost."

"Really?" Gruber asked. "You saw it?"

She nodded.

They stared at the thing until Gruber said, "Well, Rich, what do you think? Start with surface scans? Try to take some samples?"

Coulet nodded. "Makes the most sense to start there, I would say. Try and see what this thing's made of. Then we'll work our way to the tube."

"Let's get going then."

Chapter 3

Wilson walked through the corridor of entertainment level two, trying to cast the thing they'd found from his mind.

When he'd taken the position on board DARC12, the government suits had warned him the prolonged isolation a deep-space mission brought with it could easily trigger a mental breakdown or deep depression

To combat the stresses of deep space, the ship was fully equipped with hundreds of options for recreation. Each person had private living quarters furnished with televisions, musical instruments, personal computers, and video games. On every floor of DARC12, there was at least one, sometimes two, decently sized recreation rooms for the scientists and crew members to use when they needed a break.

Aside from the individual rec rooms, three levels of the massive ship were filled with nothing but movie theaters, libraries, restaurants, rec rooms, a small four-lane bowling alley, gyms, pools, and even (after several months-long debates between the higher-ups and a strict four-drink-per-day maximum was established) a bar serviced by its own small brewery. The intent was to give the crew the feeling that they were living in a small town or community rather than stuck on a giant research vessel for several years.

Wilson walked into the bar and scanned it for Collette and Rodney. It was a shift-ending ritual to meet his two best security officers at the bar for a few beers before they each retired to their quarters.

The pair were at a table near the back wall, already well into their lagers. He navigated the small room and joined them.

At six-foot eleven inches and three hundred pounds of solid muscle, Rodney Smith held the distinction of being the largest man on board the DARC12 (and the largest Wilson had ever met). He looked up as Wilson approached and said, "Hey, boss." His voice was stilted; he seemed distracted, lacking his usual happy-go-lucky attitude.

"How are you guys?" Wilson slid into an empty chair and motioned for the waitress.

Collette ignored his question. "So, what is it?"

"What is what?"

"The thing they found. What did it look like? Was it alive?"

"The scans said it was organic. Didn't look alive to me."

"So, what did it look like?"

"Looked like a goddamn rock to me," he muttered. The waitress came to the table, setting his beer in front of him and leaving them alone again.

He took up the beer, gulping down half the glass.

"Damn, Wilson," Collette said. "Something wrong?"

He smiled. Just being around her made him feel somewhat better; looking at her washed the thoughts of the ship's discovery from his mind.

She was sexy and exotic-looking, with dark hair and light brown skin. And she took good care of herself; her body was as perfect as Wilson had ever seen.

He enjoyed her company, too. Despite coming from different backgrounds, they had similar outlooks on most things. She was good at her job, good enough to be the security office's second-in-charge. Collette was Wilson's idea of the perfect woman.

If it wasn't for the fact they worked together in the same department, he'd have made a move months ago. She'd even dropped a couple of offhanded comments that led him to believe she felt the same way.

But he knew complicating a boss–subordinate relationship with sex was never a good idea, as much as his libido hated it. He'd seen it ruin too many professional partnerships to put his and Collette's friendship into the firing line.

But still… That body and its curves. Those pouting, full lips.

"Boss?" Rodney said, pulling Wilson's attention away from his daydreams.

"I'm fine. What about you guys?"

"I'm good," Collette said. "I'd be better if I could have been there to see that thing."

"Trust me—you didn't miss anything."

"If you say so."

Wilson turned to Rodney, who was staring into his beer with a deep frown etched on his face.

"What's wrong?"

Rodney looked up from his drink. "Nothing. Just tired, I guess."

"You sure?"

"Yeah. I think I'm gonna finish up this beer and hit the bed."

"No bowling? You always bowl after your beers."

"Not tonight." He dropped his gaze to his beer again. He looked almost ashamed.

"There something you want to tell me?"

The big man shook his head. He drained his glass and rose from the table. "I'm just tired, boss."

"Fair enough, then." Wilson watched as Rodney weaved through the tables and left the bar. He turned to Collette and raised an inquisitive eyebrow.

She shrugged. "He's been like that for the past hour or so. One minute he was fine, then he just clammed up."

"You think something's wrong with him?"

"He says he's tired. I'm gonna take his word for it. If it was something else, I think he'd tell me. I'm like his sister."

"Okay."

She finished her beer and motioned the waitress for another. "You seem pretty cynical for a man who just experienced first contact with alien life."

"It's overrated. Besides, I'm a cynical guy."

"I know. Because of Earth."

"Because of the people on Earth."

"That's all you ever tell me. People are evil."

"They are. You don't spend as many years as a cop as I did and not figure that out."

The waitress returned and sat two fresh drinks on the table. Collette grabbed one and slid the other toward Wilson.

"We're friends. You can talk to me about it, you know."

He nodded. "I know." He finished his first beer and took a long pull from the second. "I saw a lot of things back home. Evil, sick, fucked-up things."

"Fucked up enough to make you leave the planet. You've told me that part."

"It's quiet on a DARC. My first trip out, on DARC7… When I met you and Rodney… That was like heaven. No rapists, no serial killers, no tortured wives or…"

"Or…"

He shook his head, thinking back to his last days on the force. He tried to clear his mind of what had happened. Instead, it settled on the thing in containment room seven, and he shuddered. His thoughts, it seemed, were out to get him tonight.

"I killed a man." He blurted it out, surprised that he'd said it. He'd never talked about it to anyone. When the ship's shrink tried to bring it up, he'd always refused to discuss it. But Collette was different. She deserved to know at least some of his past. That, and the fact talking about it might pry his mind away from the alien thing they'd found.

She blinked, obviously surprised by his confession.

He forced a weak smile. "I'd done it twice before, but they were self-defense. Shootouts, you know?"

Collette didn't respond.

"But that guy, he wasn't trying to kill me. He was…doing something else."

"What?"

He ignored her question. "We walked into his apartment, and I saw him, and I shot him without a second thought. Arresting him never even entered my mind."

"Your partner?"

"Shook my fucking hand. Backed me up when I lied to the suits at the inquiry."

"That's why you quit the force and signed up for DARC missions?"

"I don't regret it, if that's what you mean. Hell, I'm proud of killing the son of a bitch. Some people don't deserve life. He was one of them. What I regret is I didn't get there a bit sooner. If I had, things might have turned out different."

"What did he do? What could have been different?"

"I don't want to talk about it. You think you want to hear it, but you don't. I've been trying to forget it since the day I saw it. It was bad—let's just leave it at that."

She stared at him in silence.

"I want you to trust me. That's why I'm telling you this. But there are some things I'm just not going to get into. I can't."

She nodded. "All right."

"I quit because of what I saw. And because I blame myself a little bit for it, I think. If I'd trusted my gut and went there the day before like I wanted to, then maybe…"

The image of the alien filled his mind, pulling him from the past and back to the ship.

"Wilson?" Collette whispered.

"I don't want to fuck up like that again. I took this job to get away from all that kind of shit."

"I doubt anything like that will happen on a DARC."

"Probably not. Doesn't stop me from worrying about it, though."

Chapter 4

Jim Sutter sat on the edge of his bed, staring at his wife through the doorway that led into the main room of their living quarters.

Elle was in her usual chair, concentrating on the book she'd been reading over the past few days.

She hadn't even asked him about what they'd found, and it didn't sit well with him.

The creature was magnificent. The moment he'd seen it, it had mesmerized him. Leaving it in the lab had been the hardest thing he'd ever done in his life.

And his wife didn't even care about it.

He stood and walked to the open doorway. "Don't you want to know about it?"

"About what, babe?" She didn't bother to look up from her book.

"What we found. The creature."

"Creature? Judith told me it was just a rock, maybe with some microbes on it."

Sutter felt a tinge of anger well up in him. "How the hell would she know? You guys run the recreation levels."

Elle shrugged. "Through the grapevine, I guess." She looked at him. "Is she wrong?"

"It's not a rock. It's alive, and it's amazing."

"Really?" She was interested now, and it brought a smile to his face.

"It's alive. It might look like a meteor, but it's so much more than that."

She put her book down. "What do you mean?"

"I can't really explain it. I just... I could feel it, you know? Its energy or something."

"Energy?"

"It just calmed me, somehow. All my cares melted away when I was around it. And..."

"And?"

"Nothing." He couldn't tell her everything, not yet. She'd think he was having a mental break, call in the shrink. Soon, when she heard it, they could share their experiences with each other. Soon, he knew, it would talk to her just like it had talked to him.

"Jim?" She put a hand on his leg.

He raised an eyebrow.

"You're smiling. What is it?"

"Nothing. Just happy, is all."

She studied him. "You're sure everything's all right?"

"I promise, hon. I'll let you get back to your book."

He leaned forward, kissed her, then rose and returned to their bedroom. He undressed and stepped into the adjacent bathroom, turning on the shower.

As the hot water danced over his skin, whispers filled the room, so quiet that, for a moment, he thought he was imagining them. Within minutes, however, they were as loud and clear as his own thoughts. It was a choir of voices, soothing and angelic.

He listened as they told him of the future they held in store for him.

Chapter 5

Lisa had never been more frustrated in her life.

They'd run a dozen surface scans. They'd taken samples. Dr. Coulet had chipped off a small piece of it when it was still in the rock-like state and run through several tests to try and determine what the thing was made of. Even the Advanced MRI had given no answers; the results were simply images of a black shadow.

It was like banging their faces against a wall. Four hours' worth of tests, all with the same results: Unknown. Unclassifiable. Unrecognized. Finally, Gruber had called for a break, and the three of them went to the floor's rec room for coffee.

Lisa was the first through the door as they returned, and she nearly cried out with excitement when she entered the lab and looked in to the containment room.

The thing had changed. The rock-like crust had vanished. Now it shimmered as if it were coated with a film of slime. It looked softer.

Gruber raced across the lab and peered through the glass. "Check the cameras."

Coulet walked to the monitors and did as he was asked, rewinding the footage the lab cameras had taken while they were gone.

"Something went wrong," he said.

Lisa and Gruber joined him. "What do you mean?"

"Look for yourself."

On the screen were four separate camera feeds: three different views of the containment room and one of the lab itself. The three of them were busy running the tests they'd done earlier. There was a flicker, a flash of static, and the screen went black. A second passed, then the screen blinked back to life and the thing in the room was in its new form and the lab was empty. Another few seconds, and then the scientists returned to the lab.

"You're kidding me," Lisa muttered.

"To hell with it, then." Gruber grunted.

They walked back to the containment room and studied the thing.

There was no mistaking the organic nature of it now. Its body looked like flesh, albeit greenish-brown. A layer of slime nearly an inch thick coated the thing's skin. The tube had vanished, apparently absorbed into the body.

"Coulet, take slides of the slime," Gruber said. "Fill up some tubes, too."

Lisa hurried to the supply station and fetched a handful of slides, four test vials, and an oversized syringe designed for taking plasma samples. It had an opening five times larger than most, allowing the thickest of liquids to pass into it. She waited as Dr. Coulet pulled on his protective suit before handing him the materials.

"Make sure the goddamn cameras are working," Gruber said to her.

She walked back to the screens and confirmed that they were operable, nodded to Coulet, and watched as Gruber punched in the password to unlock the door.

Coulet hesitated at the doorway, looking from Lisa to Gruber as if for assurance. He stepped into the room, the door closing behind him.

When he reached the thing, he froze, staring at it. Gruber pounded on the glass, shaking him back into action.

He used the syringe to fill the tubes, then applied a drop of the stuff to each slide. Every few seconds, he stopped his actions and looked the thing over as if reassuring himself of something before continuing with his task.

After several minutes, Coulet had finished, and he took one final look at the thing and, after handing the samples to Gruber and Lisa, he took off his suit and left the room.

"Lisa, check the slides," Gruber said. "We'll handle the vials."

Lisa went to her workstation and slid the first slide into the atomic microscope. She dialed in the magnification and waited for the image to focus on the screen.

It was blank. Just the white light of the scope, as if nothing was on the slide.

She frowned and increased the magnification.

At the current setting, she should have been able to see organic molecules or even molecular ions. Instead, the screen was still the same blank, brilliant white.

Again, she adjusted the microscope, dialing it up to subatomic levels.

Nothing. No atoms; not even a proton or electron showed up on-screen.

"Okay," she whispered. "Bad sample."

She reset the microscope and removed the slide, replacing it with a different one.

Now blackness filled the screen. No light at all, just darkness filling the monitor.

"What the hell?" She returned the microscope to subatomic levels.

Blackness. If it weren't for the settings displayed across the bottom of the screen, she would have thought that the monitor had lost power.

She went through the remaining slides quickly. Some were pure black, the rest the same bright, empty white.

"Doctor Gruber?" she said across the lab.

He turned to her. "Tell me you have something."

She shook her head. "I think the microscope's malfunctioning. It's giving me nothing."

"It's not the scope. I ran a vial through the particle analyzer twice. The first time it said that the vial was empty; the second time it said that the contents had a mass too high to measure. DNA sequencer came back unknown. Same with the bacterial scan."

"What now?" Lisa asked.

Gruber thought for a moment. "Run the surface scans again. Do another AMRI, too. Now that it's changed, maybe they'll pick up something else."

"All right."

She punched in the commands at the computer terminal and watched as the containment room lit up with the flashing blue lights of the surface scan.

The thing looked ethereal in the light, and panic filled her as she looked at it. Her heart raced; each breath seemed to bring in no oxygen at all. Her head spun as if she had motion sickness.

And then, as quickly as it came, the terror was gone.

She sat, deeply sucking in air as her heart slowed. There was no reason for her fear; it had gripped her and passed without any trigger she could place.

Except for the thing.

It was innocuous enough now; no real threat discernible in it.

Chapter 6

Wilson woke from a dreamless sleep and looked at the clock. His shift started in three hours. In two, his alarm would wake him.

He rolled away from the harsh digital numbers and tried to fall back to sleep, but in the darkness, all he could see was an image of the object they'd found. His memory distorted it; it wasn't a solid rock in his mind's eye, but rather a slick, slimy thing that seemed to ooze with alien knowledge.

From behind him, he heard a voice.

Soft and delicate, too quiet for him to make out the words.

He rolled over again and reached for the bedside light, switching it on in one quick motion and bathing the room in light.

He was alone, but still the whispers came.

Wilson flung back the covers and climbed out of bed, then hurried to the adjacent bathroom. He flicked on the light and scanned the small room. Nobody.

He crossed back through his bedroom and into the living area and found it empty as well. Standing there, he cocked his head to one side, listening for the source of the whispers.

There was more than one now. He couldn't pinpoint an exact number, but there were several voices speaking at once and growing louder.

They were soothing and feminine, coming from all around him and filling up his room.

From deep within him, Wilson felt the terror that had driven him off the police force and onto the DARC resurface. The what-ifs, the fear of failing again, the guilt bubbled to the front of his mind, and he broke into a cold sweat. His head swam. Nausea gripped him as he saw, in his mind, the man he'd shot so long ago.

And the voices began to speak of salvation.

They promised to take away the guilt he'd carried for so long.

Promised that he'd never again need to worry that his decision—or indecision—would jeopardize anyone.

He only needed to embrace them, accept them fully, and forget all he had been. Give himself to a greater power.

He wanted his guilt and doubt erased, wanted peace at last. He'd dreamed of it for years, and now it was here, being promised to him by some choir of unseen angels.

But he couldn't.

There was malice hidden in the voices. He could feel it, dwelling beneath the gentle promises. The words were lies, and Wilson knew it.

He repeated it over and over to himself, trying to drown out the voices with his own thoughts.

There was a moment of change in the whispers. The beauty was sucked away from them, the truth behind them becoming evident. Deep, alien voices speaking in a language Wilson had never heard. They shifted and slid around the room, almost liquid in quality. Despite not knowing the words, Wilson knew their meaning. The voices were filled with hatred, disgust. And they were threatening him.

The room fell silent; the pounding of his heart was all that filled Wilson's head.

Like a drunkard, he stumbled to his bed and collapsed on it as the room spun around him. Sleep rushed up for him, pulling him away from the vertigo.

His alarm screamed out, waking him. Wilson sat up in bed and scanned the room.

The nausea was gone, the voices a distant memory.

He switched off the alarm, got out of bed, and walked to the bathroom, where he splashed cold water on his face, trying to chase away his unease.

His mouth was dry with fear. He stood staring at himself in the mirror, trying to figure out what had happened. What had happened had felt so real, but so ethereal.

It had to have been a nightmare. A vivid dream that had tricked his mind into believing it was reality for a few minutes.

He hoped like hell that that was all it was.

Chapter 7

Sutter watched his wife stir in their bed, her thin arm snaking out from beneath the blanket to switch off the screaming alarm on her com-phone. She sat up, groggy, and glanced around the bedroom until she found him sitting on the floor in the corner.

"Jim?"

He smiled at her. She was truly beautiful. He'd been lucky to find her.

"How long have you been awake?"

"I couldn't sleep."

Elle slid out from beneath the sheets and let her legs dangle from the edge of the bed. "You're sure everything's okay?"

"Wonderful. I promise."

"Your shift starts soon. Are you going to be able to work with no sleep?"

"I'm not tired."

She frowned. "Okay. Well…I need to get ready for my shift."

"Which level are you going to be on today?"

"Rec-two. The theater screens need to be recalibrated, and we need to inspect all the small rec rooms."

She opened a drawer and pulled out her work uniform, dressing quickly.

"Have you thought about it anymore?" Sutter asked.

"About what?"

"The thing we found."

She glanced at him, confused. "No. Should I have?"

"I'd hoped that…"

"That what?"

"It's so amazing, Elle. As soon as I saw it, I just felt relaxed, happy. Then, when I was helping Lorenzo load it onto the cart, something happened. Something incredible."

"What do you mean?"

"It spoke to me."

She frowned. "What?"

"It did. In my mind. It started out so quiet I could barely hear it. It never really got above a whisper, but it spoke to me."

"What did it say?"

He could hear a hint of unease in her voice, and it hurt him. What was happening?

"Not to be afraid. All my fears, all my worries, they're for nothing. Meaningless."

"Your fears?"

"Of death. Of what happens after. There's nothing to be afraid of, it told me. I felt it."

"Jim, you're tired. I'm sure it's been an exciting time for you—"

"This has nothing to do with being tired. It's the truth."

"Are you listening to what you're saying?"

"I know what I'm saying. I finally know now, without a doubt. There's an afterlife. I know it because God himself told me."

She stood up, backing away from him. "You're scaring me. I don't know what happened—"

He slammed his fist into the wall, the report like a gunshot in the small room. "I told you what happened, damn it!"

"Jim…"

Sutter could see the fear in his wife's eyes. She was on the other side of the room now, her hands trembling. She looked pitiful, like a wounded animal. The sight of it calmed him, stripping away his anger and replacing it with shame.

"I'm sorry, Elle." He stood and took a step toward her. "I'd hoped it would speak to you, too. I just want you to understand; it's amazing. "

"Amazing is one thing. You just called it God."

He shook his head. "I didn't mean to say it. I don't know… I just…"

"I think you need to see Roberta. Now."

"What? The shrink? I just had my psych test two weeks ago. You know that."

"Something's wrong. Remember when we signed up? The class we had to take about this? How to spot a mental break?"

The rage was returning, burning in his chest. "I'm not having a mental break."

"It could be quick, they said. Maybe days, maybe hours. You're—"

"I'm fine. I'm not seeing anyone."

She left the bedroom, hurrying through the main room to the door. Her face was pale, her hands trembling. "Jim, I love you. That's why I'm giving you a chance. I'm supposed to report anything like this to security immediately, remember? Please… See Roberta. If you haven't talked to her by the time my shift's over, I'll report you myself."

"I don't need to see anyone. You have to believe me. You have to understand."

The door slid open—a jarring punctuation to his defiance.

"I'm not going to argue with you. You're scaring the hell out of me. I'm asking you as your wife. Please."

She stepped through into the hallway and vanished, the door closing behind her.

Within seconds, the whispers crept through the room, urging him toward his destiny.

PART 2

Chapter 1

Wilson couldn't stop thinking about it. The thing in Containment Room 7 had permeated his thoughts.

He was sure the two hundred forty-four other people on the craft had heard about it by now. Wilson had learned long ago that life on a Deep-space Atomic Research Craft was a lot like life in the small town he'd grown up in: news traveled fast, whether you wanted it to or not. He wondered if any of them felt the same dread that filled him.

It was a bad omen. He knew it in his gut. It made him uneasy just knowing that it was on the ship with them. And his nightmare of the voices added to his dread. Somehow, the more he thought about it, the more the dream seemed connected to the thing.

And now Jim Sutter had snapped. Not just a mild, homesick, tear-filled breakdown kind of snapped, from the sound of it.

The day's shift had been uneventful until Collette had called him for assistance, forcing Wilson to leave the peace and quiet of the nearly empty residence levels and descend to the topmost research floor.

News of Sutter's mental collapse would spread quickly, he thought as he rounded the corner. A small crowd had gathered in the narrow hallway behind Collette, Rodney, and Billy Rothberg, gazing at the door and whispering to one another. Several people were talking on their com-phones, undoubtedly spreading the gossip or beckoning their friends to come watch the show.

He hurried to join Collette in front of the door Sutter had locked himself behind.

"What the hell is going on?"

"He locked himself in there with his wife."

"We're sure it's Jim Sutter?"

"It's him. His wife was doing the weekly inspection on the room. A couple of people saw him go in a half-hour ago. The door was locked right after that. "

"Anybody else in there with him?"

"Don't know. There's a chance Judith Spitzer was helping his wife. If so, she may be in there, too."

"No clue what he's doing?"

"No clue. Someone passing by the room heard what they thought was a woman screaming and a man shouting. It was too muffled for them to make out exactly what was going on. When they couldn't open the door, they called us."

Wilson glanced at the crowd behind him and dropped his head, pinching his nose between his thumb and index finger. "Goddamn it."

Collette shrugged. "They're bored. This is the most excitement we've had on board since we left Earth."

"I like it that way. We're not really equipped for much excitement."

As his gaze drifted to the locked door, his mind wandered back to Containment Room 7 and its contents.

One of the techs who'd loaded it had been Jim Sutter. And now the poor bastard had gone crazy. It could be coincidence, of course. That was the most logical explanation.

In addition to all the relaxation options available to them, all the men and women on board had to submit to bi-monthly mental exams; if any began to exhibit signs of distress, the head of security was the first to be informed.

But Wilson had received no such distress warning. And Sutter wasn't anywhere near as alone as many on the spacecraft. He had a small circle of friends who regularly met at the bar. Wilson saw them there often, and he even had a beer with them on numerous occasions. Plus, Sutter's wife was on board with him. It seemed like that would help keep a man grounded.

But at the moment she was behind a locked door, her husband apparently holding her hostage.

"So…what's the plan?" Billy Rothberg asked, fidgeting with his repeater pistol. At twenty-one, he was the youngest of Wilson's twelve-man security squad—a baby-faced blond who reminded Wilson of his brother back on Earth. It was Billy's first trip into deep space, and he was still adjusting to life on the DARC.

Wilson glanced at the young man's weapon. "Keep it in the holster, for starters. I've never seen anyone fire one of those on a ship yet, and that's a streak I don't wanna break unless I have to."

Billy dropped his hands to his sides and shifted his weight from one foot to the other.

"Other than keeping it in the holster…what's the plan?" Collette said.

Wilson sighed and fished his keycard from his pocket. "I guess I try to talk to him."

The door was about seven steps away, but after he took three toward it, he froze, dropping a hand to his gun as the entrance let out its familiar hydraulic hiss and slid open.

Jim Sutter stepped out of the room and gazed at Wilson, the other security officers, and the small crowd watching from the hallway. A couple of hushed gasps burst forth from some of the people, but other than that, nobody made a sound.

He was covered in dark blood, some of it dried and flaking off his skin, most of it still fresh and dripping. The grotesque sight caused all four security agents to draw their weapons instinctively.

"He loves you all. You just don't know it yet," Sutter whispered.

"Shit, Jim. What the hell did you do?" Wilson said.

Sutter stared wide-eyed at him, as if surprised such a question could even be asked.

"They didn't understand. It had to be done. You can't understand it yet either, I know."

"Rodney…" Wilson said.

Rodney walked toward Sutter, slipping his handcuffs from his belt. Wilson, Collette, and baby-faced Billy Rothberg kept their guns trained on Sutter as Rodney advanced.

Sutter cocked his head to one side like a curious puppy, then held out his hands before him, accepting the handcuffs.

As Rodney put Sutter's hands behind his back and latched the shackles around his wrists, Sutter's eyes locked with Wilson's.

"You don't believe, don't understand," he said, nodding. "But you will."

Wilson stared at him for a moment, lowering his weapon. "Take him to the tanks, Rodney. Billy, you help him."

Collette and Wilson stood silent as Sutter was led down the hallway. Once the three men had rounded a corner and left their sight, Wilson shifted his attention to the room the blood-soaked man just exited. The door had closed behind Sutter, hiding whatever horrors lay beyond.

"What the hell do we do now?" Collette whispered.

Wilson frowned. This was his second trip into deep space as head of security. It was a full-time job watching over such a large ship for such a prolonged period of time, but he'd never expected, least of all seen, something like this. A fist fight here, a petty theft there, an accident to investigate—that was usually the extent of the kind of things he had to deal with.

Now, however…

He stared at the door. After a long pause, he jerked his thumb toward the crowd behind them. "Keep them back."

Collette glanced over her shoulder. "I don't think they've got any plans on moving, boss."

Wilson looked back at the group. Nobody moved or spoke. They stood like a small platoon of statues, all of them staring at either Wilson or the door.

"Right," he said. "Call the docs…the maintenance crew, too, I guess. Tell them to get the hell up here."

That said, he approached the door and steeled himself. Before taking the position on the DARC, he'd been a detective on Earth—a job that had given him more than enough glimpses into the dark side of human nature. The DARC journeys paid much more, and up to now were free from murders and rapes and riots and hostages. His time in deep space had given him a blessed reprieve from those past horrors, and now his gut burned with the knowledge he was about to be plunged back into the very kind of crime scene he thought he'd left behind. He took a deep breath and walked inside.

The metallic scent of blood hung heavy in the air. Wilson smelled the odor before he saw its source. Elle Sutter lay on the pool table in the center of the room, arms folded over her chest, her throat slit. The blood still oozed from the wound, seeping into the table's green felt and turning it a blackish red. Beside her lay a steak knife, the silver blade coated in crimson.

Propped against the wall, underneath a massive television screen, was another body. Wilson recognized the red-haired, freckle-faced woman but couldn't remember her name. She, too, had suffered a slashed throat.

The two women looked peaceful despite the violence they'd suffered.

The urge to vomit crept into his throat, and he swallowed it back. He stood rooted to the ground for several minutes, staring at the grotesque scene.

"Had to happen on my fucking ship," he whispered.

Chapter 2

Lisa Michaels stared through the glass at the brownish-green mass.

They'd worked straight through sleeping hours and the next day's shift, coffee, caffeine powder, and excitement fueling their research.

Now she, Gruber, and Coulet were dumbfounded. Over thirty hours of research, tests, and scans had given them no answers or clues to what they had discovered.

Frustration and exhaustion had set in, and the three of them were scattered about the lab, each seated at different desks but all focused on their enigma.

"I think," Coulet said softly, "that we could all use a break from this."

Gruber nodded. "The other science departments have been blowing up my com-phone, begging for a turn with it. Tomorrow I'll give it to them. The physicists first, then the botanists."

"I doubt they'll have better luck," Lisa said.

"So do I. There's really nothing they can do that we haven't done. But I have to keep everyone happy. You two get some rest. We'll meet back here in nine hours and do one more round of scans. Then I'll call in the other departments."

Coulet stood and made his way to the lab door. "I hate to be pessimistic, but are more scans even necessary?"

"It changed once already, in just a few hours. Things could be different by the time we come back," Gruber said. He crossed the room and joined Coulet at the door.

"Doctor Gruber?" Lisa said.

"Yes?"

"Where do you think it came from?"

"The hole."

"How is that possible?"

"The radiation signature. A rotating black hole. It's the only explanation."

"What is that, exactly?"

"Up until now, a near-impossibility. A black hole's gravity swallows everything, right? Nothing can escape its gravitational pull."

"Yeah."

"A white hole is supposedly the opposite; nothing can enter it, but things *can* escape it. It's all theoretical, but a few people think that if a rotating black hole existed, you could avoid its singularity and enter it, then pass through and out of a white hole in another dimension. It's like a gateway of sorts. The two are connected, existing simultaneously but separate, and indistinguishable from one another."

"And we're orbiting around one of those?"

"We've thought that for a while. But this almost proves it. There's really no other explanation."

"So that means this thing is from another dimension?"

"It's a strong possibility, yes."

Lisa nodded, studying the thing again with newfound interest.

"Lisa?" Gruber said.

She looked at him, raising an eyebrow.

"Go to your room and get some rest. Be back here in nine."

"Yes, sir."

"I mean it. Get some sleep." That said, he turned and followed Coulet out of the room.

She turned back to the thing and frowned. Although it had shown no sign of life aside from changing its appearance, the creature (could she call it that?) was the creepiest thing she'd ever seen. Sitting alone in the room with it was unnerving. She couldn't shake the feeling that the thing was watching her.

Lisa shivered and stood up, grabbing her things. It had been a hell of a long day, and she was ready for a long soak in a hot bath. A moment after she left the room, Lisa heard a sound. Wet. Slithering. She went back briefly to check and found everything was fine, but as she was leaving again, the thing in the containment room pulsated, then went still.

Chapter 3

The holding cells on the DARC12 were small eight-foot by ten-foot rooms encased on all four sides by steel. A plain metal door with a small window made of reinforced glass allowed access to each cell. The only accessories inside the cells were a cot lining one wall, a sink, a toilet, and a camera mounted in the ceiling.

The cells seldom saw use. Occasionally, a fight would break out over some petty squabble, and the combatants would end up in one of the four small cells. On rare occasions, a theft would occur, but aside from that, they were usually empty.

Wilson and Collette stood in front of the screens that covered an entire wall in the security office, watching their prisoner on the monitor. Behind them, seated at a small table, Rodney and Billy sipped coffee, staring into their cups.

Sutter sat on the cot, hands still cuffed behind his back, staring at the camera mounted in the corner of the room.

"He's kind of freaking me out," Collette said.

Wilson responded with a grunt.

"I mean it. I feel like he's looking at me."

"You know that's—"

"I know it's impossible, yeah. Doesn't change the fact that the son of a bitch is creeping me out."

Wilson's eyes shifted down several screens to the monitor displaying Biology Lab 5. The thing they'd found sat motionless in the containment room, just as it had every time Wilson checked it. Slowly, he felt the same uneasiness Collette just described wash over him. He felt like the thing was watching him, looking at him through the camera.

"He didn't say anything to you when you brought him down here, Rodney?" Collette asked.

Rodney looked up from his coffee, then shook his head. "Not a thing. I didn't try to talk to him either."

"Don't fucking blame you there," she muttered.

"What about maintenance and the docs? They finish up?" Wilson asked.

Collette shook her head. "Not much the docs can do, really. It's not like they're a forensic team or something. Clean-up guys… Well, I don't think they'll be able to clean the pool table. Rest of the room is done, though."

"The other woman?"

"It was Judith Spitzer, just like we thought. She ran the rec levels with Elle. Wrong place, wrong time, I guess."

Wilson nodded. He stood up and made his way to a door in the back corner that led to the holding cells. Beyond the door, a corridor stretched fifteen feet before ending in a perpendicular wall lined with holding cells.

Sutter stood in front of his cot when Wilson entered the room, smiling a smile that, for an instant, was identical to the insane grin of the murdering father Wilson had killed so long ago. He shuddered at the memory, then focused on the man before him.

"The handcuffs aren't necessary, Chief." Sutter's voice was calm and emotionless.

Wilson nodded. "I'll take them off when I leave, if it's all the same to you."

Sutter shrugged in response. He sat back down on the cot and stared at Wilson.

"Why'd you do it, Jim?"

"Do what?"

"You killed your wife and another woman. Judith Spitzer."

"I had to help them."

"Help them by killing them?"

"Help them and us all. It was the only way. I didn't want to at first, but He said it must be done."

"Who?"

Sutter ignored the question. "I tried to make them see, but they didn't believe. She told me I was an idiot. That I'd lost my mind."

"Who said that?"

"Both of them."

"Why'd they think that?"

Sutter shrugged. "They said He wasn't real."

"Who isn't real?"

"God."

"She told you God isn't real, so you killed her."

"I tried to tell them He was here, on the ship with us. He told me they had to die by my hand—to herald his arrival. Their lives were required for his rebirth. And now they're one with Him. Now they believe."

"God's on the ship?"

Sutter looked surprised. "Of course. You were there when we found him."

Wilson's heart skipped a beat. Immediately he knew what Sutter was talking about.

"The thing we pulled out of space two days ago? You think that thing is God?"

"It is."

"Why do you think that?"

"He spoke to me. I feel Him inside me even now. I'm the first of His Chosen Ones. He picked me above all the others on board. I am His prophet, and His presence has been announced with the blood of the nonbelievers. Soon the others He deems worthy will know His glory. Soon the cleansing will begin." Sutter's smile grew wider as he spoke. "He loves us all, wants us to be with Him, to be reborn through Him."

Wilson chewed his bottom lip. Sutter had dreamed of voices as well. But, it seemed, they'd had more of an effect on the engineer.

"He spoke to you. In a dream?"

"No. I was awake, as I am right now."

Wilson stared at Sutter, studying him. The man had obviously lost his mind. He'd have to check Sutter's latest psych evaluation to make sure, but Wilson was confident it would be normal. He'd never believed in coincidences, either. Unless he could find some other explanation, it seemed the mass they'd found floating through space had driven Sutter mad in less than two days.

"Anything else you want to tell me?" Wilson asked.

"I don't believe so. If the Great One doesn't speak to you, then there is nothing else you need to know. Is there anything else you want to ask? Maybe I could help enlighten you somehow—help lead you to His glory."

Wilson ignored the question and approached Sutter, unclipping his keys from his belt. He unlocked the handcuffs and stepped back.

Sutter sat on the bed, a calm look of euphoria settling on his face.

"I wish you knew what I know, Wilson. It's going to be glorious."

"What is?"

One corner of Sutter's mouth turned up in a smile, then receded.

A moment of silence passed while each man scrutinized the other. Wilson realized, with some unease, that Sutter really believed what he was saying. The man looked peaceful and content—happy, even.

Wilson backed out of the room. Once he was outside in the hallway, he locked the door quickly. It was only after he'd taken several steps away from the holding cell that he realized his entire body was covered in a cold sweat.

When he returned to the security room, only Collette was there. He looked at her and raised his eyebrow.

"We turned on the audio in the room. Once he started talking about killing them for God, Rodney just stood up and left," Collette said. "Billy followed him a minute later. He didn't say much. Guess maybe he got freaked out or something."

"Billy I can understand. He's still a kid. But Rodney? Hell, he was a cop in Miami for a few years. I wouldn't have thought hearing something like that would bother him after some of the shit he's seen."

Collette shrugged. "Maybe it doesn't. He might have just got tired of listening to it. But it was kinda unnerving, the stuff he was telling you."

You have no idea. Wilson thought.

"You believe any of that shit?"

He stared at her a moment, thinking about the thing they'd found. Finally, he forced a smile. "Are you asking if I believe we found God floating in outer space? That we're holding him in the biology wing for testing?"

"Not quite. Just asking if you believe Sutter really believes that."

Wilson nodded. "He certainly seems to." He made his way past her, heading for the door.

"Going to see the captain?"

"I'm sure he's already heard, but I better go talk to him about this. He's probably waiting on me."

As he exited the room, Collette said, "They're sure that thing is alive, though?"

He froze. An image of the thing flashed in his mind for a second, sending an icy chill trickling down his spine. "No more alive than a plant, from what I understand. But yeah, it is."

Before she could respond, he left the room and made his way down the hallway toward the captain's deck.

Chapter 4

No sooner had Lisa entered her living quarters than her com-phone rang. She grabbed it as she locked the door and headed for the bathroom.

"Hello?"

"Hey, Lisa."

"Roger. Hi."

"So, did you hear?"

She turned the knobs on the tub, only half-listening to Roger Han. They were good friends, which was something she'd found hard to come by. It wasn't her looks; she knew she was attractive. At twenty-seven, she still had a firm, well-built body and a delicate, pretty face. But devoting most of her life to her career had left her little time to focus on social interactions, and since her Aunt Lucy had died so many years ago, she had been left with no one to confide in.

The few men she'd tried to date had only been interested in getting her into bed, and she'd quickly told them to go to hell. Finding someone who genuinely respected her had seemed impossible, and she'd been lucky to meet Roger shortly after the DARC had left Earth. It was wonderful having someone to talk to about things not related to the lab. Roger would listen with understanding as she opened up to him about her life in Philly: the junkie mom and deadbeat dad; the kids making fun of her because she'd preferred reading over fucking and smoking pot. She'd even shared some of her deepest secrets and desires with him and had been greeted with warm understanding.

He was a hell of a good friend, and recently they had gone on a couple of romantic dates to the restaurants on the leisure levels of the ship. At first, he was nervous, appearing almost fearful that he would say something wrong. It was obvious he had little experience with women, or even with other people in general. He'd opened up quickly, however, and she truly did enjoy talking to him, even if it was about nothing at all.

But now, after all the hours she'd spent studying the mass they'd found, she had little interest in chit-chat.

"Hear what?"

"Jim Sutter killed his wife, Elle, and Judith Spitzer."

She went silent, watching the steaming water fall and amass in the tub, trying to process what she'd been told.

"Lisa?"

"I'm here. I'm just…" She trailed off, lost in her thoughts. A double murder on board a DARC? It was unheard of. And by someone as calm and laid back as Jim Sutter had always been?

"I know. Kinda scary, huh?"

"Yeah. I just saw him a couple of days ago. He and Lorenzo brought that alien thing to the lab. Put it in the containment room for us. He seemed fine."

Now Roger was silent. Lisa turned off the water. "You there?"

"Yeah." His voice had lost its usual pleasant tone. He sounded concerned. Or scared. "Yeah, I'm here. But that thing. The one you're examining."

"What about it?"

"That's sort of why I called."

"What do you mean?"

"I'm the one who was running the arm when we brought it on board. Sutter and Lorenzo were the ones who secured it and moved it to the containment room."

"Okay."

"The rumor is Sutter killed those women because of that thing. That it drove him crazy or something."

"What?"

"Are you feeling all right? I mean…you're working on that thing."

"I feel fine, Roger. Tired and a little freaked about what you just told me, but I'm fine." She paused, leaving dead air on the phone between them. "And you? You feel okay?"

There was a long silence. "I'm all right. Just freaked out, too, I guess. Murder on a DARC…it's crazy."

"Have you talked to Lorenzo?"

"No. I called you first. I'm gonna call him right now, though."

"Okay."

"Lisa… Call me if you need anything, okay?"

"I will."

"All right. Bye." The com-phone beeped twice as the connection terminated.

Lisa sat on the edge of the tub, staring at the still water of her bath, wishing Roger had stayed on the phone with her for just a little longer. A murderer on board the ship was disconcerting, for sure. But that Sutter had murdered his wife and another crew member because of the thing in the lab was unthinkable.

She shuddered.

Rumors, she told herself. Blaming an inanimate alien orb was foolish. As strange as the thing was, as uneasy as it made her, it certainly wasn't sentient. Sutter had simply snapped. Deep space could do it to a person, no matter how well-adjusted they were.

Suddenly cold, she undressed quickly and slipped into the hot water.

Chapter 5

Captain Carlson *was* waiting for him, just as Wilson had expected. He listened as Wilson reported all he knew about the murders and the man who committed them.

They stood on the captain's deck—a gigantic room that was essentially the flight deck, where most of the ship's functions were controlled. A huge window wrapped around the front of the room, looking out into the deep infinity of space. Carlson stood facing the void, his back to Wilson as he gave his report.

When Wilson finished, the captain ran his fingers through his graying hair and sighed. "We'll have to hold him indefinitely. Possibly for the duration of our mission."

Wilson blinked. "Sir?"

"There's not really another option right now. I'll send a message to Control, but you know as well as I do that when you're this deep in space, it takes days to get a response."

"You want me to keep him in holding for the next three or four *years?*"

"Hopefully Control can send a transport ship. Something small and fast. Maybe from one of the mining colonies closer to us than Earth. It'll still take over a year to reach us. I'll get Roberta to give him a psych test ASAP. See what she thinks."

"Jesus fucking Christ."

Carlson glared at him, raising his voice. "Do you have a better idea? If you do, by all means…"

Wilson shook his head. "I don't, sir. It's just that he's already crazy. I'm no shrink, but I'm sure that locking him in a little room—especially for a year—is only going to make him worse."

Carlson smiled grimly. "That's why you aren't going to let him out."

Chapter 6

Lorenzo wasn't answering his com-phone. Roger had tried to reach him several times since talking with Lisa, with no luck at all.

Lisa. He really liked her, ever since they'd first met. He hoped she was okay.

He'd lied to her, of course. He wasn't *quite* all right. They'd just started dating a few weeks ago after a long friendship, and the last thing he wanted was for her to think he was bothered by a strange object from space and a murder. What if she thought less of him for it? His entire life had been a lonely one. Now that he'd met a woman who was actually interested in him, there was no way he could fuck it up by acting like a scared little boy.

But the thing was consuming his mind. Twice while talking to Lisa he had almost fallen into a trance just thinking of it.

It was beautiful.

He'd almost cried as he watched Sutter and Lorenzo take it from the loading bridge. It was out of sight, but damn sure not out of mind.

He saw it whenever he closed his eyes. Dreamed of it while sleeping. Every bite of food he had eaten since then was cloaked in the thing's scent, clinging to the back of his throat as he ate.

And now, on two separate occasions, he'd heard a choir of voices as endless as space itself. The first time he'd heard them, they'd said nothing he could understand—just hushed whispers in another language. The voices hadn't scared him. Quite the contrary. They had calmed him, made him understand that the thing was wonderful beyond any human comprehension.

The second time he'd heard them, the words were clear. They whispered of sacrifice and glory, of eternity and love. It promised he would no longer be by himself, that he would no longer spend each hour afraid of living a solitary life and dying alone.

How could anyone refuse such gifts?

Roger wondered if the rumors were true, if Sutter really did kill his wife and another crew member because of the mysterious mass. He found it hard to believe.

The thing was perfection. The only reason to murder for it would be to protect it. But it was in no danger right now. It was safer in the lab's containment room than anywhere else.

Roger realized he was obsessing over it again and pushed the thoughts from his mind. He needed to do something besides sitting here. Something to keep his mind off the organic sphere he'd plucked from the cold void of space.

That wonderful, awe-inspiring mass. So perfect; it wasn't merely alien—it was Divine.

His heart quickened, and Roger drove the thing from his mind once more. He tried to call Lorenzo again and received no answer.

Staying in his room frightened him. He needed to find someone, anyone. Conversation might help keep his mind off the glory in the biology labs. But it was Lorenzo he really wanted to speak with. Perhaps he was feeling the same obsessions, hearing the same voices. He hoped Lorenzo shared the strange sensations. If not, then there was a good chance Roger's sanity was slipping.

He pocketed his com-phone and left his apartment, trying to keep his mind off the thing by counting his steps as he hurried to Lorenzo's quarters.

Chapter 7

"What's next, boss?"

Wilson took a sip of his beer and regarded Rodney for a moment before answering. "I'm so fucking glad we've got beer on these ships. That's the one thing I miss most about Earth."

Rodney and Collette glanced at one another.

The three of them sat in the corner of the nearly empty bar, now well into their third round of drinks.

"Not really a question you can dodge for too long, Wilson," Collette said.

His mind wandered back to the thing, dredging up the cold cloak of dread he was reluctantly becoming accustomed to.

"We just leave him locked up, then?" Collette asked.

Wilson nodded and finished his beer, then signaled the waitress for another. "You all right now, Rodney?"

Rodney's face twisted into a quizzical expression. "What do you mean?"

"You left while I was talking to Sutter. Collette said you got pissed off."

The big man glanced at Collette, who shrugged.

The waitress arrived, setting down Wilson's beer. "Last one tonight," she said with a smile, then left them alone.

Rodney stared into his glass, chewing on his bottom lip.

"Rodney?" Collette said gently.

"I just get pissed when somebody can't take responsibility for what they've done. Blaming your mistakes on someone else… I just don't like it. And blaming it on God? How many jackasses have used that line before? It's a crock of shit, and it pisses me off." He lifted his beer and drained it.

"Fair enough," Wilson said.

"I'm gonna go bowl a frame or two before I go to sleep." Rodney rose from the table. "I'll see you guys later."

"See ya," Collette said.

Wilson watched as the giant of a man made his way out of the bar. "He's not telling us something."

Collette frowned. "About what?"

"Not sure. You're a helluva lot closer to him than I am. Has he said anything to you?"

"Nothing." She studied Wilson. "You all right?"

He stared into his drink before answering.

"You know what scares me? If the shit ever goes down and something happens on this ship that endangers the whole crew, the responsibility to deal with it falls on me. I don't mind the responsibility or even dealing with a threat, but I'm worried I'll make the wrong decision somewhere along the line, and innocent people will die."

"Where is this coming from? What kind of threat are you talking about?"

He shrugged and lied. "A riot. Or a pirate attack. Hell, an alien attack, even. Or…I don't know…something worse."

"Something worse? Like what?"

"I don't know."

"You look like you've at least got an idea."

Wilson started to tell her the truth—about the ominous feelings he'd been having since that thing had been brought on board, and about his nightmare. His judgment, however, told him it was a bad idea. Better to keep his thoughts to himself for now. Sharing them would only cause Collette to worry unnecessarily.

"No… But I think tomorrow I'll go talk to Lorenzo Hill. He was the tech Sutter was working with."

"Why do you need to talk to him?"

"I've got my reasons."

"Gonna share them with me?"

"Not yet. You'd just think I was paranoid."

Wilson hoped that was true. That he was simply paranoid. But twelve years spent as a policeman had taught him his gut instincts were usually right. And right now his gut told him paranoia was the least of his problems.

Chapter 8

Roger pressed the buzzer a fourth time. He didn't think Lorenzo was going to come to the door, but it was worth a try. He needed to talk to him. If anybody else was having the same thoughts as him, it had to be Lorenzo.

Lorenzo had actually touched it, albeit with a C-suit on, but he'd touched it nonetheless. It made Roger jealous. He'd wanted to touch it, to feel it without a suit, or anything else, between it and his flesh.

As he expected, the door didn't open.

Probably out seeing a movie or having a beer, like you should be doing, Roger thought. *Or he's in there ignoring me. Thinking he's too good for me since he got to touch The Great One instead of having to use a fucking mechanical arm.*

"Fuck you then, Lorenzo!" he shouted at the door, then pounded it with his fist until two women passed through the intersecting hallway, giving him an amused look.

Roger stared at them in silence, ashamed, until they were out of sight.

Pull yourself together. He's not hiding from you. He's just…not in there.

He nodded, breathing heavily. He was scaring himself now, losing control of his actions like that.

Roger walked down the hallway, afraid to go back to his apartment but unsure of where he *should* go. He wanted to see the thing again. He needed to. It was perfect, after all. A god on a ship of mere mortals. Why shouldn't he get to be one of its disciples?

As he wandered down the corridors of the DARC12, the voices filled the ship. Hushed whispers so quiet he couldn't make out what they were saying—or even what language they were in—came from around every corner. Mingled with the hundreds of whispering souls, Roger heard the ancient alien voice in his mind, begging to be heard, demanding to be obeyed.

Chapter 9

Collette watched Wilson drain his last beer. "So…any plans for the rest of the night?"

He shook his head. "Bed, I guess. Start early tomorrow."

"You're sure you don't want to clue me in on what you're so worried about?"

"I'm sure. Like I said, it's probably nothing. Just my nerves expecting the worst."

"All right then," she said.

"I'll see you tomorrow, Collette."

"Okay."

She watched him leave the bar, then rose from the table herself. His reluctance to talk to her was unnerving.

He loathed talking about himself. It was always after a couple of beers, and only when he and Collette were alone, that he would open up and reveal more of what a wonderful person he was.

But this was different. He seemed afraid, almost.

And Rodney did as well, for that matter. If Wilson wouldn't talk to her, perhaps she'd have better luck with her partner.

Rodney was about to leave the bowling alley when she found him lacing up his work shoes. She sat down in a seat opposite him and watched as he tied them.

Without looking up, he said, "I'm fine, Collette."

"I didn't say anything."

"I know. But you're here, and it's late."

"You have been acting a little…off."

His mouth twitched—just a quick change of expression that she almost missed. It looked as if he had winced in pain. He looked up at her and smiled. His smile always calmed her. All her life she'd wanted a sibling, and Rodney was a fine surrogate older brother.

"I'm fine. Today just got to me is all. Nothing I can't handle."

"And last night?"

"I told you—I was tired."

She stared at him.

"I promise."

Collette nodded. "What about Wilson?"

"What about him?"

"Did he seem weird to you?"

Rodney shrugged. "He's got a lot on his mind, I guess."

"It's like he knows something, though."

"He was a cop for a long time. Intuition can be a bitch. He may be expecting something just so he can be ready for it. Or he may be trying to figure out how to deal with the fact that we have to keep Sutter in a cage smaller than my bathroom for years."

"I guess."

Rodney stood up and grabbed his rental shoes, motioning with his head for Collette to accompany him. She did so, walking beside him as he made his way to the shoe counter and returned the bowling shoes.

"Listen, Wilson's fine, I'm sure. I've only heard of one other murder ever happening on a DARC. It's a fucked-up thing, and Wilson's the kind of guy that blames everything on himself, even if it's something he had absolutely no control over. You remember your first trip out?"

She nodded.

"You remember Rooney? The maintenance guy who was working in the power room cleaning the reactors?"

"Yeah. He forgot to switch on the failsafe when he went to swab the inside of one of the chambers. The system kicked on and cooked him alive."

"Right. Do you remember how bad it fucked up Wilson? He blamed himself for that for a week and a half, and he was *asleep* when the poor bastard got killed. Asleep, twenty floors above the power room—a room that security hardly ever deals with."

"Yeah," Collette said. "I remember."

"It's the same thing. He's blaming himself for those women getting killed."

They left the bowling alley and started up the hallway toward the elevators.

"All right. But you're sure you're okay?"

"I'm positive. Now, let's get some rest. Don't worry, all right? Tomorrow you'll wake up and everything will be fine. I promise."

Chapter 10

Sutter sat silently in his cell, staring into the blackness of the room. The lights had been turned off long ago, but it was impossible to sleep.

Not because of the dark, however—not anymore.

For his entire life, it had always taken him hours to fall asleep if his bedroom was silent and dark. He needed music, or a movie, or some form of distraction to lull him into slumber. Without it, his mind drifted inevitably to death—that final darkness.

He'd never believed in God or an afterlife. Those notions were impossible. But without them, there was only one alternative remaining: the end of consciousness.

The emptiness of it terrified him; to return to that silent, unimaginable ether from whence he'd come was too much to bear. He'd pushed himself into several panic attacks thinking of it.

But no more.

God had spoken to him, shown him the error of his beliefs, and promised to guide him through the darkness when his life ended.

The moment he'd helped load the Great One onto the ship, he'd heard the whispers. He hadn't understood them at first, but he soon began to hear and comprehend the love and peace and glory they held.

They were speaking to him now.

The words wrapped themselves around him like a womb, filling the dark room with the love of the Great One. They promised him salvation—protection from the hellish blackness that so terrified him. He'd done well thus far; the sacrifice had proven his newfound devotion. God was pleased.

A part of him missed his wife, of course. They'd had a good life. He knew that, even though he could hardly remember the details of it. But those details were trivial—minor occurrences in the grand scheme of his existence. The Great One had promised him that their separation would only be a temporary one, a necessary one. These deaths would help God renew himself, help Him regain His power.

And even with his wife gone, Sutter was not alone on the ship. Even now, others were learning of the glorious being on board the DARC, and they were joining His fold.

Already, the first of the Great One's miracles was beginning.

God's will would be done, and the nonbelievers would suffer before giving up their lives to Him. With every life, the Great One would grow stronger.

In the dark, Sutter smiled.

Chapter 11

DARC12 was sleeping. The second security shift and some main-tenance workers still roamed the vast ship, but most of the personnel had retired. Working in normal day/night shifts was easier on the body and mind.

The lift doors slid open on Residence Level 1, and eleven people crept into the hallway. They split into groups and made their way to the doors leading into the crew members' living quarters.

Lorenzo Hill stepped to the first door's control switch and deftly bypassed the locking mechanism, his years of engineering training mak-ing it simple for him. He went down the corridor, unlocking each door with barely a sound.

His companions waited patiently, their steel blades glinting in the harsh hallway lights.

Chapter 12

In Biology Lab 5, Containment Room 7, the shimmering body of the thing shuddered and changed. Tiny red follicles sprouted from it, and the slimy surface lost much of its luster. Something inside the mass squirmed.

In the darkness of the ship's morgue, bare feet slowly made their way across the cold tile floor.

PART 3

Chapter 1

Wilson had done this before, somehow. There was a preternatural quality to every step he took. *Déjà vu* coupled with the unshakeable feeling that some unknown entity was watching him as he approached the house. Something studied him.

He led the way up the narrow, ramshackle steps to the cluttered porch. Ronnie Dutch, his partner of four years, followed him.

The windows were covered with newspapers taped to the inside of the glass. Even outside the house, the smell was overpowering, like rotten fruit and a sewer mingling together.

He knocked on the ramshackle door, but it was unlatched and swung in as he did. The stench exploded from inside and assaulted Wilson. A whirring and rattling echoed through the decrepit home. He fought back the urge to vomit and stepped into the house.

Trash covered the floor; there was more refuse than furniture. Maggot-laden food was scattered across the sole table in the living room, and the couch was crawling with them as well. Drug paraphernalia and empty liquor bottles littered the house.

Wilson drew his sidearm and crept through the home, searching for the source of the noise. He reached an open doorway and peered into the next room.

It was the kitchen, which was even more disgusting than the living room. The refrigerator door stood open, empty save for a rotten hunk of meat and a few spilled cartons of milk.

Standing over the sink, his back to Wilson, was Harold Mills—their chief suspect in a dozen crimes. He was naked, emaciated, and covered in filth and gore. Blood dripped from the countertop and pooled at his feet.

As if he sensed the police, he stepped to the side, turned toward the doorway and locked eyes with Wilson with a wide grin. It was a hellish, Cheshire Cat grin that shone with insane glee.

In his hands was the mangled body of an infant boy, one leg gnawed away to the hip and the other crammed into the growling garbage disposal.

Wilson's gut boiled with a rage he'd never known before or since. He couldn't speak. There was no thought behind his actions—just pure instinct born out of his rage. He raised his gun and splattered Harold's poisoned brains onto the kitchen wall.

The insane man still grinned from ear to ear as he collapsed onto the floor.

And then everything around Wilson changed. He was plunged into a darkness so pure that he couldn't see anything at all.

But something was still there; he could feel it. The same presence he felt while searching through the house where he'd lost a piece of himself so long ago.

Watching him.

A moment passed, and something appeared in the distance. A small dot, moving toward him steadily.

It took only a minute for him to realize that it was the mutilated form of a baby. crawling toward him on malformed stumps.

Again, whispers wrapped around him, filling the darkness. Childlike voices taunted him for his failure. Feminine ones promised him salvation. Deep, guttural ones told him of agonies he could only imagine.

He couldn't move. Fear and shame paralyzed him. He tried to scream, but the darkness swallowed the sound of his voice.

The baby grew nearer, its milky, dead eyes accusing him.

The whispers reached a dizzying, fevered pitch. He couldn't discern one from another. They bled into one loud, hellish cacophony that split Wilson's head in two.

And then he was awake, his com-phone ringing on the nightstand beside his bed.

Heart pounding and head groggy, he switched on the com-phone. "Wilson."

"Boss?" Billy Rothberg. His young voice was shaky and hesitant. "We've got an issue."

Wilson rubbed his eyes. "What kind of issue?"

"The women Sutter killed… They're gone."

He was wide awake. "What do you mean, gone?"

"Gone. Just…vanished. Doc Reynolds called it in a little while ago. I think you need to get down here, boss. I don't know what the hell to do."

Wilson was already out of bed and half dressed. "I'm on my way. Don't let anyone else in the morgue until I get there."

He tossed the phone onto the nightstand and pulled on his boots, suddenly unsure as to his next course of action.

Chapter 2

The halls of the ship were practically empty. It was far too early for most of the people on the ship to be awake. The day shift didn't start for another three hours. Wilson passed a few people during the ten-minute journey from his room to the morgue.

Billy stood in the hallway, leaning against the wall beside the morgue door.

"You look like shit, Billy."

"Yeah, well, a murder yesterday and now missing corpses. It's been a fucked-up couple of days."

"I won't argue with that." Wilson opened the door.

The ship's morgue was small—about forty feet by forty feet. A desk with a small computer sat in one corner. Two steel tables were situated in the center of the room, each paired with a steel cart holding surgical tools. A large stainless steel door sat in the middle of one wall. On the opposite wall was a doorway that led into a smaller room with a single table at its center.

A middle-aged man wearing a lab coat stood against the wall opposite the steel door, studying the room.

"Doctor Reynolds?" Wilson said.

The doctor didn't even glance toward them. "I don't understand who the hell would want to take the bodies."

"Where were they when you left them?"

"On the tables. I was going to put them in the freezer this morning, then head to the lab."

"The freezer?" Billy asked.

"You never wondered what happened when somebody died in deep space?" Wilson said.

Billy shook his head. "I try not to think about stuff like that."

The doctor took his cue. "We freeze them. Really, this room doesn't see much use. A couple of accidents each trip out, maybe a heart attack. On a rare occasion, somebody slips through a psych test and commits suicide.

"We usually lose one or two people in the course of a mission." He pointed to the large metal door. "There's a cryogenics unit in that room. We freeze the bodies and keep them in there until we get back to Earth. Then we turn them over to their families."

"What about that room?" Billy asked, gesturing through the open doorway.

"Autopsy room. If we need to do one, we do it in there. Then we prep them for the freeze here."

"So why didn't you just freeze them last night?"

"It's a bigger process than just cramming them in a freezer, kid. I didn't get the bodies until after my shift in the medical bay ended. I came down here when I got the call, filled out the paperwork, and left. I was tired."

"And now they're gone," Wilson said flatly.

"Yeah. Now they're gone."

"Any clue why somebody would want a dead body?"

"None that I'd want to think about for too long. It's kind of bothering me, to be honest with you. When you find whoever did it, do me a favor and let me know." The doctor headed for the door.

"You're leaving?" Wilson asked.

"I've got a normal position on this ship. I'm only here when I need to be. I'm heading to the medical bay. I can get an early start today now that I don't have to run the cryo-freeze. And then there's the fact that a fucking corpse thief on the ship is creeping me the hell out. There's not much more I can do for you, anyways."

He turned and passed through the door. It closed behind him, leaving Billy and Wilson alone in the morgue. Wilson knew as soon as Reynolds saw someone else that he'd share what he'd seen with them. The rumor mill would begin early today, and Wilson doubted he'd be able to slow it once it started.

"Any ideas, boss?" Billy said quietly.

Before he had time to answer, Doctor Reynolds started to scream.

Chapter 3

Collette woke in a cold sweat, her heart thudding in her chest. Terror coursed through her veins, but she couldn't remember the dreams that had brought such fear to her. She lay in bed for a moment, the darkness of the room so profound that it only served to add to her horror. She had the uneasy feeling something was watching her. Some unknown thing that lived in the blackness and had but one purpose: to consume her.

She forced her arm from beneath the covers and flicked on the bedside lamp. Light flooded the room, driving away the unseen evil.

Her heart still racing, she climbed out of bed, the cold floor beneath her bare feet helping to shake her out of the panic that had gripped her. She made her way to the small bathroom and turned on the faucet, splashing cold water on her face. She'd had nightmares from time to time, but nothing had left her so uneasy before.

As her heart steadied itself, she studied her reflection in the mirror. Considering she felt like she hadn't slept at all, she looked pretty good. Her dark hair was barely out of place, and her eyes were bright and rested.

Nerves steady and her fear forgotten, she returned to the bedroom and began to dress.

The security staff worked alternating twelve-hour shifts but stayed on call around the clock in case of an emergency. Collette had never followed the schedule, however, and generally worked whenever she was awake. Unlike a lot of the other crew on board, she enjoyed the long jaunts in deep space. Of course, aside from the scientists, most of the crew were on board because they had no other choice. Poverty was rampant on Earth, and the DARC trips paid well. A five-year trip into deep space would give even a maintenance worker enough money to live on for seven or eight years when they returned home.

Collette's life before signing on for DARC security could have been summed up in a word: mundane.

She'd grown up in the suburbs of Chicago in an average, middle-class family, the daughter of a college professor and a nurse. Her grades in school had been average. Her teenage years weren't filled with much rebellion, aside from a few drunken nights with her friends and sneaking out a few times to see whatever boyfriend she was with back then. Despite the fairly close proximity to such a large city, her life had seemed dull.

During high school, she'd considered a job as a police officer in Chicago, as well as the military. Both of those prospects had horrified her parents, who begged her to find some safer means of employment. She'd eventually relented. Not because of their fear, but because, in her senior year, the first DARC mission was announced and launched. The news captivated her.

The excitement of being a police officer or soldier was enticing, to be sure, but millions of people before her had done the same thing. However, a five-year voyage as a security officer on board one of the most technologically advanced (and controversial) spacecrafts ever built, heading farther into space than most people could even fathom? If ever there was a way to break out of such a humdrum life, a DARC mission was it.

She had signed up as soon as she turned eighteen, and she graduated the training program at the top of her class, her motivation to be accepted driving her grades and exam scores higher than they'd ever been. Her first trip out had been everything she'd hoped for—exciting, amazing, and far from average. She'd seen supernovas and nebulas, blue and purple gasses swirling like a galaxy-sized work of art, and star systems and planets never before seen by anyone.

On that first trip out, she hadn't paid much attention to what the physicists were studying in space. Instead, she was fascinated by the experiments being performed in the labs of DARC7. As a rookie security officer, she was assigned certain sections of the ship, but she had somehow ended up being partnered with Rodney and assigned to the labs that were normally off limits to most on board.

She'd been amazed as the scientists grew new human fetuses from mere cells and created comatose but living bodies that held dozens of transplant organs. She glimpsed men and women with four hearts beating in their chests, breathing with machines instead of their missing lungs. She knew the experiments were illegal on Earth, and very controversial, but in her mind, if creating mindless, soulless husks of human beings could save the lives of countless others, it was an avenue worth pursuing.

She'd also met her two best friends: Rodney and Wilson. It had taken her and Rodney two days to bond, and they became like siblings. The older, stronger man kept an eye on her throughout her first voyage, showing her all he knew and answering any of her questions.

She had been immediately attracted to Wilson. He was a good-looking man—fit and smart—with an aura of mystery surrounding him. Rumors passed through the staff about his police history and just why he had signed on for DARC employment. All he'd ever said was he had been a detective back on Earth. She'd heard several officers ask him, in nonchalant ways, just why he left the force for the far more mundane job on board the DARC, but Wilson had always ignored the question and quickly changed the subject. The mysterious past hidden behind his smoky blue eyes only deepened Collette's attraction to him, and near the end of their first journey together, she sensed he harbored similar feelings for her.

There had been little action on that first trip out, aside from a couple of fistfights and one near-encounter with a small pirate craft, but the trip itself had been adventure enough to leave a lasting impression.

She'd managed four months on Earth before yearning for a return to deep space. Due to psychological concerns, the company required a six-month layover before anyone was eligible for another voyage. Those last two months she spent waiting seemed to take forever, and she'd immediately signed up and requested to once again be assigned with Wilson and Rodney's crew.

They were the only two officers on board DARC12 that she'd served with on her first jaunt, but they were the only two she wanted to be journeying back into space with. She and Rodney had remained close while on Earth, chatting over their computers. But Wilson hadn't contacted her, and she'd been embarrassed with herself when she started missing him.

Now, back in space with the two of them, Collette felt at home. And Wilson's attraction to her was apparent now, as well. There were no official rules about coworkers dating, and she was unsure as to why he hadn't brought it up yet. She hoped he'd act on his desire soon. If not, she might have to make the first move.

His unease last night had been disconcerting. She hoped it had been the shock of what had happened that was making him uncomfortable.

Dressed and calm, smiling at the thought of her and Wilson as a couple, Collette slipped her repeater pistol into its holster and headed out into the corridors of DARC12 to see what the day held in store for her.

Chapter 4

Lisa sat in bed, staring out at her darkened room. Her dreams had kept her awake most of the night. She'd dreamed of the thing in the lab, its glistening skin pulsating and glowing. She saw it swell in places, as if some living thing held prisoner inside of it was trying to push its way free. And in her dreams, she heard screams and voices chanting in languages that she knew weren't spoken on Earth, reaching a feverish pitch that made her heart pound so loudly and her blood run so cold that she had awoke with a scream.

That had been hours ago. She'd tried to fall back to sleep, but every time she passed over the threshold of rest, those alien tongues filled her brain and jolted her back to consciousness.

The clock told her she had about two and a half hours before her shift started, which meant she might as well get up, drink some coffee, and shower. She'd have to request some energy pills from one of the docs if she was going to make it through the day.

She swung her legs around, dangling them off the side of the bed, and reached for the lamp.

Something on the other side of her room moved.

She froze, hand halfway to the light as her eyes scanned the darkness. Focusing now, she thought she heard breathing coming from somewhere in the blackness. Was she hallucinating from lack of sleep? It was possible. She'd always been a woman who needed her rest in order to function at full capacity.

It came again. A slight movement, barely noticeable. It had left her bedroom and was in the other room now—the main section of her quarters.

She grabbed the lamp, fumbled with the switch. The intruder's footsteps quickened with her movement, then her door opened. The light from the hallway spilled into the main room, briefly casting a shadow of her visitor across the floor. Then the door closed, leaving Lisa alone, accompanied only by her fear.

Chapter 5

Wilson charged through the door, drawing his repeater pistol. The screams had fallen silent, but the guttural growling of a hungry animal drew his attention to his left.

Thirty feet from him, just at the intersection of hallways, lay the body of Doctor Reynolds.

Squatting over him like a feral animal was Elle Sutter. She was naked, her blonde hair hanging wildly about her face. One hand was buried in Reynolds's abdomen, while the other ravenously shoved a chunk of the doctor into her mouth. Her slit throat gaped like a maw, and bits of the flesh she consumed slid out of it, falling back onto Reynolds's body.

Wilson was dumbfounded as he tried to process the horror—the impossibility—of what he saw.

"Oh, what the fuck?" Billy said as he caught sight of the scene.

At the sound of his voice, Elle—or the thing that was once Elle— jerked its head upward. Yellow eyes glared at Wilson and Billy while she clutched a large piece of meat in her mouth. She leaped from her meal and charged down the hallway at them, snarling like a rabid dog.

Wilson raised his pistol and fired.

The bullets were tiny things, a little smaller than a pea. The rounds were held in a clip much like a standard pistol, but thanks to their small size, each clip could hold over one hundred shots. Upon firing, they would pierce the skin and unleash a jolt of electricity, paralyzing nerves and muscles and usually knocking the victim unconscious as the shock reached the brain. A small dial on the butt of the gun could adjust the magnitude of the charge. In extreme circumstances, a security officer could press their thumb against a small plastic print reader just above the handle, which would read the thumbprint and unlock the highest setting, dialing up the voltage to a lethal level.

The bullet slammed into the woman's chest. Her body twitched as the charge passed through it, and she dropped forward onto her knees.

Wilson watched as the current ran its course, expecting her to collapse completely. Instead, as the charge tapered off, she jumped to her feet and charged forward again.

Before Wilson could fire a second time, she leaped and slammed headfirst into Billy, tackling him.

They'd barely hit the floor when the naked monstrosity clamped her teeth onto Billy's cheek and pulled, ripping it from his face and leaving most of his jawbone exposed in a hellish version of a grin. His screams gurgled as he choked on his own blood.

Wilson twisted the small dial to its highest non-lethal level and fired two more shots, both into Elle's head. Her body convulsed wildly, but her jaws were clenched onto Billy's throat, tearing the flesh from it as the charges forced her to jerk. Wilson rammed the gun barrel against her ear and rapidly squeezed off three more shots.

Finally, the rounds did serious damage, and the woman fell forward and rolled to one side, falling in a gory heap next to her victim. Grayish liquid mixed with blood trickled from her ears.

Billy's dead eyes stared up at Wilson, a dark crimson pool steadily spreading from beneath his head, creeping across the hallway floor.

Crying as much from anger as from sorrow, Wilson screamed into his com-phone for an emergency medical team. He thought about pulling off his shirt and using it to try and stop the bleeding, but he knew it was too late to save Billy.

Wilson tried to calm himself as he waited for the medics to arrive. Elle Sutter had been dead, goddamn it! He'd seen her body, checked her pulse.

How was this possible? Some kind of virus?

Or was the thing they'd pulled from space responsible somehow? Some kind of radiation emanating from it that had contaminated the ship?

Jim Sutter called it God. Was it trying to prove him right?

Wilson pushed the ridiculous thought from his mind. Conjecture was a waste of time right now. The truth was Elle had come back to life a ravenous killer.

That meant Judith Spitzer was up and stalking through the ship right now.

Chapter 6

"Look... I almost didn't tell you about it," Lisa said. "After the night I had, I may have been imagining the whole thing."

"Imagining your door opening? You said you saw someone's shadow in the hallway light," Collette said.

Lisa nodded. "I think I did. I mean...damn, I may have just been dreaming." She shivered. "Jesus, just the thought of somebody in my room, watching me in my bed..."

"I'll look into it. Only so many people could know how to get past the electronic locks on the doors. I'll start with the engineers and technical officers. Do any of them know you personally? Would anyone have any reason to do something like this?"

Lisa shook her head but stopped. "Roger Han. We're good friends, and we've gone on a couple of dates. He called last night and sounded a little...strange. But he wouldn't do anything like this."

"You never know. Weird shit's been happening on this ship lately. I'm sure you heard about Jim Sutter?"

Lisa nodded.

"You're probably right, but just in case, I'll talk to Han soon. We'll try to run an extra patrol sweep down your wing for the next couple of nights, too."

"All right. Thanks, Collette."

"No problem. And call me if anything else happens, okay?"

Lisa nodded and forced a smile as she turned and headed down the hallway to her lab. She hadn't planned on reporting the incident, though she wasn't sure why. Sure, there was what appeared to be an obvious threat present and she'd been terrified in the heat of the moment. But looking back on it, she hadn't felt as if she were about to be attacked. Of course, a peeping tom was a peeping tom, and Lisa wondered if something was wrong with her. She should still be horrified.

Unless it had been a dream.

She was still trying to write it off as her imagination. It was the most rational explanation. The electronic locks on the ship were sophisticated. And why the hell would anyone just stand in the dark and stare at her while she lay in bed?

It was only when she chanced to meet Collette on her way to work that she decided to mention it, taking care to stress the fact she had slept little and had been plagued throughout the night by nightmares.

She'd also called the head of maintenance to replace her lock and add a second one. She assumed that was action enough. Now, all she wanted was to get into the lab and start her shift. The thing in the containment room creeped her out, but it would undoubtedly keep her mind off the intruder in her living quarters—be he real or imagined.

She entered the lab and was surprised to find she was the first to arrive. Dr. Gruber was usually in the lab at least an hour before the shift began, but ever since they had pulled the alien object out of space, he'd been coming in even earlier. She'd expected to find him in the lab on this morning particularly, since today was the day other departments took their turns examining the thing.

She stopped dead in her tracks as she looked into the containment room.

The thing had doubled in size to almost seven feet in diameter, filling half of the room that held it. Its newly grown red follicles protruded like porcupine quills. The coating of slime had vanished, replaced by a dull orange surface that resembled human flesh. The gray tube had returned, larger now. It extended four feet from the body of the thing and slowly slid back and forth on the floor.

It no longer looked like a benign lump of space shit to her. It looked menacing.

Lisa hurried to the monitor, intent on seeing the change on video.

Static filled the screen. She ran the recording backward, seeing nothing but static. The video returned to normal in time for her to see herself exiting the lab.

As soon as she had left the room last night, something had happened to the cameras—a short circuit, an error with the recording software or hardware. *Something* had happened that prevented her from seeing the thing changing its form. Again.

She left the monitor and approached the glass wall of the containment room, embarrassed to find herself too frightened of the thing to get very close. She stopped several feet from the glass and stared wide-eyed at the thing.

Looking past the forest of quills that had grown from it, she could see the orange skin was almost translucent, and beneath it, she could just make out a dark shape silhouetted by the lights, moving ever so slightly. It reminded her of her dream and planted a cold fear inside her gut.

She was so enthralled by the thing that she didn't notice the figure crouching in the far corner of the room, hidden in the shadows of the computer towers.

Chapter 7

The elevators on the DARC were too damn slow, Wilson realized, as he impatiently shifted his weight back and forth between his feet.

But at least he was alone. It was hard enough to concentrate on what to do without having an elevator full of people to distract him. Indecision wasn't usually a problem for him, but the situation he was facing was more than he'd ever dealt with. There were too many variables, too many unknowns. But he couldn't waste too much time. The safety of the ship was paramount. He had to act quickly.

Under the circumstances, he thought he'd done the right things thus far.

He'd ordered the emergency doctors to get the bodies into the morgue and call whoever else knew how to run the cryo-freeze equipment. He wanted the bodies frozen quickly; no point taking any chances on them getting up like Elle Sutter. It had taken a half-hour for Jacoby and two of his cohorts to arrive and begin prepping the bodies. Once they were in the freezer, Jacoby could contact the biology department and Dr. Gruber and let them try to figure out how the hell the dead had come back to life.

A maintenance man was cleaning the blood from the floor when Wilson left. He'd left two of his men in the hallway to search for Judith

Spitzer and to try and keep other crew members from seeing the carnage. The last thing he needed was news of walking, feral corpses to spread across the ship. Panic on the vessel could do more damage than anything. The rumors would spread no matter what Wilson did, of course, but if his crew could find Judith before she did any damage, the rumors would stay rumors instead of turning into pandemonium.

With Billy dead and two security officers guarding the halls outside the morgue, Wilson was left with only nine others to help him track down Judith and deal with any other problems.

He had called Collette and Rodney just before boarding the elevator and told them to contact all the other officers (even those who had just worked the second shift and were now supposed to be off duty) and have them all congregate in the security office.

He was still trying to formulate a plan when the elevator doors opened. Wilson ran down the hallway, thankful that no one passed him. Blood stained his shirt and hands, and that would be enough to start the panic mill turning.

Finally, he reached the office, and when he entered, he was relieved to see that all his officers had already arrived. Unlike the rest of the ship's passengers, who were all assigned living quarters on two designated levels, the security officers were housed on the same level as the primary security office, so that in the event of an emergency like this, they would be close by. An emergency security office and additional quarters were one floor below, but thankfully Wilson had never had to use them.

Although the DARC was a behemoth of a ship, Wilson had always felt like a dozen security officers and one head officer were overkill on a ship filled with scientists and engineers. They seldom had anything to do. Now, looking at these nine men and women, he felt woefully understaffed.

"What the hell is going on, boss?" Rodney said, eyeing the dark stains on Wilson's hands.

Wilson paused, trying to think of a good way to explain it. "Elle Sutter killed a scientist…and Billy Rothberg."

The room was silent; nobody moved. Wilson saw the color drain from several faces, wide-eyed shock replacing it.

Someone whispered, "What?"

"I know how it sounds. But I saw it. I shot her in the head three times with my repeater before she dropped. We don't have time to talk about how that's possible. Judith Spitzer's body is missing, too. Which means she's probably up and moving around, as fucking weird as that sounds."

Nobody spoke. Everyone simply stared at Wilson expectantly.

"We need to pair off in twos and hunt her the fuck down before she kills somebody. I'm honestly surprised that she hasn't already. She should still be on the same level as the morgue—Elle sure as hell didn't look like she could use an elevator—but if she's found the stairs…" There were too many variables…too much he didn't know.

Shaking his head, he continued. "Maybe I'm wrong. Maybe she isn't…whatever the hell Elle was. But we've got to find Judith."

Whispers ran through the room, and Wilson heard someone say, "Bullshit."

"It may be bullshit," he said loudly. "Believe whatever the hell you want to believe. I don't give a fuck right now. I want her found. That's all I care about. You can make up your own mind as to what she is once you see her."

Wilson pointed to one of the younger officers. "Kennedy, you don't partner up. I want you to get over there behind those screens and stay there. Watch them all. You'll have as good a chance as seeing her as we will—maybe better."

The group quickly paired up, few words passing between them as they did. He could tell that some of the officers didn't believe what he was telling them and were just following orders. He was surprised at how easily others had accepted what he'd told them as fact; he'd been expecting arguments, disbelief. Perhaps the rest of the crew was feeling the same sense of dread and unease that he'd been experiencing.

Wilson was glad to see Collette had joined up with Rodney. No matter how strange he'd been acting lately, Rodney had always treated Collette like a sister. The big man would take care of her.

Wilson quickly delegated them to different parts of the ship.

"What do we do if we find her?" Collette asked.

"Aim for the head. I think the only reason I stopped Elle was because my rounds went through her ear and into her brain. Set your repeaters to the highest level. Otherwise, they don't do shit."

The officers all pulled out their pistols and changed the charge setting.

"No," Wilson said. "Use the scanners. Lethal levels." He followed his own order, turning the tiny control dial to its last setting.

There were a few hushed murmurs from the officers, and a few surprised glances exchanged.

"Do it," he said.

He watched as they pressed their thumbs to scanners on the gun handles and dialed up the voltage.

"Find her. The shifts start in a few hours, and the halls are gonna be full of people. Don't let any of them know what's going on. A bunch of panicked people is *not* what we need right now."

"You don't think we should warn them?" an old bearded officer named Turner said.

"No. Not yet, at least. Most of the crew are still in their quarters, anyway. If we can't find her before they're all up and moving, we'll warn them then."

"You aren't partnered up," Collette said. "What are you going to do?"

"I've got to talk to Carlson. We may have to cancel shifts today and put the ship into lockdown."

"I thought you said you didn't want people to panic."

"I said we *may* have to lock it down. If we can find Judith, we probably won't need to, but I need to tell the captain what's going on and let him know we should consider it. Panicked and in their rooms is better than panicked and wandering around the ship.

"That's all I know to say right now, so go find her."

The officers quickly filed out the door, leaving only Wilson and Kennedy in the room. The younger man was already standing at the wall of screens, surveying them closely.

"If you see her—or anything else—let everyone know," Wilson said.

"I will."

Wilson left the office and headed for the front of the ship, trying to decide how to discuss the situation with Carlson. Telling his subordinates was one thing, but explaining to his superior—especially a hard-headed son-of-a-bitch like the captain—what was happening on the ship would be another matter entirely.

He doubted that Carlson would believe a word of it.

Chapter 8

The thing shuddered, a spasm quaking through its body. The movement startled Lisa, and she took a step back from the glass.

"It's amazing, isn't it?" a voice behind her said, eliciting a surprised scream.

She whirled around to see Roger walking toward her from across the room. His eyes were locked on the creature in the containment room, and she wasn't sure if he was talking to her, to himself, or to the thing. Her heart quickened when she noticed the steel bar in his hand, the end of it stained dark with something she prayed wasn't blood.

"What are you doing here?"

He ignored her. "When I loaded it onto the ship, I knew it was something special. But now...look at it."

"How did you get into the lab?"

"I'm an engineer. Bypassing a standard electronic door lock isn't very hard for me to do."

"How long have you been here?"

"Just a little while. Since I left you."

It *had* been Roger in her room. A shiver danced up Lisa's spine. A flash of anger coursed through her, then turned to fear as she thought of just what he was now capable of. This wasn't the Roger she'd known.

He'd broken into her living quarters and stood there staring at her in the dark for God knew how long. And now he was here in the lab, entranced by some alien creature that was doing nothing to her but filling her with fear. And the metal pipe…and the stains on the pipe…

Lisa stepped to her side, away from both the containment room and the advancing man. "Roger…you need to go. This lab's a restricted area, and Doctor Gruber will be here soon. When he gets here, he'll—"

"He's already here. He got here right after me."

Lisa glanced around the room, scanning everywhere. She'd never realized how large the lab was until now, or how many nooks and crannies the equipment created.

Her focus settled on a shadowed crack between a storage cabinet and a computer processing tower against the far wall. A shoe was visible; above it, an ankle and nothing else. She stifled a scream.

Roger frowned, his gaze dropping. He looked sad. "I didn't want to. He was going to make me leave. I just…want to be with it. I told him I'd be quiet and wouldn't bother him. He told me I had to go or he'd call security."

"Roger…"

"Please believe me. I need to be here…with it," he pleaded, like a child begging for a cookie. He looked like he was about to cry. "I've spent my life wanting to be wanted, to be part of something more than just my shitty fucking life. Now this is here and…" He fell silent and walked closer to the containment room, transfixed by the thing.

Lisa scanned the room, trying to decide whether or not she could escape. The door was thirty feet away. If she were lucky, she'd be halfway there before Roger even realized she was running. But if he caught her, odds were she'd end up like Gruber—just a foot or hand poking out from the shadows of some hastily improvised hiding place. She looked for some kind of weapon—anything within reach she could defend herself with.

"Tell me all you know about it," Roger said, startling her.

"What?"

"You've been studying it since we found it. What did you find?"

"Nothing."

For the first time since making his presence known, Roger turned his gaze away from the thing. He glared at Lisa. "You're fucking lying to me. You don't want me to know what you've learned."

He took a step toward her, pointing the bloody pipe. "I thought you liked me. Thought you were my fucking friend. But I should have known someone like you didn't really want anything to do with me. You're just like Gruber, aren't you? You fucking bitch! You want to keep me away from it. Want to take your samples and run your tests and get closer and closer to it and keep it for yourself and keep me away and laugh about how you fucked me over."

"No!" She took a step backward, toward the door. "We really don't know anything, damn it! The microscopes, the gene sequencer, the mineral detectors… None of them recognize anything."

"When did it change? How did it change? It didn't look like this when I loaded it onto the ship."

"We don't know." She took another step back as his face tightened in anger. "It happened when we weren't in the room. The cameras went out last night, so we don't even have it on film. I swear I'm telling you the truth."

"What has it said to you?"

"What?"

"It must have spoken to you by now. What did it say?"

"I don't know what you mean," Lisa whispered, choking back her fear.

He stared at her, chewing his bottom lip. She could tell he was weighing her fate, deciding whether or not he could believe her. She kept her eyes fixed on the steel bar he clutched. The moment he raised it, she would run.

But instead of attacking her, he dropped his arms to his side and nodded.

"Let me go," she pleaded.

He smiled. "Not yet. I want you to do something for me."

"And you'll let me go if I do it?"

"I promise."

"What do you want?"

"I may be an engineer, but I can't do shit to this containment room without a key or a password. The safeguards can't be bypassed."

Her heart skipped a beat as she realized what he wanted.

"I need the password from you."

"Roger…"

"Something as perfect as it doesn't deserve to be locked up in a glass prison. I want you to open the door."

Chapter 9

"You believe him?"

Collette glanced at Rodney. "Wilson isn't really the kind of person who'd make up something like this."

He sighed. "I know. It just sounds crazy."

They reached the first door on the entertainment level. It led to one of the three restaurants on the ship. One entire floor of the DARC was devoted to cold storage. It was a massive freezer holding several years' worth of food to stock the trio of eateries. It amazed Collette just how much went into the operation of a DARC, and how most on board simply took the amenities for granted.

Technology had jumped in massive leaps over the past thirty years, and she'd heard stories from the old-timers back on Earth of how horrible the first deep-space missions were; no theaters or restaurants or even private living areas. Just a handful of labs and a hundred people locked together in a steel box, hurtling through the void. No wonder so many had lost their minds back then.

Collette paused, hand hovering above the door control button.

"Rodney…you all right? I know what you said last night, but you really seem different. You can talk to me. It's okay."

"I'm fine."

"You're not fine, and you're a shitty liar. I've known you long enough to know when you're trying to hide something. I'm asking because I'm worried."

He sighed. "I just…look, don't tell Wilson, okay?"

She nodded.

"I just keep having weird-ass dreams about that thing they found. I can feel it—like it's watching me. I never see it; I just know that that's what it is. I can't sleep, and I've had a really bad feeling ever since it was loaded onto the ship. Hell, I can't even work out at the gym anymore. Anytime I'm alone, I start hearing voices."

She eyed him carefully. "What kind of voices?"

"I don't know. Quiet ones. I can't even really tell what they're saying. It's in another language or something." He shrugged. "I'm just tired, maybe. And looking for a walking, murdering dead woman isn't exactly something that'll settle your nerves, you know?"

Collette nodded.

"I hope the boss is wrong. Maybe she wasn't really dead."

"I don't know, Rodney. Maybe…hell, probably. It's been a fucked-up couple of days, for sure. But if Judith Spitzer *is* running around the ship, I doubt we'll find her here. I imagine it would be hard for a corpse to use an elevator or the stairs."

He grunted. "I'd imagine it would be hard for a corpse to do much of anything."

Collette smiled and pressed the button. The door slid open, and the two of them entered the restaurant.

The dining room was dimly lit by the small safety lights in each corner of the room. A thin sliver of light crept from beneath the door leading into the kitchen. The shadows were menacing.

Rodney slid his hand across the wall, trying to find a light switch, but he was unable to do so.

Collette flicked on her flashlight and let the beam slice through the darkness, revealing dozens of dining tables and chairs and nothing more.

From the kitchen, a clanking sound rang out, and then silence. Collette could feel Rodney tense beside her.

"Early crew. They've got to prep for breakfast," she whispered. "Try not to scare the hell out of them, and remember to keep quiet about the whole walking dead thing."

They crossed the room to the kitchen door—an old-style, double-hinged one—and pushed it open.

Beyond the door, a makeshift hallway, formed on one side by three large stoves and on the other by a tall shelf filled with food stuff and seasonings, stretched on for fifteen feet. The room smelled of cooking bacon, but no one was in sight. The clanking noise rang out again, just around the corner of the shelf, followed by a wet, slurping sound.

Rodney took the lead, several steps ahead of Collette, as they slowly made their way into the kitchen. He reached the end of the shelving unit and stepped beyond, his gun pointed in the direction of the sound.

Collette watched as his face contorted with horror. She quickly stepped past him, her gaze following his.

Just ahead of them, the naked corpse of Judith Spitzer squatted over two bodies. A carving knife protruded from her chest, just above her left breast. A large yellow blister covered her face and neck while dozens of smaller ones dotted her arms and body like hellish freckles. She was chewing ravenously, bits of flesh dangling from her lips.

The monstrosity didn't notice Collette and Rodney. Its focus was locked on its meal—a young man wearing a black chef's outfit. His throat had been torn out. Beside him, a middle-aged red-haired woman, similarly dressed, lay face down in a deepening pool of blood mingled with cooking oil.

As the creature fed, it rocked sporadically from side to side, its foot on the handle of a large frying pan on the floor, eliciting the clanking that had drawn them to it.

Rodney and Collette were rooted in place, staring at the horror, too shocked to do anything. As Judith leaned over and buried her face in the open throat wound, Collette raised her weapon and fired.

The bullet slammed into the top of the beast's head and lodged in the skull, the silver end of it still exposed above the scalp. A blue spark danced through Judith's hair as she spasmed violently.

As the electrical charge dissipated, Judith leaped to her feet, snarling at her attackers. She lunged forward with a scream, but her feet slipped on the oil coating the floor, and she slammed face first into the tile.

Collette used the opportunity to squeeze off another shot. Rodney followed suit.

The corpse flailed about as the charges passed through her, splashing in the blood and oil as her deep-throated growls filled the room. Slowly, she crawled forward, pulling her naked body through the sickening puddle and leaving a thick crimson trail behind her.

"Fucking hell!" Collette shouted as the corpse regained its footing, rose from the ground, and charged toward them.

The officers both side stepped the attack. Rodney spun toward the corpse as it passed him, and he dove headfirst into its back, tackling it. He landed hard on top of the thing, driving a belch of blood from its mouth. The knife in the corpse's chest plunged through its back, missing Rodney by inches. He pinned the nightmare to the ground, using his massive size to his advantage as the thing beneath him flailed and screamed.

"Kill it!" He struggled to maintain control over the corpse as it fought his grip.

"How the fuck do I do that?"

"The head! The boss said the fucking head!"

Collette scanned the kitchen, quickly spotting a small paring knife on the counter beside a pile of oranges. She grabbed the weapon and lunged toward the corpse, driving the blade into its temple.

It fell still beneath Rodney. He kept his grip tight for a moment, panting for breath.

"Is it dead?"

"I…think so," Collette said. She gripped the countertop with trembling hands, pulled herself to her feet, and vomited into the nearby sink.

Chapter 10

Even when things on board DARC12 were operating normally, the topmost level was slightly unsettling to Wilson. Perhaps, he figured, it was its stark simplicity compared to the other floors. Instead of the labyrinthine layout of corridors leading throughout the remainder of the DARC, there was only one large U-shaped passageway. The lifts were situated at the midway point on either side. At the start of each passageway were the doors to the stairwells. At the base of the U was the entrance to the deck, where Wilson stood, deciding how to give his news.

He pressed the control switch, and the door to the captain's deck slid open. Wilson stood in the doorway, examining what lay beyond. The vast room appeared to be empty, except for the dozens of guidance systems, control panels, and other equipment far too high-tech for Wilson to understand.

He knew the guidance system was mostly automated, but the machines still had to be monitored. A skeleton crew was employed during the second shift—just a few people ensuring everything ran as expected.

But now the deck was a tomb. The computers still beeped and whirred, but there was no sign of human life. Beyond the huge glass wall that formed the front of the room, the cold blackness of space stretched into infinity.

Wilson eyed a door just behind a large bank of computer screens and control panels. It led directly to Captain Carlson's living quarters; the close proximity allowed him to reach the deck in a matter of seconds in case of an emergency.

Hesitant, he drew his repeater pistol and stepped into the room, wincing as the door slid closed behind him. Dread knotting up in his stomach, he kept a steady pace as he made his way toward the captain's quarters.

Halfway across the room, he saw blood. It spread out on the floor from behind a communications desk.

"Shit," he whispered. He'd wanted to be wrong, prayed that more wouldn't go wrong on DARC12, but now, staring at the thick rivulet of blood, he knew he was right. The ship was going to hell. And quickly, at that.

Wilson slowly approached the blood, giving the desk a wide berth so he could see around it quicker. The trickle broadened into a pool, which he followed with his eyes until he saw the hand that was attached to a young woman. Someone had scooped out her eyes, the empty sockets fixed toward the ceiling.

Wilson walked to the woman, his eyes taking in the rest of her body. A wound in her chest was the source of most of the blood. He bent down and gingerly pulled open the tear in her shirt, recognizing the clean signature of a stab wound. The blood around the wound was thick with coagulation. She'd been killed some time ago.

He didn't think Judith Spitzer had attacked the woman. The raving corpse would have ripped her flesh like a wild animal. But why the hell would someone take her goddamn eyes?

Wilson caught sight of another body, this one slumped in a corner against the gigantic window. He recognized the face of Henry Peterson, one of the older crew members on the ship. Dark blood soaked the man's white beard. Two other bodies lay face down on the floor between him and Peterson, dark pools of blood spreading out from each of them.

Sutter was in the holding cell, which meant there was another killer on board the ship, in addition to a walking, marauding dead woman.

The ship was going to have to be locked down. And now there were more dead. Fear and panic welled up inside him. More dead could mean more dead coming back to life. Now, like whoever was murdering the people, they were a threat to be assessed and dealt with.

Wilson hurried across the room to the door, pressing the buzzer to call the captain. An eternity passed with no response. He glanced around the room and frantically pressed the buzzer again. A minute ticked by, then another.

"Fuck it," Wilson said as he pulled his keycard from his pocket. While his security officers could access most of the doors on the ship, only he and Captain Carlson had full access to the ship. Their cards alone could lock or unlock any door, and as a security precaution, every door on the ship except for the living quarters could be locked from either side. Now there was no time to waste waiting on the captain to answer, especially if he shared the same fate as the four second-shift crew members lying dead on the deck. Wilson scanned the card and pressed the control for the door, heart racing as the entrance slid open.

Carlson's room was dark and silent. Wilson's breaths sounded too loud as he entered. He slid his hand along the wall until he found the light switch and flipped it on. The darkness retreated, but the illumination did nothing to calm his nerves. The living area looked much like Wilson's—sofa, television, an extensive collection of books and movies on a shelf in the corner.

"Captain?" He didn't expect an answer, but he called out anyway. "We've got a big fucking problem. We've got to lock DARC12 down, sir."

He stood still, listening intently. No response came. He headed deeper into the living area, walking to the center of the room and peering down the short hallway toward the captain's sleeping quarters. He went down the corridor and flicked on the light in the captain's room.

Captain Carlson lay in his bed, a peaceful look on his face. Like Elle Sutter and Judith Spitzer, his throat had been slit. As gruesome as the scene was, as uneasy as it made him, Wilson wasn't shocked at all. After the slaughter on the deck, he was expecting something like this.

He stared at the dead man, considering what to do next. His heart was pounding, his mind racing. He felt lost. With Carlson gone, there was no one he could defer responsibility to. Securing the ship would fall solely on his shoulders.

The captain's second-in-command would take over for him, of course, but Thomas was practically a kid. He'd reached his post by acing his classes throughout school—not through years of experience. Hell, this was his first trip out. When it came to dealing with whatever was happening on the DARC, Thomas wouldn't have a clue. The standard protocol that he'd been taught in classes addressed how to deal with riots or pirate and terrorist attacks, not serial killers and the living dead. The rookie would be fine running the ship's technical side, but that was a small matter at the moment. And that was if there would even be a ship left to run. At the rate things were going, the entire crew was going to be…

The door! Carlson's door had been locked, and he'd been asleep. Whoever killed him had bypassed the lock.

A realization shot into Wilson's head like a bullet. Lorenzo had been helping Sutter move the alien thing into the containment room, and Sutter had killed two women shortly after that. It stood to reason Lorenzo might have followed his partner into madness. Not to mention, Lorenzo was one of the ship's technical engineers. He'd have no trouble bypassing the simple electrical locks on the captain's door. And that meant he could do the same to almost any other door on the DARC. It was doubtful he'd acted alone, however. One man couldn't have killed the captain and the crew on the deck. There was no choice now; he had to warn the entire ship.

Wilson turned and hurriedly exited the living quarters, running for the communications desk.

The equipment was mainly used to contact other ships and send messages back to Control on Earth, but it also had an intercom system to broadcast messages to the entirety of DARC12. Reaching the desk, he scanned the buttons for the intercom control.

Before he could find it, his com phone beeped loudly, startling him. He fished the phone out of his pocket from underneath one of the guns and switched it on.

"Wilson."

"Boss," Collette said. She was breathing hard, her voice cracking with fear. "We found her. It was fucking awful. I've never seen anything like it."

"I know. Did you kill her?"

"Yeah. Again, I guess. You were right about the head."

"Good." A wave of relief washed over him. With any luck, if the bodies were put in the freezer soon enough, at least one of the horrors on board would be taken care of.

"But she killed two people."

"Shit. Call the morgue. Tell them to send somebody for them as fast as they can. Tell them I've got five more up here as well."

"Five more?"

"Yeah."

"What the hell is happening to this ship?"

"I don't know, but it isn't good. Carlson's been killed. Four of his skeleton crew, too."

"Oh my god. The captain?"

"Yeah. We've got to get the bodies into the freezer fast. I don't know how long it took Elle and Judith to come back, and it looks like the ones here died a while ago. Whatever is doing this—radiation, a virus, whatever—I don't want to fuck around by leaving the bodies unattended for too long. The quicker we take care of them, the less chance there is of them getting the hell back up."

"I'll call the docs to the morgue now."

"After you do, call the rest of the team and let them know you found her, and they need to switch gears and start looking for Lorenzo Hill. I'm pretty sure he's the one doing the killing. I'm about to get on the intercom and tell the whole ship to follow lockdown protocol. Then I'm calling back to Earth and getting somebody sent out here ASAP." Wilson switched the phone off and returned his attention to the communications array.

It took him a moment to locate and flip the switch that set the microphone to broadcast over the intercom. His mind raced, trying to think of just what to tell the crew. Too much information would undoubtedly panic them; too little and they might simply ignore the order to group up with others and lock themselves in their living quarters. He moved to press the ON button for the microphone and—

—a groan erupted from the other side of the communications board. Another moan followed, and a bloodied hand shot upward into Wilson's view, gripping the edge of the desk opposite him.

Wilson stepped back from the console as the dead woman pulled herself up with one swift motion, leaping to her feet and turning to face him, her empty eye sockets as dark as the space outside the ship's window. A trickle of dark drool spilled from the corner of her mouth as her lips curled into a hellish grin. She took a clumsy step forward and bumped into the communications desk. The obstruction elicited an angry snarl from her.

As he backed away from the corpse, the rubber sole of his shoe squeaked across the metal floor.

She screamed and dove across the desk toward the sound, crashing clumsily over the communications controls and setting its lights flashing wildly. Static blasted from the speaker as the woman fell headlong onto the floor.

Wilson ran to the door as the woman righted herself and gave chase, like a blinded rabid dog pursuing the sounds of its quarry.

He reached the exit and pressed the door control, turning to check on the woman's progress. She was close, so he raised his repeater pistol and fired off six shots. Most slammed into her body, but one managed to pierce her cheek. The charges erupted from the rounds, and the woman jerked to the floor in a convulsion at the same moment the door behind him slid open.

Wilson backed through it, watching as the electrical bursts subsided and the corpse climbed back to her feet. The door closed between them just as she resumed her charge. A second passed, then there was a sudden thud as the woman plowed into the door. Through the metal, Wilson heard her let loose another cry. It was an inhuman howl, mercifully muffled by steel.

Panting for breath, his hand trembling from the adrenaline pumping through his system, Wilson fumbled with his keycard and slid it through the door control, thankful that this corpse was blind. The fact Judith Spitzer had been found on the leisure levels meant these thing could use the door controls, but the sightless thing he had just fled from would have a harder time finding the button, which had bought him the precious seconds needed to lock the door. He'd never locked a door on board a DARC before—never needed to. It was a security protocol intended, like most of the other security measures, to help defend against riots or pirates.

The light switched from green to red, announcing the door's newly established locked status, and Wilson backed across the hallway. There, he leaned against the cold wall, his mind reeling with confusion, disbelief, and fear.

Chapter 11

Kennedy stood at the bank of screens, hurling obscenities at them. Ten minutes after the rest of the security team had left to hunt down Judith Spitzer, every monitor flashed sporadically, plunged into darkness, and then returned to life, displaying nothing but black-and-white static.

Without the screens, Kennedy felt useless. The rest of the crew was spread out through the ship, and he was supposed to be their extra set of eyes. Now the technical problem had rendered him ineffective. He'd checked the small antennas that sent and received the wireless signal through the ship via a series of signal transponders. All of them seemed to be connected properly. Any other repairs were beyond his limited knowledge of technology.

Kennedy had put in a call to the technical engineering department, and now he stood waiting for someone to arrive and help him. It was his first-ever trip out as an officer on a DARC, and he didn't want to let down his comrades.

The door to the security office slid open, and a thin, dark-haired man stepped through.

Kennedy turned his attention from the security monitors to examine the visitor. "Can I help you?"

The man looked over Kennedy's shoulder at the static-filled wall of screens, then back to Kennedy.

"I'm here to fix the screens. The whole damn ship's been having electronic problems."

Kennedy breathed a sigh of relief and turned back to the monitors. "Thank God. They just…died. Then they came back on like this. I don't know what the hell is going on, but I need them working again fast." It registered with him suddenly that the technician was empty-handed. "Don't you need some tools or something?" Kennedy looked over his shoulder just in time to see the man pulling something from behind his back.

A knife. He was sliding a knife from the waistband of his pants. Kennedy spun around, drawing his pistol.

He should have paid more attention to the man when he walked in instead of worrying about the damn security monitors. Now that his attention was focused, Kennedy saw the blood covering the man's hands and arms and the distant, wild look in his eyes.

"Stay where you are!"

The man only grinned and continued crossing the room.

Kennedy pointed the repeater pistol at his attacker. "I'm serious, man. This thing hurts like a motherfucker!"

The man responded by speeding up his advance, breaking into a plodding run and brandishing the knife in front of him. Kennedy fired twice, his nervousness sending both shots past the crazed man, slamming harmlessly into the wall behind him.

He tried to retreat, but the dark-haired lunatic was too quick and was on him in an instant. With his free hand, the man grabbed Kennedy's shooting arm and forced it downward with surprising strength.

Kennedy fired another round into the floor as he felt the blade slip through his ribs and into his lung. He dropped to his knees in agony, screaming as the man withdrew the knife and plunged it into his chest again, and then stabbed him a third time.

He tried to catch a breath, but it felt as if he were drowning. Gurgling came from deep within his chest. As he fell forward onto the floor, the dark rushed up to greet him.

Chapter 12

The dark-haired man stood over his kill, watching to make sure the younger man was dead. After a moment, he wiped his blade on the corpse's pants, slipped it back into his waistband, then rolled the body over and rifled through the pockets. A smile flitted across his face as he pulled a keycard from the officer's breast pocket. He started to turn but paused to pry the repeater pistol from the dead man's hand.

Examining the weapon, he turned it over and over in his hand as if it were a puzzle in need of solving, then contentedly dropped it into his pocket.

The theft completed, the dark-haired man crossed the room to the holding cell doors and used the keycard to gain entry. He walked purposefully down the short hallway to the holding cells, stopping in front of the only locked one. After scanning the keycard again, he watched the door slide open.

Sutter stood in the center of the holding cell, staring through the open door with a smile on his lips.

"Lorenzo," he said to his rescuer. "Good to see you, brother."

The dark-haired man grinned and nodded.

"The cleansing?"

"Done."

"And the others?"

"They're waiting in the hallway for us."

Sutter stepped through the cell door and took a deep breath. He smiled and made his way out of the security office to join his brethren.

Chapter 13

"I swear, Roger. I can't open the door," Lisa said again. She knew that he wasn't going to believe her, but she was telling him the truth.

"You're a fucking liar." He pointed at her with the metal bar.

"Really, I can't. Only Gruber knew the password, and the only other way to open the doors is with a level-four card. Only Captain Carlson and the security officers have those."

"That's bullshit. I've seen the doors in the other labs opened by anybody that works in them. You're Gruber's right-hand girl—"

"In the other labs!" Lisa cried out.

Roger stared at her, his eyes blank.

"They're holding animals, Roger. Monkeys and pigs and rats… Have you even noticed how thick the damn glass here is compared to the other ones?

"Remember, I told you Gruber reassigned me to this one a few days ago, when we found the thing? There's a reason we didn't put it in one of the other labs. The containment rooms in this one were specifically designed to be used if we ever found alien life."

Roger remained silent, his knuckles turning white from his grip on the bar as he stared at Lisa.

She continued her plea, pointing to the thing. "These containment rooms are completely secured. They're even airtight, for God's sake. We're pumping air in through vents on the off-chance it breathes like us. I can't open them. It's a security protocol."

He ground his teeth so violently that Lisa could hear them scraping together. "You can't open the doors."

She shook her head.

"You've been studying it since we found it, and you don't know a goddamn thing about it."

Her gaze dropped to the bloody metal bar Roger clutched, expecting him to attack her with it. Instead, he turned away from her and looked at the creature again, nodding. "What do you think about it?"

She swallowed audibly, confused. "What?"

He shot a scornful glance over his shoulder at her. "You've been closer to it than anyone else except Gruber over the past couple of days. What do you think about it, personally? Can you tell me that fucking much, or is that inconclusive like your goddamn tests?"

"Roger…"

What had happened to him? He'd been one of the nicest men she'd ever met, even somewhat timid, and now he was a murderer. Somehow this thing in the containment room had changed his personality completely. And now he wanted to know her thoughts about it. Should she try to answer with what he wanted to hear or simply tell him her true feelings about the thing?

He glared at her, waiting for a response.

"You want my personal opinion on it?"

"Yes."

The truth, then, she decided. If he attacked her, she'd have to be ready; it was better than standing here waiting for an assault that could come at any time. Better to bait him and be expecting his attack. At least then she had a chance of defending herself. In all likelihood, it would be another hour before anyone else showed up at the lab, and by then, it could be too late. She had to do something.

She sighed. "Fine, then. I don't like it. It scares me—makes me uneasy. And more than that, I think it's done something to you. You're different now. You're a murderer because of that thing. You're obsessed with it."

He blinked, his face turning red with anger. "I had to kill Gruber. I need to be with it, to protect it. I need to prove myself worthy of it! It wants me to share it with other people on the ship. But I can't share it! I should be the only one it loves. It's perfect. Can't you see that? A God." He brandished the bloody bar at her again, punctuating his words with a violent thrust of the weapon. "No…you can't. Because you're a goddamn fool."

"Roger…"

"Do you know what I did for you? I stood in your room for hours, watching you sleep. I could have killed you in a fucking instant and shown it how devoted I am. How worthy I am. But I didn't. I want to give it freedom instead of your life. And you can't even appreciate that!"

As scared as she was, this revelation Roger had watched her at her most defenseless, that he'd entertained thoughts of murdering her in the name of some alien being, infuriated her. It terrified her to know she'd been so close to death. But more than that, knowing he'd invaded her living quarters and stood in the dark like some perverted lunatic filled her with rage.

She wanted this confrontation to end. She wanted to hurt him for what he'd done. And she had a better chance of doing so by baiting him into action.

"If it were up to me, I'd shoot the damn thing back into space where it came from!"

His eyes grew wide with shock, and just as she'd expected, her words pushed him over the edge.

"You can't do that!" Roger screamed as he drew back the metal bar and swung it toward her head.

He moved slower than she'd thought he would, or perhaps it only seemed that way because she'd been planning for him to attack. She ducked beneath the bar and kicked upward with all the force she could muster, connecting solidly with his crotch.

He let out a muffled yelp like a wounded dog and dropped to his knees, cradling his manhood in his hands. The pipe fell to the floor, and Lisa instinctively scooped it up before running for the door.

She pushed the button and waited for the steel door to slide open, turning back in time to see Roger charging across the lab toward her.

The door slid open as he neared her, and Lisa swung the metal bar toward him. There was a crack as it slammed into his face. His jaw jerked oddly to one side. Blood gushed from his disfigured mouth, and he collapsed onto the floor, screaming in pain.

Lisa hurried backward through the opening, staring at Roger's thrashing body as the door slid shut in front of her.

She stood in the hallway, trying to process what had just happened. The adrenaline made her dizzy. Her heart thumped in her ears. She'd never been in a fight, even a screaming match, with anyone. Even in her teenage years, she'd always walked away from the many confrontations she'd been faced with. And now she'd smashed in someone's face. That fact alone had her mind reeling.

She needed to find Collette Garcia, or *someone* on the security staff. Not just so they could deal with Roger, but so she could tell them about her fear of the thing in her lab—tell them she thought it had changed Roger into the madman he now was. What if he wasn't the only one being driven insane by it? She doubted they would listen to her, but she didn't care at the moment.

Clutching her weapon, she set off toward the lift and the security office.

Chapter 14

Jacoby shivered in the morgue, a chill gripping him as he slid a second tube into the vein of Billy Rothberg's corpse. There were a total of six tubes pumping the chemical agents required for the freezing process, each inserted at a specific place on the corpse. Once the chemicals were injected, the body would be placed into the massive freezer on the opposite side of the room. It was taking him longer than he'd expected. He'd never done a freeze alone before. The three times he'd been on board a DARC when someone died, Reynolds had handled the duties, with Jacoby assisting twice.

But now Reynolds lay naked in the nearby autopsy room, next in line for the freezing process. They'd fill up the freezer at this rate.

The rash of deaths on board the ship made Jacoby nervous. He'd been having the most unnerving dreams lately. He'd awoke the past two mornings unable to remember them but cursed with the unshakeable feeling that the nightmares were harbingers of something evil pressing down on him. As a scientist, he'd written the feelings off as ridiculous remnants of the nightmare still imprinted on his consciousness. But now, with so many dying (and coming back to life, if he could believe Wilson), Jacoby was starting to wonder if they *were* more than mere dreams.

Reynolds had told him last night of the dead women in the morgue, of the deep wounds in their throats. If Reynolds believed they were dead, then they had been dead. Which meant they'd gotten up, dead as they may have been, and killed Reynolds and the young security officer.

The living fucking dead. On a DARC, no less.

It was too absurd to believe, but the evidence was overwhelming. Wilson was right. Better to get the corpses in the freezer as quickly as possible, just in case. The fewer that knew of the situation, the better; rumors could fill the crew with worry and impede their productivity. Jacoby understood that, but he sure as hell hadn't wanted to be *alone* while he prepped out the corpses.

He worked quickly, his mind running through a list of what the hell could cause the dead to rise. Wilson mentioned the thing they'd found in space a couple of days ago being a possible cause—a virus or radiation, or something similar. Jacoby supposed that was possible, but the thing had been scanned, rescanned, and then scanned again. The scan should have picked up any—

A grunt from the autopsy room snapped him out of his theorizing. He cocked his head toward the open door and listened. Another grunt, followed by something wet slapping the cold tile floor.

Jacoby put down the cryo-tubes and walked slowly to the open door, peeking into the room.

Dr. Reynolds walked across the room toward the door, most of his intestines dangling out of his stomach and trailing between his legs like some bastardized tail. Coagulated blood smeared the tile like dark red gelatin.

Jacoby ducked his head out of view and backed along the wall into the furthermost corner. Wilson hadn't been lying. The shock of seeing it had rendered Jacoby unable to even take a breath. He stood listening, watching the door of the autopsy room.

Reynolds's footsteps resumed, and within seconds he shambled into the room. Jacoby didn't move. Reynolds's corpse was focused on the door leading out of the morgue and to the rest of the ship.

Thank God, thought Jacoby. Let the abomination leave the room; then he'd call Wilson and let him and his security squad deal with it.

Hopefully, they could get to it before it attacked anyone in the hallway, but if it did...well... *Better them than me*, he figured. He could always freeze them before they had time to reanimate like Dr. Reynolds.

The thought of freezing another corpse reminded him of what he'd been doing moments earlier: prepping a body that had been killed at the same time as Reynolds. The realization came too late, and by the time he turned around, Billy Rothberg charged across the room toward him, cryo-tubes dangling from his arms and chest.

Instinct kicked in, and Jacoby broke into a run, fleeing the room and heading for the morgue door. Reynolds turned to greet his old colleague, then ran headlong toward Jacoby with a snarl. Jacoby sidestepped Reynolds at the last moment, just as the corpse lunged at him, high-stepping over the entrails following Reynolds.

Jacoby reached the door and pressed the button frantically, glancing over his shoulder at the oncoming horrors chasing him. The door slid open, and he ran through just as both corpses pounced upon him, tackling him into the hallway and ripping into his body with their hands and mouths.

From the corner of his eye, Jacoby saw a maintenance worker fleeing up the corridor, staring wide-eyed over his shoulder as he ran. The thing that had been Billy Rothberg leaped to its feet and rushed down the hallway in pursuit.

Jacoby screamed as he watched Dr. Reynolds begin to eat his flesh, his cries of agony echoing off the steel walls of the ship. Mercifully, it took death mere seconds to claim him.

Chapter 15

Yes, the dead were getting up and attacking the living.

Wilson forced himself to accept it. Somewhere in his mind, he'd been holding onto the hope that Elle Sutter and Judith Spitzer were anomalies—crazed women who'd survived their assault and were now ravenous lunatics. He'd been too busy trying to secure the ship to give much thought to just what he was securing it from. But after being attacked by the blinded woman on the captain's deck, the horror had been driven home, and he had no other option but to accept it as absolute fact.

Wilson stepped onto the elevator and pressed the button for the floor of the security office. He'd stood outside the lift for twenty minutes or more, accepting what was happening and trying to decide what should be done, cussing himself for his indecision. His fears were coming true. The ship was going to hell, and dealing with it fell on his shoulders. He hoped to God that his choices weren't going to cause any needless deaths. That worry aside, Wilson knew he needed to be quick about things, but there were too many problems and not enough people on his crew.

He'd managed to decide on a plan to help prevent any more of the walking dead. The ship had to go into lockdown while a door-to-door sweep was made. After the sweep (or during it, with a bit of luck), with the rest of the crew in safety, they could find the murdering bastard prowling the ship. Not to mention deal with the dead on the captain's deck.

Now, as the doors closed and the lift began to move, he redialed Collette's number.

"Garcia," she answered.

"Collette. We're too fucking late. They came back. They already fucking came back."

"Wilson? Calm down."

He paused. He sounded hysterical, spitting out sentences like that. If he sounded panicked, his officers wouldn't follow his lead, which was something he didn't need. He took a deep breath and tried to sound calm. "The corpses on the captain's deck came back before I could use the intercom. I locked them in there. I just tried to call Jacoby in the morgue and tell him not to send anybody there, but I didn't get an answer. Have the docs been by to get the bodies out of the restaurant?"

"Yeah, they just left with them. Only two docs showed up, so Judith Spitzer's body is still here.

"Shit. Try to catch them. It sounds god-awful and fucked up, I know, but…I want you to make sure the bodies don't come back."

"What do you mean?"

"I mean…crack them in the head. Stab them in it, something. That seems to be what kills them—kills them again, I mean. So do it before they get up and do any damage."

"Fuck. That's crazy."

"I know. But everything that's been happening is goddamn crazy. I don't want any more of those things loose on the ship, and I don't know of any other way to do it. I'm flying by the seat of my pants here."

There was a pause on the line. Wilson could hear Rodney and Collette talking amongst themselves. Finally, she came back on the phone. "All right. We'll do it. But then what?"

"Call me. I'm heading back to the security office now to check the cameras myself. I tried to call Kennedy, but he isn't answering either. I don't like the fucking feeling I'm getting about all this."

"No shit," Collette said. "What about lockdown? The shifts are about to start, but I'm not seeing too many people out in the halls."

"Like I said, I didn't get on the intercom and give the order."

"Well, something's going on then. I've passed three people on their way to their stations, but normally there should be a shitload of people out and about."

She was right, Wilson realized. He should have passed somebody by now, as well, but the halls and elevators had been as empty as space itself. The morgue docs, security crew, and a couple of the cleaning and maintenance staff were the only people he'd seen since Billy Rothberg had called him to the morgue.

"I'll call the rest of the team and have them start going door to door and check on everyone, plus give the lockdown order that way," Wilson said. "I've got a feeling Lorenzo's our murderer, so I need you and everyone else to keep an eye out for him."

"And the things on the captain's deck?"

"We'll deal with them later."

"Sounds like a plan, I guess."

"Not a very fucking good one, but it'll have to do. Call me when you deal with those bodies."

"All right."

That said, Wilson disconnected, then dialed the number that turned the com-phone into a walkie-talkie, allowing him to talk to all his officers at once. The elevator doors opened, and he made his way down the hallway to the security office while he explained to his men what he wanted them to do.

They were to knock on every door and inform each person to partner up into groups and lock themselves into one living quarter. If there was no response, the officers were to use their access cards and investigate each apartment. It was a breach of privacy, to be sure, but one that Wilson felt was necessary.

He finished with his instructions just as he reached the security office, pocketed his com-phone, and entered the room. The wall of static-filled screens flickered with nothingness.

"Kennedy?" he called out, drawing his gun. He'd already seen enough today to know that if the rookie wasn't answering his calls, Wilson should expect the worst. The malfunctioning monitors only served to reaffirm the feeling. Slowly, he made his way into the room, peering over the desks and equipment as he walked toward the screens. He only took a few steps before he spotted Kennedy's body.

"Son of a bitch." Wilson crossed the remainder of the room and squatted next to Kennedy, examining the youth's wounds. The blood was still wet and warm. The murder hadn't happened long ago.

He scanned the room again, his attention falling on the door leading to the holding cells.

"Fucking hell." He left the body and headed down the hallway to check on his prisoner.

The door to Sutter's cell stood open. It was a slap in Wilson's face. Had another walking corpse freed Sutter? He doubted it. They could open doors and work the lifts, but unlocking a holding cell seemed a bit much for them. And besides that, Kennedy had been stabbed, like those on the captain's deck. Most likely, it was the other killer lurking somewhere on the ship.

Whoever had released Jim Sutter only added to Wilson's growing fear that he was quickly losing control of the situation—and he wasn't sure if he could get it back again.

His mind reeled with doubt. He knew all that had happened on the ship wasn't his fault, but his decisions hadn't stopped the DARC from continuing on its downward spiral into Hell. He hadn't acted on the ominous feelings and nightmares the thing they'd found triggered in him. He hadn't even asked his colleagues if they shared his thoughts. As usual, his gut instincts had proven right. But he'd fucked up by not following that instinct earlier, and now a lot of people had died. More than had ever died on a single DARC mission, as far as he knew.

And unless things changed quickly, Wilson feared that a lot more were going to die on this ship, hurling through space millions of miles from their homes. A wave of nausea swept over him, and he choked back the urge to vomit. Despite what had happened thus far, he had to do what he could to save what was left of the ship, no matter what it took.

Steeling himself, he headed back down the hallway, returning to Kennedy's body and standing over it. After a moment, he squatted beside the dead youth and withdrew his repeater pistol.

He pressed the barrel against Kennedy's left ear and fired three times, the body convulsing with each shot, then falling still.

Wilson stood, hoping that he'd done enough to keep Kennedy dead.

He'd head to the morgue. He could meet up with Collette and Rodney and ensure that the docs didn't try and stop them from finishing off the dead bodies. And then he could join up with them and the rest of his officers in instituting the lockdown, speeding up the rate at which they could find Sutter and his murdering friend. Then they could deal with the dead on the captain's deck.

His mind made up, he crossed the security office, reaching the door just as it slid open.

A pretty blonde woman burst through, dressed in panic and a lab uniform. Blood spatter stained her white suit and speckled her bare arms. He noticed she clutched a steel pipe coated in blood. Her eyes met his, and he saw some of the fear drain from her face, replaced by relief.

"You have to help me!"

He nodded. " What happened?"

"Roger Han! He's lost his mind. He's obsessed with that thing we found. He killed Doctor Gruber!"

Feigning shock wasn't required, after all. He *was* surprised, and he knew that she could tell from the look on his face. Maybe Lorenzo wasn't the killer after all.

She continued, not waiting for a response from him. "He's obsessed with that thing we found. He's in the lab. He's lost his mind, and he tried to kill me when I told him I couldn't let it out of the containment room. I hit him in the face with this bar. I think I broke his jaw. I know it sounds crazy, but I think we need to get that thing off the ship." She spoke quickly, her words blurring together as she did so.

Wilson was glad that Kennedy's body was obscured by tables and desks. The woman was doing all she could to hold it together, and all things considered, he supposed she was doing a pretty good job.

Meeting up with Collette and Rodney could wait. He may have found the murderer who'd been leaving a trail of dead bodies on the ship. He hoped his two officers could take care of the corpses without incident.

The crew's safety was paramount; they would be safest if the lockdown happened quickly and smoothly. The more men he had taking care of that, the better. Besides, he could probably handle Roger Han alone, especially if he'd been clocked in the face with that steel bar.

"All right," Wilson said. "Biology Lab Five, right?"

The woman nodded.

"I need to get down there as quickly as I can. Can you head back to your room on your own?"

"Hell no."

Wilson stared at her.

"I know you won't believe me and that I sound crazy, but there's something going on. I've been having nightmares about that thing, and then Roger kills Gruber and tries to kill me. You can't leave me alone right now."

"Your room—"

"No. I don't want to go back there. He was in there with me while I slept. He might come back for me."

He studied her, pondering what to do. "You know I'm going right back down where you came from?"

"I know. But I don't want to be alone." The last sentence came out as desperate, her pleading drawing her ever closer to the verge of tears.

Wilson had heard similar words many times on Earth, victims telling him that they didn't want to be cast into solitude after their attack. On Earth, he'd had someone who could stay with the victim—another cop, usually. Sometimes a psychiatrist or social worker. Here, he had no one to leave her with and no time to find someone. And he couldn't blame the girl for wanting companionship.

Wilson nodded. "Fair enough." He held out his hand, and she shook it. "I'm Wilson. Head of security."

"Lisa Michaels."

"You going to hold onto that metal pipe?"

She nodded, tried to force a smile, and failed. "If it's all right with you. Just in case."

"Fine by me. After I arrest Roger, I'll take you to the residence levels and get you into a friend's room or get somebody to join you in your own. The ship's getting put into lockdown, so you'll be with at least one or two other people. That work for you?"

"Why is it being put into lockdown?"

"Like you said, something strange is going on right now. Just a safety precaution."

She nodded. She was starting to calm down already. Wilson supposed it was most likely just because she wasn't alone anymore.

"Good. Let's go before he leaves the lab."

"I don't think you need to worry about that," she said as the two of them headed down the hallway for the elevators. "He doesn't want to leave that thing's side."

Chapter 16

"Hold up, guys!" Collette called out, her voice echoing off the steel walls. The sound made her wince as it cut into her ears, her own words sounding alien, foreign. Eerie. One hundred or so feet away, at the end of the hallway where it forked like a capital T, the two doctors stopped pushing the gurneys and looked over their shoulders. Even from the long distance, Collette could see the confusion on their faces.

She fumbled for the right words, trying to think of the best way to explain what she and Rodney needed to do.

The big man beside her did it for her. "The boss gave us some extra orders. First off, there's no need for you guys to go up to the captain's deck. It's locked down tight. Nobody in or out. Second, Wilson wants us to stay with you guys and make sure these bodies don't get up like the other ones did."

The narrow hallway carried his voice easily down its length, and Collette was glad to hear him speak. He'd barely said a word to her since leaving the leisure levels or while heading for the morgue. He almost seemed to be in a trance.

One of the doctors laughed uneasily. It was obvious he was trying to conceal his fear. "I'm not going to turn down having you guys around, considering what's going on. But I've got to tell you, we're putting them straight in the freezer with the others, so I don't think they'll get a chance to get up.

"Not sure how long we've got until they reanimate," Collette said. "Wilson wants us to take extra steps."

"Extra steps? What do you mean?"

"We'll explain once we get them into the morgue."

The doctor walking in front of the other shrugged and returned his attention to the gurney, but before he could disappear around the corner, he froze, his eyes growing wide with fear. The sound of someone running echoed down the hall.

"Oh fuck no!"

Still a fair distance from the two doctors, Collette halted and placed the back of her hand on Rodney's chest, stopping him as well.

The doctor in the rear turned and ran back toward them, a string of obscenities rushing from his mouth. The other doctor tried to follow him but was slowed by the gurney his partner had abandoned. A corpse leaped into view from the left fork of the hallway. It slammed headfirst into the doctor, knocking him out of sight down the right fork.

The screams only lasted an instant.

Before the cries of agony finished, a second corpse rounded the corner in a dash, this one's stomach torn open and dragging its guts. It careened into the gurneys, spilling the dead bodies onto the floor. It ran down the hallway in pursuit of the fleeing doctor, with its entrails bouncing along behind it like puppies chasing their master.

Collette raised her gun and fired, missing with all but one shot. She wasn't surprised that the rounds did little to slow the attack. Beside her, Rodney stood like a statue, staring at the oncoming monster.

"Rodney!" she screamed, slapping him on the shoulder. He glanced toward her and blinked rapidly, as if waking up from a dream.

The doctor's speed was no match for the attacking terror. It was on him in a matter of seconds, jumping onto his back and dragging him down as it tore at his face and neck and shoulder with its gore-stained teeth and fingers. Its eyes locked on Collette as it did so.

Without pausing to savor its kill, the thing rose back to its feet and charged toward the two officers. Behind it, the two bodies it had knocked from the gurneys moved.

Collette was the first to break and run for the elevator. When Rodney regained his senses, he followed close behind. The door had already closed, and Collette frantically pounded the control switch. A centuries-long second slipped by, and the door slid open just as the dead man reached them. It lunged forward, growling and grasping for Rodney, but it couldn't manage to get a hold, as the big man spun backward in anticipation of the attack.

Rodney gripped the corpse by its shoulders as he spun. His massive muscles and the momentum of the charging nightmare flung it past him and Collette. The monstrosity fell onto its stomach and slid several feet down the hallway. The intestines snapped under the weight and friction of their owner as he careened down the passageway, and the guts rolled into a heap to one side of the hall.

Collette and Rodney filed into the elevator and pressed the control buttons. The door slid shut just as the corpse regained its feet and charged. Collette collapsed against the back wall of the lift, sliding down it until she was sitting on the floor.

"What the fuck are we going to do? How are we going to fight those fucking things?"

The big man was silent for a long time. "It's going to kill us all."

Collette stared up at her partner. "What?"

"The thing we found. It's responsible for all this—the murders, the corpses getting up and attacking us. My nightmares, the voices I've been hearing. I know it's all because of that fucking thing."

"We need to tell Wilson, then."

Rodney nodded. "There's something else." He paused, visibly straining for the words he wanted. "I think it's driving me crazy."

"What do you mean, crazy?" Collette stood back up.

"Since we left the restaurant, I've been hearing those voices again—a lot more clearly now than they have been. They're in my head, and I can't shake them off."

"Are they still in another language?"

"Yeah. But they make me think things. It's like, somewhere in my mind, I understand what they're telling me, and I want to obey them. I start to, and then I manage to stop myself." Rodney's lip quivered as he spoke, his voice cracking as he fought back tears. "I'm getting fucking scared. What they're saying isn't good. I don't know if I can keep controlling myself."

"What do they make you want to do?"

"For a second, after those corpses attacked us, they were so loud I couldn't hear anything else. I wanted to just let that thing take me."

Collette's eyes widened in shock and horror. The big man was crying now, staring at her like a child about to be punished.

"Before that, they were just whispering to me. I wanted to skip out on going down to the morgue and go somewhere else."

"Where?"

"To *It*."

"The thing we found?"

"I wanted to go to the lab it's in and let it out of the containment room… I can still hear the voices right now, whispering to me, telling me where to find it. To come to it."

Collette stared in silence, fear knotting up inside her gut.

"God help me, Collette. You may need to lock me up."

Chapter 17

The journey to Lisa's biology lab was unsettling. Wilson and Lisa passed no one as they made their way through the ship. The occasional beep of a computer, or the quiet hiss of oxygen pumping through the ship's vents, were the only sounds accompanying their footsteps.

Reaching the lab door, Wilson turned to Lisa. "Are you still going to wait here?"

She glanced over her shoulder, then down the hallway past Wilson. "Honestly… I think I'd rather go in with you. I'm kinda creeped out right now."

"I don't blame you. Let me go in first and make sure he's not up and ready to attack somebody."

"Okay."

Wilson drew his repeater pistol. It might be useless against those things, but it would damn sure bring down a normal man.

The door slid open, and he stepped through, scanning the room. A few feet from the door was a small puddle of blood, but the lab it-self appeared empty. Except for the thing in the containment room.

Wilson's focus his attention on the creature, and he was instantly transfixed.

"Wilson?" Lisa said from the hallway. She repeated herself, louder this time.

He wrestled his gaze from the thing and looked back at her.

"Is it safe to come in?"

He looked around the room again. "I don't see him anywhere."

Lisa walked through the doorway, pointing to the puddle of drying blood. "He was right there. He has to still be here."

"I doubt it. I'd say he ran. He probably knew you were going to get security."

"You don't understand. He's obsessed with that thing. He tried to kill me. He *did* kill Gruber."

"Oh shit." Wilson had forgotten there was a dead man to contend with. "Where is Gruber?"

Lisa pointed. "Over there."

He made his way across the room, stopping in front of the corpse. Gruber's skull had been bashed in. The entire top of his head was grotesquely misshapen, caved inward. There was little blood. Matching streams had flowed from his ears and were now dry. A thick band of crimson had seeped from Gruber's head down over his face. The tip of his tongue protruded from permanently pursed lips.

As horrible as the death of the chief science officer was, it was relieving to know that he wouldn't be returning to life. Roger Han had made sure of that.

Wilson left the body and rejoined Lisa near the door. The woman stared at him with wide, expectant eyes.

"He's dead."

"I told you that. But you need to find Roger."

"I know. I will; trust me. He knew you were running for security. He ran out of here as soon as he was able to stand up."

"And I'm telling you he didn't go far."

Wilson returned his attention to the containment room. "Because of that."

"Yes. He wants to let it out."

"What?"

"That's why he tried to kill me. I told him only the captain and the security staff had the cards that would open it."

Awestruck, Wilson took a few steps closer to the thing. "It's changed so much since we found it."

"Yeah. A little bit at a time."

The intestine-like tube swayed back and forth. The dark shape within the thing writhed slowly as the forest of quills twitched. It seemed to respond to Wilson's attention, the slight movements like a silent greeting. After a moment, the thing fell still, the grotesque swaying tail its only sign of life.

"What is it?"

"All I know is it's not good. It's doing things to people's minds. Like I told you before, I think we need to shoot the damn thing back into space."

Wilson didn't answer. A wave of warmth washed over him. The problems with the ship were slowly melting from his mind, to be replaced with happiness, with peace. This being was all that was right and good in the universe. It was pure—perfect. A God made flesh, and it was here to help deliver them all into salvation. Freeing it made sense. It could make right all the things tearing apart the DARC12. It could make right everything in Wilson's life. It was weak still, but with freedom, it could grow so strong—strong enough to fix everything in the universe. It only needed to be released. And Wilson had the keycard that could give this being its freedom.

"It's amazing," he whispered.

A nervous edge crept back into Lisa's voice. "That's what Roger said, right before he tried to kill me."

The statement snapped his attention away from the thing. The peaceful feeling left as quickly as it had arrived, leaving him cold and fearful. The events of the past few hours had been terrifying, but he'd stayed strong. Now, after being enveloped in whatever power the thing was emanating, Wilson was horrified. He could see how Roger and Sutter had fallen under its spell.

The question of what was causing hell to break loose on his ship had been lingering in his mind since Billy Rothberg's death. He'd assumed the dead were rising because of some virus or strange radiation. But he'd never believed in coincidence, and after feeling the power of the creature, he was certain of one thing: this being was far more than he or anyone else could have ever imagined. There was no doubt in his mind that it was causing everything that was happening on the ship.

"We have to run the purge command and launch it back into space," Lisa said.

"You can't just shoot things out into space for the hell of it. The purge command has to be authorized by the captain after he's gotten clearance from Control to do it. His card's the only one that will override the security lock for it."

"I know all of that. But Carlson will see what's happening. You've got to talk to him."

"Shit." Wilson thought of the blinded corpse he'd locked in the captain's deck. By now, Captain Carlson had probably returned from the dead and was wandering around his room, waiting for someone to slaughter.

"So call the captain," Lisa said. "Tell him what's going on."

"I can't."

"Tell him to come down here if he doesn't believe it! He'll see that thing and know, too. Call him."

Wilson didn't want to tell her about Carlson. She'd already dealt with enough; to worry her with his death seemed wrong.

"I'll deal with it. First, we need to get you somewhere safe. We'll group you up with the rest of the crew, and then I'll get his clearance and shoot this fucking thing back into space where it belongs."

"And what about Roger?"

Wilson sighed. "I was hoping I could get down here before he could run. He's hiding somewhere. But the important thing is he can't open that containment room, and once everyone is in lockdown, it'll be a lot harder for him to hurt anybody. Don't worry. I'll find him."

Lisa looked at the thing again, studying it. She returned her gaze to Wilson and nodded. "Let's go, then."

He led the way out of the lab. A moment after the door slid closed behind them, the beast inside the containment room began to pulsate like a giant, deformed heart.

Chapter 18

Turner pressed the call button again and stepped back from the door, glancing beside him at his comrades. None of the other security officers were getting any response, either.

They'd split up the residence floors: he, Jenkins, and Smith were on the first residence level, the remaining officers on the other. It was a simple enough task to instruct each crew member to assume lockdown protocol, but after several minutes of trying to get them to answer their doors, Turner was growing impatient.

And nervous. He had his doubts about what Wilson had told them; the walking dead was a little too farfetched for him to believe. But something had scared the hell out of the chief, and there was no denying that Sutter had lost his goddamn mind. Now, alone except for the other two officers, Turner's skin was crawling. Three rooms and no response from anyone?

"Fuck it," he whispered.

"You want to go in?" Jenkins asked.

"No choice. Boss said if we had to, we had to." Turner slid his key card through the lock and watched as the thick, metal door slid open.

The room beyond was a dark, silent void.

Turner drew his repeater and watched as Jenkins and Smith opened their respective doors.

"Looks empty," Smith said.

"We've gotta check it out," Turner said flatly.

He'd been on more DARC missions than anyone on board, and he'd be damned before he'd let them know the whole situation was beginning to scare the hell out of him. Gritting his teeth, he stepped into the darkened room, sliding his hand across the wall until he found the light control.

The light filled the room, eliciting a sigh of relief from Turner. Nothing had been waiting in the dark to pounce on him. None of the grinning, cackling corpses Wilson had warned them about.

"Hello?" he called out, making his way toward the bedroom.

Turner's stomach churned when he flipped the light on. A man, dressed only in a pair of boxers, lay face-up on the floor, one leg still on the bed. His throat had been slit from ear to ear, and his dead eyes were wide in horror.

He hurried from the room, back into the hallway, running to the next door just as it opened and Jenkins dashed out, his face pale. "She's dead."

Turner nodded. "Goddamn it."

"Looked like she put up a hell of a fight, though. The whole bedroom's torn apart."

"Some son of a bitch broke into their rooms while they were sleeping."

"We've got to check the other rooms. He couldn't have killed everyone."

"I'm not so sure just one guy did this."

Before the two men could say anything more, the adjacent door slid open, and Smith careened into the hallway, clutching his left shoulder as a steady stream of blood seeped between his fingers.

"He fucking bit me! The son of a bitch bit me!"

"Smith—"

Turner fell silent as a blood-drenched figure appeared in the doorway behind Smith. Several dark circles on his pajamas suggested he'd been stabbed multiple times. His face was twisted in a hellish sneer, made all the more hideous by the fresh blood coating his mouth. The man lunged at Smith at the same time Jenkins charged toward the gory figure.

Jenkins was quicker, tackling the dead man to the floor and landing on top of him, wrestling to pin the rabid nightmare down. Turner joined the fray, slamming the butt of his repeater pistol to the corpse's head. After four solid blows, the skull split open, bits of coagulated blood and brain spilling from the wound. The creature fell still.

"You hurt?" Turner asked Jenkins.

"No."

Smith leaned against the wall, staring at his two partners and clutching his wounded shoulder. His blood continued to run from beneath his hand and drip down his chest. Turner could tell from the sheer volume of blood Smith had already lost that he wouldn't last long without medical attention.

"He took a hell of a chunk out of me."

Turner nodded. "Jenkins, call the docs. Tell them you're bringing down Smith, and they should meet you at the elevator."

The door behind Smith opened, and the corpse Turner had just seen lying half-in/half-out of its bed stepped into the hallway. It caught sight of the three men and charged toward them before Turner could even grasp what he was seeing.

The monster leaped onto Smith's back and wrapped its legs around his waist in a grotesque version of a piggyback ride. Smith let loose a scream as the creature bit into his ear, ripping it from the side of his head and sucking it into its mouth as Smith collapsed.

Jenkins drew his weapon and fired, missing his target and hitting Smith instead. The security officer's body convulsed as the electrical charge tore through him. Before he stopped twitching, his assailant bit into the back of his scalp and jerked its head upward, ripping away hair and flesh and exposing the skull beneath. Jenkins fired again, the shots finding their intended target this time but doing nothing to stop the carnage the monster was inflicting.

"Run, goddamn it!" Turner yelled, turning from the horrific scene and running down the hallway for the other elevator. He put thirty feet between himself and the monster that was eating Smith when a door near the end of the hallway slid open. Turner froze, watching the doorway.

A couple entered the hallway, he in a pair of pajama bottoms and she in nothing but a thong. Like the marauding corpse behind him, each of their throats had been slit. Their dead eyes locked with Turner's and they broke into a run, sending Turner fleeing back the way he came.

Jenkins hadn't moved; he stood rooted to the floor, firing his repeater pistol at Smith's attacker. From between gritted teeth slipped a steady, near-silent scream. Smith lay dead in a growing pool of blood. The creature that was astride him twitched with each of Jenkins's rounds. Half of the shots missed. Jenkins was mad with panic, and his aim suffered for it.

Turner yelled his name as he approached, drawing Jenkins's attention. Jenkins stopped firing and watched, stupefied, as Turner ran past him and the still-convulsing corpse.

The elevator the three officers had arrived in was a mere twenty feet from Jenkins, and Turner dove toward the control button, pounding it with his fist as he glanced over his shoulder.

The young couple had overtaken Jenkins. He lay silent beneath them, staring at Turner with wide, unblinking eyes as they tore the flesh from his body. The other corpse had climbed off of Smith and shifted its attention to Turner. As it did so, a door near the middle of the hallway opened and released yet another walking corpse.

My god, Turner thought. *Someone's killed them all.*

He'd barely finished processing the thought when the door closest to him opened and a blonde woman walked out, her nightgown a bloody mess. Catching sight of him hammering on the elevator call button, she snarled and rushed toward him with all the fury of hell itself.

Chapter 19

Collette stared down at Kennedy's body, her stomach churning. She and Rodney had found their colleague's corpse moments after arriving at the security office. They'd tried three times to reach Wilson on the com-phone, and each attempt was met with nothing but electrical hisses and pops.

"Sutter's gone," Rodney called out from the holding cells. "Looks like somebody let him out."

Collette nodded to herself. She'd expected as much, given all that had been happening. It all started with Sutter, so in the midst of hell overtaking the DARC, it made sense that the murdering engineer was freed.

Rodney joined her at the wall of useless screens. "Should we make sure he's not going to come back? Crush his head or something?"

"No." She pointed to a thin thread of blood that had trickled from each of Kennedy's ears. "Looks like somebody else already did."

"Wilson?"

She nodded. "That'd be my guess."

"But he didn't let Sutter out."

"I really doubt it."

Rodney regarded the static-washed screens. "What do you think happened to these?"

Collette didn't even bother to look at the monitors. "Same as the phones and the crew and the rest of the ship—they're fucked."

"So what now?"

"I guess that's up to you, big guy. We were coming here to talk to Wilson and lock you in a holding cell. Wilson obviously isn't here, so that leaves locking you up. Do you really think I need to do that?"

A long silence hung in the air as Rodney stared at his friend and pondered the question. He gnawed his bottom lip so fervently Collette expected it to bleed.

"You need me. I can't leave you alone with everything that's happening."

"Rodney—"

"I know… You can take care of yourself. But we don't know what's happening on the ship or just how bad shit's really getting. If you lock me up and something happens to you, I'll spend the rest of my life blaming myself and feeling like shit. So let's find Wilson and figure out what the hell to do."

"All right."

"But I *do* want you to keep an eye on me. If you have to do it, don't hesitate for a second to take me down with your repeater."

"Okay."

"I'm serious. If I start acting like I'm going to hurt you or anybody else, stop me."

"I will. I promise."

"So, like I said, what now?"

She shook her head slowly. "I don't know. We still need to find Wilson."

"He sent the rest of security to enforce the lockdown. Maybe he's on the residence levels with them."

"So we go to the residence levels?"

"Unless you've got a better idea."

"How about we call him again?"

"You can try, but I'd be willing to bet that the phones are gone."

Rodney dialed Wilson's number on his com-phone and waited a

moment. Disappointment twisted his face, and he switched off the phone, returning it to his belt.

"That's what I figured," Collette said.

"All right then. Let's go."

The two officers left their fallen comrade, making their way out of the security office and into the cold, dead hallway.

They walked to the elevator without speaking, their slow, steady footsteps echoed like thunder in the empty passageway.

As they waited for the elevator, Collette studied her partner. His face was pale, with miniscule beads of sweat clinging to his forehead. He was chewing his bottom lip and staring at the elevator doors.

"Rodney?"

He jerked his head toward her, eyes wide with surprise.

"You all right?"

A slight nod. "Yeah. Just nervous, I guess. I've got a bad feeling we're about to walk into a shit-storm."

"No voices?"

"No. Not since the morgue."

She nodded. She'd never imagined she would see Rodney so nervous, so scared. Collette clung to the hope everything could be resolved. That it wasn't too bad just yet.

Rodney had given up hope. He looked like a man trying to come to terms with the fact he was going to die soon.

The elevator arrived and its doors slid open. Collette took a step toward it and froze.

The interior of the lift was awash with blood. The back wall was smeared with it, the floor a wall-to-wall pool of the stuff. Another of the ship's security officers, Jack Thompson, lay slumped in the corner, grimacing. He had cut the bottom leg of his pants off and tied it around his right thigh as a tourniquet. Despite the makeshift bandage, blood still seeped from around the cloth. Beside him was a barefoot body, lying face-down and clad only in a pair of pants. Its skull was cracked open just above the right ear. Jack's blood-covered pistol lay on the floor beside it.

"Fucker…got me good." Jack panted. "Wilson wasn't making it up.

They're everywhere."

"Where is Wilson?"

"How the hell would I know? I tried to call for backup when I found the first body, but my com-phone is on the fritz."

The elevator door began to slide shut, but Collette stepped into the doorway, catching it with her foot. "What happened?"

"Everyone's dead—but not dead. They're up, just like Wilson said."

"Everyone?"

"The first room I checked was empty, so I'm sure whoever killed them didn't get everyone. But it doesn't matter. Those things were able to open their own doors, which means they can probably use the elevators. It's only a matter of time."

"Can you walk?" Rodney asked.

"I fucking doubt it. This guy took a hell of a chunk out of my leg, all the way down the bone. Besides…where the hell would I walk to? I told you—we're screwed. I seriously doubt those things will stay on the residence levels for too long."

"Come on," Rodney said as he entered the elevator, his feet slipping on the blood-slick floor. He put his hands underneath Jack's armpits. Grunting, Rodney lifted him, the wounded man using Rodney's arm to support most of his weight.

"Great. Thanks. Now where the fuck are we going, exactly?"

As the two men exited the elevator, Collette retrieved Jack's repeater, plucking it from the bloody floor with only her index finger and thumb, trying to shake the blood from it.

She joined them in the hallway and offered the blood-soaked weapon to its owner. Jack regarded it with disgust before accepting it.

"I don't know," Collette said as she wiped her hand on her pants. "We were heading up to the residence levels to try and find Wilson, but I guess there's no point in that."

She walked back to the elevator and pulled out her key card. She slid it through the control box and entered a four-digit code on the keypad. The box beeped once, and a small red light blazed to life on the side of it.

"If those things *can* use the lifts, at least that's one less for them," she said.

Rodney nodded, then turned his attention back to Jack. "Anyway, it looks like we need to get you to a doc."

Jack shook his head. "Don't bother. Half of them are probably walking around with slit throats right now." He jerked his thumb toward the elevator. "Pretty sure that's Doctor Landa back there, now that you mention it."

"I'm sure at least a couple of docs are on the medical or biology levels," Rodney said. "And if your leg is as bad as you say it is—"

"Didn't you hear me, goddamnit?" Jack spat. "Trying to find a doctor is a waste of fucking time!

"So what, then? You want us to just leave your ass here for them?"

"You might as well. It's not like we've got anywhere to run."

"If you don't want to try and get to a doc, then we need to secure this level," Rodney said.

Jack chuckled. "What good will that do?"

"Buy us time. If we can keep those things from getting to this floor, then we can try to figure out what to do next."

"What about any other people still alive? What about Wilson? We'll be locking them out, too," Collette said.

"We need a safe place to bring anybody alive, right? We'll secure this level and then try to find everyone else."

Collette thought for a moment. "There are six lifts that run to this floor, right?"

"Yeah. And the stairs."

"So we lock the lifts, and then we lock the staircase door. If Wilson lucks out and tries to get here by the stairs, all he has to do is unlock the door with his card. If we get in touch with him somehow, we can send him here."

"We can only lock the lifts if they're on the same floor we're on," Rodney reminded her. "If any of them are on the lifts, we'll be calling them to us."

"I know. But we can't leave the elevators running if those things can use them, right?"

Rodney nodded.

"Once we get this level secure," Collette continued, "I'm going to try and find him."

"You in love with the boss or something?" Jack asked. "You're gonna risk dying to try and find him on this big-ass ship?"

Collette shot an annoyed glance toward him. "I'm—"

"Let's worry about the elevators for now," Rodney interrupted.

"Before you start all that," Jack said, "how about taking me to the office so I can fix my leg up?"

"I thought it was pointless," Collette snapped.

"Running through the ship trying to find a doctor is pointless. Me grabbing a med-kit and taking care of this bite isn't. This tourniquet slowed down the bleeding, but it damn sure didn't stop it. And besides that, it hurts like a motherfucker."

"But we're right here, damn it," Collette said, gesturing toward the elevator they had yet to lock down.

"I'm worthless right now. I need to get fixed up. Just help me to the office, and then you can deal with it. What's five minutes?"

"Could be a lot, with these things."

"Please."

"Fine," Rodney said. "But you better walk fast: I want to lock down this level quick."

Chapter 20

Sutter glanced over his shoulder and smiled at the eleven men and women following him up the corridor. They'd done well thus far, and the Great One would be pleased.

They were The Chosen—brothers and sisters born anew by a God. All of them washed in the blood of those sacrificed in His honor.

No one spoke as they approached the door to Biology Lab 1; they had no need to. They each knew what the Great One desired, and to speak of it was pointless.

From the Great One, Sutter knew that The Chosen were still missing two of their brethren. Sutter didn't know who it was that had yet to join their ranks, but he thought it odd anyone would refuse or resist such an honor. Those who had yet to join with them had missed the first Cleansing, and they would now fail to be a part of the second. Sutter pitied them. To do the Great One's bidding was a blessing, and the rewards would be wondrous.

That pity was matched by a slight twinge of envy for the other Chosen. Like the other Chosen, Sutter had heard the Great One's call for them to join together and carry out The Cleansing. But he had been unable to do so because of the heathen bastard of a security chief. He'd been locked away in the holding cells while the others had carried out the first act of Cleansing. Lorenzo had told him about their systematic slaughter of the crew members, of how most had been sleeping as their throats were slit. Of how the ones who were awake put up great struggles but were outmatched by The Chosen. The killing had taken much time but had gone smoothly. Those who weren't in their living quarters when The Cleansing began would be dealt with soon enough, either by The Chosen themselves or by those the Great One would breathe new life into.

This second Cleansing would not be as great or as meaningful as the one he had missed, but Sutter was nonetheless grateful to be a part of it. And besides, he took great comfort in the knowledge he was the firstborn of the Great One. He had heralded His coming, and he would be forever held in higher regard than his brothers and sisters, no matter his part in the first Cleansing. He heard the Great One's voice incessantly, heard and understood the hushed whispers of all those Chosen who had come before him, Chosen who had given themselves eons ago, on distant planets that Sutter's mind could barely begin to fathom. He felt the love and purity the Great One held, and felt all of Its desires. It was a connection the others did not feel as strongly. The Great One spoke to them as it did to Sutter, but for all those who had not been called on, God would speak through Sutter and Sutter alone.

He was the Firstborn. The Prophet.

Reaching the lab door, Sarah stepped to the front of the group and slid her access card through the door control. The group entered the biology lab and walked to the center of the room, gazing around at the failed experiments.

The lab was larger than most of the others on the ship, the containment rooms smaller and far more numerous. In the center of the room, the three largest glass cells held several animals—four baboons in one, six chimps in another. A group of six dogs of various breeds lay in the corner of the last room.

Biology Lab One was designated as mainly a holding room for the results of the cloning department, which operated next door in Bio-Lab Two. There were three other rooms filled with animals that had been brought from Earth, all waiting their turn to be used by the scientists for whatever purpose suited them. While standard cloning was a fairly simple task, the scientists recently began undertaking radical gene-splicing experiments. Sutter was unsure of just what they were attempting to achieve by mixing various creatures together, and he didn't care.

Dozens of smaller rooms lined the walls, filled with the various abominations the cloning techs had created. There were pitiful beasts with the basic shape of a dog but the long upper arms of a chimp, dragging themselves around their cages like a paraplegic without a wheelchair. A half-dozen large, hairless primates that looked much like men, albeit with the malformed features of an ape or baboon, sat in individual cells, staring out at The Chosen with unblinking eyes.

Dozens of limbless larvae-like things with human faces or the snout of a dog floated in small aquarium-sized tanks. Something that reminded Sutter of a pig covered with thick fur paced back and forth in a larger containment room. A massive pink tumor with the vague features of a human face slid over the floor beneath it, looking like some half-formed Siamese twin. Smaller creatures that resembled nothing Sutter had ever seen were everywhere—some alive and moving about, some dead and floating in fluid-filled rooms.

Sarah walked to a computer terminal along the back wall and pressed a sequence of buttons. That done, she moved to the containment room holding the baboons and flipped open a small flap to reveal a red button.

She pressed the button, and instantly, the baboons began to gnash their teeth and screech, jumping back and forth and slapping at the walls. The fervor lasted a few seconds; then, one by one, they fell to the floor like stones.

"Are they dead?" Sutter asked.

"Yes. The gas works quickly. It's a last resort in case an animal becomes too violent to work with anymore. I've already armed the gas in all the other rooms. We just need to activate each one."

The Chosen dispersed, each making their way to a containment room, flipping open the safety cover and pressing the kill switch. Like the baboons, the other animals broke into a short-lived panic before succumbing to the gas. It took several minutes until all the creatures were dead. Then The Chosen regrouped in the center of the room, surveying their handiwork as Sarah walked to a computer and used it to vent the gas from the rooms. A few moments passed before she opened the doors to all of the containment rooms. Then, she left the computer and rejoined her brethren.

"The Great One will be pleased," said one of the men.

"The Great One *is* pleased," responded Sutter.

All of The Chosen smiled as they left the lab in single file, heading for the next biology lab and the doomed creatures it held.

Chapter 21

"Damn it!" Wilson switched off his com-phone and thrust it into his pocket.

"Still nothing?" Lisa asked from beside him. As the two of them walked up the hallway to the nearest elevator, he had tried twice to reach someone on his phone.

"It's out. First, the goddamn security cameras, and now the phones."

"The camera in the lab went out last night, too."

"Doesn't change the plan. My men will be on the residence levels when we get there. I'll talk to them then."

Lisa knew that Wilson wasn't telling her everything. She'd asked him several questions about what was happening since they'd left the security office, and he had thus far failed to give her a straight answer. Not that she could blame him; she knew she had been on the verge of losing her cool when she'd first barged into the security room, and he was most likely trying his best not to push her back into a panic.

She stopped her advance up the hallway, standing and watching as Wilson also stopped and turned to face her.

"What is it?"

"I want to know what's going on. *Exactly* what's going on."

He only stared at her. She could tell he was trying to find a way to get out of answering.

"I've got a right to know, and I'm not moving until you tell me. I know I was freaking out when I first found you, but I've pulled my shit together."

"It isn't good—"

"I figured that out for myself. But I want to know the whole story. I promise I can handle it. I grew up hard, goddamn it. I worked damned hard to get where I am, and I've seen a lot of bad things along the way.

"You're not telling me what's happening because you think I'm going to lose it. I understand that. But if it's as bad as I think it is—and judging from the way you've been acting, it is—then I need to know now so I'm ready for whatever it is if we run into it."

Wilson was silent for a moment, then nodded. "All right. But I'll tell you while we move. I need to get to my officers."

"Fair enough."

They resumed their trek up the hallway, Wilson telling Lisa all he had seen so far.

She listened without interrupting, processing everything that he told her. It was bad, just as she'd thought. Worse than she'd expected, actually. It seemed far-fetched, insane even.

But it was all true. As impossible as it sounded, she knew Wilson had no need to invent such a terrible story. She'd demanded the truth, and now she was getting it.

When he finished, she said, "So you think that thing is the cause of all of it?"

"Yeah. Driving Sutter and Roger crazy, bringing the dead back to life, the cameras and the phones shutting down—everything. That's why we've got to get it the hell off the ship."

"With the captain's card."

"Exactly."

"What about the things you locked up with him?"

Wilson shook his head. "I'll have to deal with them when I get there."

They rounded a corner, and a pair of elevators fell into view fifty feet from them, at the end of the hallway. Before they'd managed two steps, the elevator door began to slide open.

Lisa loosed a cry as Wilson grabbed her by the shoulder and pulled her back around the corner before the doors opened completely.

"Wait," he hissed.

Lisa watched as he peered around the corner, allowing only the slightest portion of his head to protrude into view. He looked for only a second, then pulled his head back behind the wall.

Lisa questioned him with her eyes, and he shook his head in response. Annoyance surged through her. He'd already told her what was happening. Now she had a chance to see for herself, and she was damn well going to take it. She stepped around him, lightly pushing his shoulder until he moved over and let her take his place.

She mimicked his actions, peeking down the hallway while carefully exposing a minimal amount of herself.

Two of the things were thirty feet away, walking up the center of the hallway. The nude one was hideous; a large cavity had been torn into its stomach and its contents emptied out. Its face was masked with blood, and its dead, glazed eyes stared down the hallway. Lisa recognized its companion thanks to her red hair and black outfit: Susanna Tucker, the head chef of her favorite restaurant on board the DARC. The left half of the woman's face had been torn off, her jawbone and teeth exposed in a grotesque grin, but it was still unmistakably the same person who had so often prepared absolutely astounding French cuisine for Lisa.

Stifling a gasp of horror, she retreated behind the wall, crossing back over Wilson so he was closest to the approaching nightmares.

She wished she hadn't looked. Although she'd been told about them, no words could have prepared her for the sheer hellishness of the walking corpses. It wasn't the blood and gore that the things wore all over them; she'd dissected hundreds of animals throughout her career. It was the complete loss of humanity that disturbed her. These had been two people, one of whom she had known. Two people now reduced to walking husks, driven by some ungodly force to wander the dying ship with no purpose save for slaughtering anything not undead like them. Now, as these two evils steadily advanced toward them, Lisa wrestled with her panic.

She closed her eyes, willing her heart to stop its thunderous pounding, gripping her steel pipe so tightly her hands hurt. Seconds passed, seeming more like eons, and she finally opened her eyes to look at Wilson.

He wasn't eying her with a "told you so" expression like she'd expected. Instead, he was staring straight ahead at the wall on the opposite side of the corridor. For the first time since finding him in the security office, Lisa saw fear written on his face. But it was more than fear, she knew. Concern. Sadness.

Lisa recognized the look. She had seen it many times before as sirens cut through the night in the neighborhood of her youth—on the faces of mothers and brothers, sisters and lovers. On her own face, reflected in the hospital bathroom mirrors, as her aunt slowly slipped away. He was worried about someone. Someone he cared about.

His eyes met hers, and the expression disappeared. His face hardened again, resolve and confidence wiping away any other emotion. He pulled his repeater from its holster and held out his free hand toward her.

"Calm," he mouthed.

Wilson gave her no time to respond to him, stepping toward the hallway intersection and peering around the corner again.

He quickly jerked his head back, giving Lisa a confused look.

"They're gone."

"What?"

"Must have gone into one of the labs. We need to run. Now."

"But what if they come out?"

"I'll try to fight them off. But we have to go now, before the elevator leaves the floor. For all I know, those things are hunting for a fucking meal, and right now is our chance to get by them without a fight. Trust me, damn it, and just run!"

That said, he darted around the corner and broke into a mad dash toward the elevators. Lisa forced her legs into action and followed him down the hallway.

It seemed to be the longest run of her life. There were eight doors between them and the lifts, four on each side of the corridor. As she ran, she expected one of the corpses to leap out from a room and devour her.

She glanced over her shoulder as she fled, unable to shake the feeling Susanna's sneering remains were pursuing her.

But no door opened. They reached the end of the hallway, and Wilson opened the elevator. The two of them entered the lift and turned, staring back down the empty hallway until the door slid closed.

Wilson pushed the control button and sent the elevator into motion.

"They can use the fucking elevators?" Lisa asked.

"Yeah. The doors, too."

"How?"

"Couldn't tell you. Maybe that thing's controlling them; maybe they just remember how to do certain things. It doesn't really matter how. All that matters is that they can."

They fell silent, both of them pressed into the back corners of the elevator.

"How are you going to get to the captain?"

"I have no clue. Once I've got you secured, I'll meet up with my officers and figure it out. Hopefully, if we outnumber them, we can get the upper hand."

"That's it? Just charge in there and hope you kill them? What if you don't get the upper hand? Then what? Don't you have a better idea?"

"No, goddamn it! I don't!" Wilson snapped.

They stood silent, staring at one another.

"Sorry," Lisa said, holding her hands up apologetically.

Wilson didn't respond at first. When he did, his voice was calm. "You've got every right to question what I'm doing. You have to believe me. I'm trying to save the DARC and everyone on it, but this is some shit I've never been trained for. I have to do whatever seems right as I go. I've probably fucked up a couple of times already, but I'm doing the best I can."

"Okay." She nodded. "I'm sorry."

"Me, too."

Lisa's gaze drifted to the elevator buttons that lit up in turn as the lift passed upward through the DARC, toward the residence levels. Dread filled her stomach, as dark and profound as the black hole the ship was orbiting around.

Chapter 22

"We need to secure the lifts," Rodney said as he shifted his weight impatiently from side to side.

Jack sat behind a table in the security office, tending to his leg with the med-kit. "Then go, goddamn it. If you're in that big of a hurry, go fucking deal with it. I'll meet up with you when I'm done with my leg."

"We shouldn't split up," Collette said.

"I'm the one with a fucked-up leg here, not you two. How much help do you really think I'll be anyway?"

"He's right," Rodney said. "We're wasting time waiting on him. Even after he finishes, he'll slow us down."

Collette sighed. "All right. If you're sure."

"I am."

"Go," Jack said.

She nodded and headed for the door.

"Hold up," Rodney said. He hurried across the room to a locker in the back corner and slid his card through it. The door slid open, revealing a dozen riot batons. Collette smiled. She'd forgotten the weapons were even there—they were backup weapons for emergency use and close-quarters incidents. To her knowledge, nobody had ever utilized the batons on any DARC mission, and she had only heard them mentioned years ago when she'd undergone her training.

Rodney grabbed three and clipped one onto his belt. Then he returned to Collette, placing one on the table in front of Jack as he passed by.

He offered her one. "Just in case."

She took it. It was lighter than it looked, so much so that she doubted it would be useful.

"Don't let it fool you," Rodney said. "It's graphite and titanium alloy. You could bust concrete with one of these and not leave a scratch on the baton. There's a clip on the left of your belt that it fits."

"Thanks," she said as she attached the bludgeon to her hip.

They left the room without another word and rushed down the corridor, returning to the lifts where they'd found Jack.

"Ready?" Rodney asked as he prepared to press the call button.

"Yeah."

Collette watched the numbered lights above the elevator as it descended toward them. The doors of the adjacent lift were locked open, revealing the horror inside—a reminder of what they could be greeting when the elevator opened. She and Rodney stood ten feet from the door, their guns at the ready.

Despite the coolness of the hallway, sweat beaded her face. Her hand trembled slightly, and she tried to control it. She knew that the lift could open its doors and unleash more of the horrors she'd already seen, and her focus was on fighting them off. But a small part of her anxiety was locked on Wilson and his well-being. It was more than just her growing fondness for the man; his help here would be invaluable. His years of police work on Earth meant he was a more-than-capable security chief. After serving under him for two DARC missions, it was hard to imagine pulling through this calamity without his leadership.

She and Rodney had made it this far alone. And he, too, had been a cop back home, albeit not for as long as Wilson. But Rodney was fighting back his demons, and he could end up locked in a holding cell at any time.

And if that happened, it would leave her as the only healthy defense for the security level, with a crippled smart-ass as her backup.

She glanced at Rodney. "You all right?"

"I'm fine." His eyes never left the elevator, and he used his gun to gesture toward it. "Worry about the lift for now."

Her worry not assuaged in the least, Collette returned her attention to the lights as they counted down the three floors above, then stopped.

The doors opened, revealing an empty elevator. The two officers rushed to it, and Rodney used his card to lock it down.

The floor was splattered with blood, a series of streaks running through it lengthwise toward the door. A small chip of something lay in the middle of one of the lines. It took Collette only an instant to recognize it was a fingernail.

She shuddered. "Let's go."

He nodded, and they rushed down the hallway.

Out of breath, they reached the second pair of lifts. The right elevator was already making its way up through the ship.

"Press the button," Rodney said.

"You sure?"

"That's what we're doing, right? Either something called that lift or something is already in it."

"Or *somebody*," Collette said. "If somebody on a floor above us called it, then stopping it here is going to trap them up there."

"And if one of those things is riding inside, not stopping it here will let them spread through the ship. Press the button."

"Fine." Collette walked to the elevator, pressed the call button, and then backed away in horror. "Oh fuck."

The other elevator was moving now as well, dropping down from the upper levels.

She glanced toward Rodney as he took the riot baton out of its clip, holding his gun in one hand and the club in the other.

Collette's breath caught in her throat as the left elevator finished its descent, coming to a stop in front of them.

The door slid open, and she scarcely had time to count before three bloodied figures charged toward her.

She fired three shots from her repeater, and a woman in a maintenance uniform dropped to her knees, twitching.

At the same time, Rodney took a quick step forward and swung his baton toward the closest attacker. The weapon slammed into the side of the man's head, and he collapsed to the floor.

As the woman fought to rise back to her feet, Collette squeezed off two more shots, both of which missed the third corpse as it leaped over Rodney's victim and crashed into the security officer. Rodney stumbled backward from the impact but managed to keep his footing as the nightmare clung to his shoulders and tried to force its face close enough to bite the big man's throat.

Her attention drawn to the struggle, Collette barely heard the woman she had just shot dart toward her. She whirled around to face the oncoming corpse but was too late. The hideous woman collided with her and tackled her to the floor, her head slamming into the cold steel.

The impact sent a bright light flashing through her mind, and Collette could hardly focus her thoughts through the pain. Her vision blurred, but she could make out gnashing teeth trying to press their way toward her. She instinctively threw up her hands and pressed back against the woman's face, trying to wrestle her way out from beneath her attacker as she did. All of her movements felt sluggish, as if she were underwater. The woman was stronger than she was, and even dazed, Collette knew she couldn't fight her off for long.

Sudden pain seared through her hand. So intense that it somehow brought her mind back from the haze it was trapped in. Collette's vision pulled into focus just in time to see the corpse finish ripping her pinky and ring finger from her left hand and sucking them into her mouth, chewing feverishly. Her blood gushed from the wound, splashing onto her face and into her eyes, blinding her.

She struggled for a moment until a loud crack resounded in the hallway, metallic within the close confines of the corridor. The weight of the cannibalistic woman was gone. She sat up and scooted backward, using the heel of her good hand to try and wipe the blood from her eyes.

Collette's attacker tried to rise to her feet. Rodney stood over her with his baton extended in front of him. He brought the club down onto the woman's head, sending another wet crack echoing down the hallway. The woman collapsed face down on the floor and lay unmoving, but Rodney slammed the weapon into the back of her head twice more, splitting it like a rotted melon, splattering the floor with coagulated blood and gray matter.

A few feet away, slumped against the corridor wall, lay the corpse that had leaped onto Rodney, its head a similarly disgusting mess.

Choking back the urge to vomit, Collette turned her attention to her wounded hand. The two fingers had been bitten off at the lower knuckle; a steady stream of blood spilled from the stumps and pooled in her lap. She clutched the wound with her right hand, using the palm to apply pressure to stem the bleeding.

"Shit," Rodney said.

Collette looked up to see the big man looming over her, his eyes wide and staring at her hand.

"We've gotta get you back to the office, to a med-kit."

"What about the elevators?"

"If we don't stop the bleeding, you'll die before we can deal with them. Can you walk?"

She nodded. "At least take care of that one."

Rodney glanced over his shoulder at the elevator that had unleashed their attackers "All right."

Navigating past the twice-killed corpses, Rodney hurried to the control box and locked the lift.

Returning to Collette, he hooked his hands beneath her armpits and pulled her into a standing position.

"The other one went past us, didn't it?" Collette asked.

"Yeah. It stopped on the upper residence level."

"What if it comes back full of those things?"

"I don't know. But you can't fight them like this. Come on."

The return to the security office seemed to take an eternity. Jack sat across the room, his leg wrapped in gauze and propped up on a second chair. On the table beside him sat an open med-kit, a syringe, and a couple of small glass bottles alongside it. His repeater pistol was in hand, pointed toward the doorway, but once he recognized his fellow officers, he lowered the weapon.

"You scared the shit out of me."

Without responding, Rodney helped Collette into a chair and hurried to the storage locker, returning with a fresh med-kit

"What the hell happened?"

"What do you think?" Rodney said, rifling through the med-kit and withdrawing what he needed. He placed each item on the table beside Collette as he found it: two needles, three small bottles of liquid, a bottle of alcohol, a package of Wound Seal, and a roll of gauze.

Collette watched as he readied everything, still clutching her hand. Blood saturated her uniform. It spilled out onto the floor at her feet and formed a steadily widening pool. The pain had turned to a dull, steady throbbing instead of the disorienting, burning agony like when it first happened. She wasn't sure if it was her mind adjusting to the wound or if she was beginning to suffer mentally from the loss of blood.

"You ready?" Rodney asked, filling the needle from one of the bottles.

"Yeah."

"Let's see it, then."

Collette placed her hands on the table, steeled herself, and removed her right hand. Some of the blood had coagulated into a thick paste, but crimson still seeped from the wounds.

Rodney held her wrist and plunged the needle into her hand, in the space between the two mutilated stumps. Almost instantly, the pain abated.

Working with skill, he poured most of the alcohol onto the wound, then opened the Wound Seal. It was a paste-like substance, yellow in color, and reminded Collette of petroleum jelly. Rodney smeared the ointment across each knuckle, coating them with a thick layer of the stuff. The Wound Seal began to harden.

He filled a syringe from the second bottle and injected it in the same spot as the first dose, and then set about wrapping the stumps with gauze.

With the wound dealt with, he took the remaining needle and filled it from the final bottle.

"This is the plasma/platelet/adrenaline mix," he said as he squatted beside her. He slid the needle into her bicep and injected the liquid.

All security officers had to undertake emergency medical classes before being hired, something for which Collette was now grateful. Serious wounds happened occasionally, usually accidents with the heavier equipment on board the ship, but there always seemed to be a doctor close by to contend with the injuries. She'd seen the PPA mix injected into someone before but had never imagined she'd be on the receiving end of it.

It was designed to combat blood loss by coaxing the body into producing blood more rapidly, and while she wasn't sure of all of the science behind it, the moment Rodney injected it into her, Collette was glad it had been created.

The adrenaline was a wave washing over her, moving up from her bicep and enveloping her body. Her heart thudded as if trying to burst from her chest, and her mind snapped back into focus, clear and sharp. Despite the pounding in her chest (or perhaps because of it), she felt renewed.

She sat still and silent, her eyes closed as she let herself grow accustomed to the adrenaline raging through her veins. Her entire body trembled, and her skin tingled. Euphoria overtook her, easing her concerns about the terror spreading through the ship. She was still well aware of the problems confronting them, and still very scared of what might happen, but she wasn't on the verge of panic by any means at all. Collette understood why there was a burgeoning black market for the stuff back on Earth.

"You look better already," Rodney said.

"Yeah," Jack said from across the room. "Not as pale. Shit works miracles, huh?"

She opened her eyes and took a deep breath. "Just give me a minute, and I'll be good enough to head back to the lifts with you."

"I don't know if that's a good idea," Rodney said.

"I'll be fine. We've got to do it, and I'll be damned if I let you do it alone. Just let me get used to this, and we can go."

Rodney glanced over his shoulder at Jack. "What about you?"

Jack shrugged. "Drugs took care of the pain, same as her. Blood loss, too, I guess. But my leg's pretty goddamn numb right now. I doubt I can walk all that good on it, to be honest. If one of those things comes at us, all I'll be is an easy meal for them."

"Well… Can you do anything helpful, or are you just going to sit here and hope shit gets better?"

Jack chuckled. "I told you, man. Shit ain't going to get better. But I guess I can try to get these monitors working again. I used to fiddle around with tech stuff in my free time back on Earth."

"You think you can really get them working?"

"Probably not. But I'll at least give it a shot."

"Fine, then. Collette, when you're ready, let me know."

A few moments passed in silence as Collette collected her thoughts. Jack pulled a chair to the wall of empty screens and began to examine them one by one. Rodney stood like a sentry in the open doorway, watching the empty corridor.

Collette rose to her feet. "Let's go."

Rodney eyed her. "You sure you're ready?"

"As I'll ever be, considering the fucking circumstances." She held up her mauled hand and smiled. It was true; she felt pretty good thanks to the PPA shot.

"All right, then."

The two of them stepped into the hall and began the trip back to the elevators, following the trail of blood that Collette had spilled on her way to the office.

Chapter 23

The elevator door slid open and revealed Hell. Turner lay on the floor a few feet in front of the lift, his abdomen a pit of shredded gore. His throat had been ripped open, and his left arm was gone. Looking down the corridor past Turner, Wilson could see two more of his officers lying motionless on the floor. Both had been torn apart and devoured by the living corpses.

Wilson pressed himself against the side of the elevator and thumbed the "close door" button. Opposite him, Lisa mimicked his actions, with her back against the side of the elevator, just out of the open doorway. She was holding her weapon like a baseball bat, ready to swing it at whatever passed into the lift.

Her eyes widened as the sound of bare feet slapping against the bloody floor grew closer to the elevator. Wilson held a finger to his pursed lips and raised his repeater, careful not to let it fall into view of the hallway.

The door slid closed before the approaching nightmare reached them, and Wilson pushed the button for the security level. The elevator lurched into motion.

"Everyone's dead," Lisa whispered.

"We don't know that."

"You saw that. And you're not bothering to take us up to the other residence levels. You know as well as I do, everyone else is dead."

Wilson stared at her. "We're going back to the security office because that's the safest place for you right now."

"A few minutes ago, you said the safest place was in lockdown in my quarters."

"I know. Obviously, I was wrong."

"Stop being so fucking calm!" Lisa screamed. "Those things are everywhere! For all we know, we're the only people left alive on the whole fucking ship! And you're talking to me like everything's fine!"

"We have to stay calm. That's the only chance we've got to survive this."

Tears welled up in her eyes, and Wilson could see that she was fighting to hold them back. "How the hell are we going to survive?"

"I don't know," Wilson whispered.

He thought of Collette and hoped she was alive somehow. He'd most likely doomed her and Rodney by sending them to the morgue.

The remainder of the elevator ride passed in silence, and Wilson used the time to consider his few options. The situation was out of his control; his hopes of containing the outbreak of murder and mayhem, of living corpses trying to overtake the ship, had vanished. He had no way of knowing just how many of the ship's occupants had been killed by now, but he guessed it was probably most of them. And every dead person on board was likely to rise up and become one of those abominations.

The security level was the best place for them to go. It would most likely be empty, and it would be simple enough to lock down the elevators and stairwells leading to it. He could secure the floor so that Lisa would be safe and then try and figure out the best way to retrieve Carlson's keycard.

The elevator slowed and stopped, and Wilson aimed his gun toward the door. A breath, and it slid open.

Rodney and Collette stood twenty feet from the elevator, Collette with her repeater pistol leveled at Wilson, Rodney wielding one of the riot batons they kept in the office. Scattered across the blood-stained floor were three bodies.

Wilson lowered his weapon. "Holy fucking shit."

Collette grinned. "Wilson!"

He stepped off the lift, glancing over his shoulder to make sure Lisa followed him. Her crying had stopped, and she seemed to have pulled herself together again. She walked behind Wilson, staring at the corpses on the floor with a blank expression.

"The ship's gone to hell," Rodney said as Wilson and Lisa navigated their way past the dead bodies.

"I know. I just came from the residence levels. It's swarming with those things."

"Jack said everyone up there is dead. Somebody killed them in their sleep. I think we're all that's left of the security crew." Rodney's voice was quiet, and he stared at the floor as he spoke.

"Where's Jack?" Wilson asked.

"Trying to get the monitors in the office working again. They're shot to shit."

Wilson nodded and turned his attention to Collette. Knowing she was alive made him feel slightly better. It gave him a bit of hope that at least someone—someone he cared about—had managed to survive.

"What happened to you?" Wilson asked as he stared at her bandaged hand. "You look like shit."

"One of those fucking things took off two of my fingers."

"Goddamn."

"I'm all right now. That PPA shit is a miracle, even if I do feel wired as hell." She looked at him, their eyes locking. "I'm really glad to see you."

He nodded. "Me, too."

"Sutter's gone."

"I know. Don't worry about it. He's probably dead by now." He looked at Lisa, standing beside him in silence. "You know Lisa, right?"

"Yeah," Collette said. "I talked to her this morning."

"I don't think I've met her," Rodney said.

Lisa forced a smile. "Lisa Michaels. Biology department."

"I'm Rodney. Good to meet you, all things considered."

"Yeah."

"So what now, Boss?" Rodney asked.

Wilson glanced toward the elevators. "Looks like you guys had the same idea as me. We keep the lifts from running and secure this floor. When that's done, I've got to get back onto the captain's deck and get his keycard."

"Why?" Collette asked.

"To get that thing off the ship."

Collette and Rodney exchanged a glance between them. "You think it's what's causing all this?" Rodney asked.

"I just came from the lab it's in. I can't explain it, but that thing is…" Wilson tried to find a way to tell his friends what he had felt in the thing's presence.

"Evil?" Rodney finished for him.

"Yeah. Evil." Wilson studied Rodney and Collette as they shared a glance. "You have something to tell me?"

Rodney dropped his gaze to the floor and turned his back to Wilson. After a moment of silence, he walked to the elevator and used his keycard to lock it.

Wilson glanced at Collette and raised his eyebrows.

"Rodney…" Her voice was that of a mother or sibling trying to coax a youngster into telling a secret.

He turned back to Wilson and sighed. "There's… something that's been going on with me since that thing came on board."

Wilson listened as Rodney told him about the voices that had been tormenting him, and about his fear that he would eventually harm somebody because of them.

"How long since you heard them?"

"I don't know. Thirty minutes, maybe? I was hearing them when we found Jack on the lift. They haven't been loud—haven't shut down my mind like they did before. But when it's quiet, I can still hear them whispering to me."

"Whispering. I didn't expect that, but it kind of makes sense."

Rodney blinked, surprise smeared across his face. "What? How?"

"That thing hasn't left my mind since we found it. It's like an obsession or something. I've been wondering if anyone else was feeling anything, especially after you started acting weird once I started questioning Sutter."

"You've heard them, too?"

"No. But if you are, that might explain why Sutter—and whoever else is helping him kill people—snapped."

"The voices told them to?" Collette said. "That's an old line."

"Sounds like it's true this time."

"Why Rodney? Why aren't we all hearing voices?" Lisa asked.

"I'm still trying to figure that out," Wilson said.

"So, what do I do?" Rodney asked.

"That's up to you right now. I need your help, but if you think you're going to snap and try to feed us to those things the next time we run into them, then maybe we should lock you up. And we *are* going to run into them as soon as we head back up to the captain's deck."

The big man frowned, his focus darting around at his companions as he pondered his options.

"I'll be all right. I've controlled it this long, and I can't let you guys do this alone. If I start feeling like I'm losing it, I'll tell you, and we'll go straight to the cells. Like I told Collette: just try to keep an eye on me. If I look like I'm losing it, don't hesitate for a second. Zap my ass with a repeater and take me down."

"All right, then. We've got four more elevators to deal with, right?" Wilson said.

"Two more. We already dealt with the two on the opposite end of this hall. We just have to take care of the two freight elevators and the stairways, and we'll have it all buttoned up," Collette said.

"Let's get on it, then," Wilson said. "We'll lock it all down, then figure out the best way to get back to the C-deck."

Rodney looked at Lisa. "What about you? Do you want to wait in the office or—"

"I'd rather just stay with you guys. Safety in numbers, you know?"

"Let's go, then," Wilson said.

"Hold up, boss," Rodney said. "Collette, why don't you let him have your baton? With that hand, you'll be better off just using your repeater, and he can hit those bastards a lot harder than you can."

Collette nodded. "Here, Wilson." She held out the baton to him, and he took it.

"These things work better than you'd think," Rodney said, gesturing to the club. "Collette can slow them down with her gun. Then we bash their fucking heads in."

Chapter 24

The Chosen filed into the elevator in silence, the second Cleansing complete. They had visited each biology lab and used the gas to usher the animals into the void. Sutter knew that, inside the labs, the bodies of the fallen creatures were being reborn as the Great One breathed new life into them. He wished he could watch the miracle but knew it was far too dangerous for him. Once reborn, the Great One would have no control over his children and their unceasing hunger. It was the gift and curse of free will that came with all life.

For the same reason, they had to tread cautiously now, despite their eagerness to be with the Great One. With the Cleansing completed, He beckoned them. Each of the Chosen felt Him calling for them to assemble before Him. But His Reborn scurried throughout the ship, driven by divine hunger, unfaltering in their hunt. The Risen would show no quarter to any mere human, Chosen or not.

It was a dangerous pilgrimage, but one that filled Sutter with excitement. The others shared his anticipation; the air in the elevator was electric.

The doors slid open, revealing a cold, empty corridor that stretched for two hundred feet before splitting into a four-way intersection. Lorenzo started to step off the elevator, but Sutter held a hand up, halting him.

"Listen."

Two distinct sets of steady footsteps echoed through the hallway, distant but growing closer.

"The Reborn," Sarah whispered.

The rest of the Chosen nodded. Sutter knew how they felt. It was awe-inspiring to be so near to one of the Great One's creations, no matter how deadly the Reborn were.

"Quietly now, Brothers," Sutter whispered as he led the group off the lift.

They stepped lightly, listening to the sounds of the Reborn wandering somewhere ahead of them. The group had walked a hundred feet down the hallway when the hiss of a door opening sounded behind them, followed by the thundering of feet.

Sutter turned and saw a woman dressed in a chef's smock charging toward them in a snarling fury. The Chosen broke into a run, but it was too late. The creature slammed into the rearmost member of their group—a Frenchman named Georges Le'don.

She wrapped her arms and legs around him in a grotesque piggyback ride and bit into his neck, tearing a mouthful of flesh from it. Blood gushed from the wound, and he collapsed, screaming, under the weight of the Reborn.

Sutter reached the intersection and turned left, another Reborn racing down the hallway to his right. He ran the last fifty feet to Biology Lab Five and pressed the control switch.

The door slid open, and Sutter ran inside, the others following him. He pressed the control switch, and the door began to slide shut just as their pursuer reached them, its bare feet sliding across the floor as it turned to face them. With a primal scream, it dove forward but collided with the closing door and fell back into the hallway.

Lorenzo slid the keycard he'd taken off the dead security officer through the door control, locking it.

Sutter turned toward the center of the room.

The Great One sat in the containment room, glory incarnate. Sutter dropped to his knees, unable to pull his eyes away from the god. It had grown so much more magnificent since he'd first seen it. It pulsated like a giant heart, and Sutter could feel each beat of it inside his very soul.

The rest of the Chosen knelt before their god, bowing their heads in silence and listening as the Great One whispered his desires to them, filling them with his love and glory.

Chapter 25

Roger pulled himself to his hiding place in a fog of pain, his jaw mangled and throbbing from Lisa's attack. Wrapping his shirt around his face to keep the blood from leaving a trail for anyone to follow, he had concealed himself from sight behind a large computer tower. Nausea and vertigo swept over him, and within seconds, sleep found him.

His dreams were of God. It told him it was the god of all gods: the Great One. It sat in darkness, beckoning him. It had a far greater purpose for Roger than anyone else on the ship. It told him some of its secrets and that all would be revealed to him soon. He alone was unique from the others the Great One had chosen, and his path to salvation and rebirth would be far different from theirs. He wasn't to share the Great One with them, for he would be separate from them. They were merely Chosen. He was to be The Blessed. It whispered promises of love, glory, and righteous truth to him, and he knew that his place in the Great One's plan was far more important and meaningful than anything he'd ever dreamed of being a part of.

The frenzied entry of a dozen people woke Roger, snatching him out of his dreams like a baby ripped from the womb.

His face throbbing, he watched as the group fell to their knees in front of the containment room. The whispers from his dream still wove their way through his mind, instructing him, and he heeded their call, wrestling himself to his feet.

Dizzy, his vision blurred from Lisa's attack, Roger stumbled from the shadows and slowly made his way to the cluster of people, standing on unsteady legs before them. All of them looked up to him in silence.

Roger held out his hand to Lorenzo, who pressed the stolen key-card firmly into Roger's palm and then lowered his head again.

Turning his back to The Chosen, Roger approached the containment room with his attention fixed on the Great One. Reaching the glass wall, he slid the card through the door control and disengaged the lock. He pressed the control switch, watching as the barrier between him and God slid open, and the ancient scent of divinity filled the room.

There was a long, immaculate silence, the only movement that of the Great One's pulsating body and segmented tube swaying above it. A delicate sound similar to rice paper rustling crept out of the containment room as the forest of crimson bristles vibrated like wheat in the wind.

A flash of movement shot out of the containment room so quickly that Roger didn't see what it was until it slammed into his face, forcing its way into his mangled mouth and burrowing down his throat.

The tube-like appendage writhed and squirmed, joining Roger to the Great One like an infant to its mother. He collapsed onto his back and watched as the pale umbilical cord darkened, starting near the Great One and slowly turning black along its length, pulsing as some manner of sustenance pumped through it.

Euphoria gripped him as the blessings of the Great One welcomed him into paradise. A warmth spread through his guts, trickling through his body and melting away all of his worries and pain, physical and otherwise. His shattered jaw no longer throbbed; his desires were all sated.

He was a true servant of the Great One now—a living temple and testament to the power of God.

Blessed.

PART 4

Chapter 1

Sutter watched as Roger convulsed, the Great One's tube quivering as it finished with the man and withdrew itself from his throat, receding back into the wondrous body it was attached to.

Roger lay still for a while, then stirred, rolling onto his stomach and pushing himself to his feet. He turned and faced The Chosen, thick black fluid dripping from the corner of his disfigured mouth, mixing with the coagulated blood from his earlier wound.

Sutter forced himself to smile and nod in respect toward Roger, masking his disdain. He didn't deserve such a blessing.

Roger returned the smile through his broken jaw, the cracked teeth and black liquid giving him a grotesque quality.

"I've much work to do, brothers and sisters," Roger said. The words gurgled, forcing dark bubbles to froth from his lips as he spoke. He left the room without another word, walking like a man reborn and in love with the universe.

Sutter watched as he left the room, then he turned his attention back to the newly freed god. It sat just as before, unmoving save for a steady pulsing in its center mass and the barely noticeable twitching of its crimson bristles.

None of The Chosen moved for a long while. They either stared at the Great One or continued to kneel with bowed heads.

Finally, Lorenzo rose and approached the containment room, rifling through his pockets as he did. He pulled a pair of eyeballs from his pocket, strands of nerves and tissue dangling from them, and placed them at the doorway of the room. Lorenzo bowed to the god.

"An offering, oh Lord," he said with a trembling voice, then retreated to his place amongst the Chosen.

Sutter glanced at Lorenzo and saw disappointment on his face. It didn't surprise him at all. He'd tried to tell Lorenzo the Great One had little want or need for such petty things when Lorenzo had freed him from the holding cells and   shown him the eyes. Lorenzo had almost grown violent, accusing Sutter of trying to convince him not to present the gift to their god so that he could curry more favor. It had taken Sutter several minutes to calm the man down. He'd dropped the matter thereafter but had expected the result Lorenzo had just received—apathy from the Great One toward the offering.

He knew all of the Chosen felt the voice of their god coursing through every fiber of their being, but that not all felt it as strongly as he did. The Great One had his favored children.

While not even Sutter knew much of God's grand design or plans, it seemed Lorenzo knew far less.

Sutter smiled at Lorenzo's dismay. It was further proof that he was held in high regard by the Great One.

As if reading his thoughts, the primeval voice swelled up in his mind again, sweeping him away from his thoughts and enlightening him as to more of the Great One's plans.

Soon, very soon, they would all know the blessings of God.

Chapter 2

They'd secured the final elevators without incident, locked both stairwell doors, and returned to the security office to check on Jack's progress with the monitors. They also wanted to finalize their plan for returning to the captain's deck.

"How many are locked up there?" Collette said.

None had bothered to sit down. They clustered near the door, except for Jack.

"Five counting the captain, as far as I know," Wilson replied.

"And one of them's blind?" Rodney said. "Those aren't *horrible* odds. Hell, me and Collette took out three of them ourselves."

"We got lucky, Rodney," Collette said. "I lost my fingers, remember? Those things are fast and strong and hard as hell to stop. Plus, two of us are injured, Lisa is a biologist, not a security officer, and—no offense— you're hearing voices telling you to join that thing's side. That sounds like shit odds to me."

"Yeah," Wilson said. "You guys did get lucky. Besides, it's not just the five of them on the deck that bothers me. I'm just as worried about the trip up there."

Wilson looked across the room to Jack, who was still crouched behind the monitors, fiddling with something on the back of one. "No luck, then?"

"None. I think maybe the cameras short-circuited."

"And the com-phones, too?" Collette asked.

"It's that thing," Lisa said quietly. "Shutting down what it wants to."

The group fell silent.

After a moment, Collette said, "Are you sure it's that thing, Wilson? I mean, heading to the captain's deck, fighting off those corpses to take the card, and then going all the way back down into the lab is a lot of risk to go through if it isn't."

"You haven't been around it. Trust me—it's that thing."

"Why just the phones and cameras? Why not all the door locks, or the lights, or the air supply? Why is it talking to Rodney and Roger and Sutter and not me?"

"I don't know," Wilson admitted. "All I know is that the goddamn thing is evil."

Rodney nodded. "Wilson's right. Just the way I've been feeling should be enough proof. What else *could* it be?"

"So what is it, exactly?" Jack asked.

"Lisa? You're the scientist here." Wilson said.

Lisa looked at the others before answering. "I don't know what the hell it is. Roger seemed to think it was God—"

"That's what Sutter called it, too," Collette said.

Lisa continued. "It's obviously a living creature, but like nothing we've ever seen. Gruber believed the hardened form we found it in was like a cocoon or an egg, and once it was brought on board, it began to evolve according to its environment."

"It's an alien, then. So how could it be doing everything you guys think it's doing?" Collette asked.

"I don't know. Maybe it converses through some kind of telepathy or with some kind of sound waves that we don't understand. That may be why it's driving some of the crew crazy, making them deify it and kill in its name.

"The reanimated corpses… My guess would be some kind of airborne virus, but it's been locked in an airtight containment room since we brought it on board. Maybe it stimulates the electrical synapses in the dead brain the same way it gets into living crew members' heads. That may explain why head trauma kills them.

"The short-circuited security screens and com-phones could be because of some kind of ultra-frequency waves we've never encountered. It may be broadcasting its will throughout the ship, like a radio signal."

"But why just the phones and security screens? Why not the doors or lights?" Collette asked.

Wilson spoke up. "The phones and the screens operate on a wireless digital signal. All the door locks, the lights, and the lifts are hardwired into the ship. Maybe it's interfering with the wireless signals."

Lisa nodded. "That makes sense. I'm just giving you one idea, anyway. I could be completely wrong. For all I know, Roger's right and the damn thing is God."

"You don't really think that, do you?" Wilson asked.

"No. But it's as good a guess as any I've got. I don't know how old that thing is, what it's made from, what it's capable of—"

"Or how to kill it," Rodney finished for her.

"Or how to kill it," Lisa confirmed. "That's why Wilson's idea of activating the containment room purge control and shooting it back into space is our best option."

"What's to stop it from breaking out of that room, though?" Rodney asked.

"Triple-thick shatterproof glass with titanium fiber in it. It's nearly impossible to break. Of course, I don't know how strong that thing is. But Roger wanted me to let it out. And if Jim Sutter is as affected by it as Roger was, he probably wants to see it set free, too."

"Can they open the door?"

"Not without a level-four card or the password."

"All right." Collette sighed. "So let's go get the captain's card, and then get that thing the hell off the ship."

Jack limped from the screens and sat down at the nearest table. "I'll hold down the fort."

"I figured as much," Wilson said. "Collette, is your hand all right?

Should you stay here with him?"

"Hell no. I'm going with you guys."

"Lisa?"

"I'm not staying here."

Jack chuckled. "I'll be fine, boss. Sounds to me like my odds for survival are a little better here by my lonesome. If it comes down to it, I'll lock myself in one of the holding cells."

Wilson glared at Jack, then left the room, followed by his three companions.

"I've never liked that fucking guy," Collette said as the four of them made their way down the hallway. "He talks too much shit."

"He's a smart-ass, for sure," Wilson said. "But he's always done his job, until now, I guess. Besides, if he came with us, he'd only slow us down. He'd have a hell of a time on the stairs with that leg."

"Speaking of which," Rodney said. "You sure you don't want to use the elevators instead of the stairs?"

Wilson nodded. "I don't know how smart those things are. They may see the lights and know that the lift is moving. I'm already hoping like hell they haven't filled up the stairs. I don't want to have to worry about the elevators, too."

They walked in silence until Rodney asked, "So then… What's the plan when we get there, Boss?"

"From what I've seen, they'll charge straight at us, so we just have to be ready for that. Me and Rodney will try to take them out as they reach us. Collette, you try to slow them down with your repeater, and Lisa… I want you to hang back from us some. If any of us get into trouble, do what you did to Roger, only a hell of a lot harder."

Lisa glanced down at the pipe in her hand and nodded. "Okay."

When they reached the stairwell door, Wilson slid his card through the lock, and they all filed through; then they clustered tightly together on the landing. The door closed behind them, the sound echoing off the bare walls. Wilson slid his card through the door control and locked it.

He crossed the landing and peered over the railing, the sheer distance below them unnerving. The stairs saw little use. They were a safety precaution and an alternative to the lifts most on board ignored. Wilson knew a couple of the more health-conscious crew members tried to use them instead of the elevators. Aside from them, he doubted anyone on the DARC had ever set foot in the stairwell. He only did so because it was required as part of the twice-daily security checks.

Looking down the chasm at the center of the stairwell gave Wilson a perspective of how large and amazing DARC12 was. From the security office level, it was like looking hundreds of feet down a skyscraper's stairwell, and they were still several floors below the topmost one, where the captain's deck was located.

In single-file, Wilson led the group up toward the captain's deck.

They'd managed to make it up half the first flight of stairs before a door opened above them. The sound of footsteps rang out. Along with this came a strange sound—a whisper-quiet hiss, like something sliding across the floor. Grunts and soft snarls drifted down as the footsteps descended.

Wilson motioned for the others to stay put and walked the last few steps up to the landing. Rodney disregarded his order and joined Wilson. Below them, Collette readied her gun, pointing it where the base of the next flight of stairs joined the landing.

The noises grew louder, and within minutes their source fell into view. As soon as the two corpses rounded the bend in the stairs and caught sight of Rodney and Wilson, they let loose a pair of nightmarish screams and charged forward.

Wilson timed his swing perfectly, bringing his baton straight down from above his head and splitting open the skull of one of the creatures.

The remaining dead man leaped over the fallen body of its companion, diving head first for Wilson. The security chief sidestepped the attack, pressing his back against the stairwell wall. Missing its prey knocked the corpse off balance, and Rodney swung his weapon at the thing, connecting with the side of its face and sending it staggering toward the railing. He swung again, connecting solidly this time. The force of the impact sent the thing careening over the metal railing and plummeting down through the center of the stairwell. A distant thud drifted up the chamber, as it hit bottom.

In the silence that followed, a series of thumps replaced it. It sounded like something falling down the stairs. Something slid onto the landing above them, and then the thumps came again, accompanied by the same low snarling they were growing accustomed to.

Bloodstained hands came into view, reaching around the stairway and curling around a step. The creature slid into view and looked down at Wilson and Rodney. It was a corpse, lying on its stomach, torn in half just below its chest. A mess of gore trailed behind it as it pulled itself down the stairs.

Rodney met it before it reached their landing, crushing its head with a single swing of his weapon.

The stairwell plummeted back into silence as the group listened for another attack. When no new threats emerged, they made their way around the sickening corpses and continued up toward the captain's deck.

They passed through the door into the top level of the DARC, and it slid closed behind them.

Chapter 3

Roger walked up the stairs, his steps slow and deliberate. None of the elevators had responded to his calls, and he'd grown impatient. The Great One's needs were far too pressing to spend much time idle.

He remembered little of his past, and the bits he could recall seemed like a dream instead of a life lived. He knew who he was and who he'd been, but the details of his existence up until now were gone, and he didn't miss them in the least. All that mattered was serving the Great One.

There were still unfaithful people on board the DARC—ones who were resisting the Great One. Those who wanted to send God back into the black ether of space. It was obvious they had disabled the elevators somehow and were using the stairways to move about while trying to achieve their heretic goals. They would know Hell, and they would know it by his hand.

He reached the door to the biology and cloning labs level, stepped into the corridor, and walked down it without pause.

After reaching the first of the labs, he slid the door open and looked inside. Just as the Great One had said, the animals had been reborn. An ape thundered across the room toward him, followed by two more. There was no sign the animals had died, save for the clouded eyes and the blackening of their lips. The animals stopped five feet from him and regarded him with their dead gazes and their teeth bared menacingly. Thin ribbons of dark drool dangled from their lips.

He looked at them with indifference, then looked past them at the rest of the room. Limbless, pathetic beasts flopped across the floor toward him like fish out of water, snapping their jaws as they did. All around were reborn creatures, many of them bearing some hellish genetic deformity.

They all hurried toward Roger, then froze, staring at him as they realized their mutual God had blessed him. One by one, they passed out of the room and into the corridor beyond. His brothers had been given the task of ushering these creatures into the void but could not stay to help them spread through the ship. The hunger of the Reborn was too great. The blessing the Great One bestowed upon him was powerful beyond all measure, and the mere presence of it coursing through his body was enough to keep him safe amid the creatures.

He stood in the doorway and watched as all the animals exited. Then he joined them in the hallway. Already the beasts were dispersing, darting through the corridors in search of prey. Roger maneuvered through the slower ones, stepping over a legless thing that resembled a pig as he made his way to the next lab.

When he'd finished releasing the creatures from the labs, he walked through the hallway, now filled with the sounds of animals newly reborn, and went to the nearest stairway door.

He opened the door, then propped an arm against the wall for balance as he kicked the control box hard, knocking the casing from the wall and leaving the entire mechanism dangling from several colored wires. Roger grabbed the control box and ripped it free of the wires, then retraced his steps to the other stairwell door as several of the Great One's children poured through the entrance out onto the landing behind him, heading up and down the stairwell.

He repeated the process when he reached the other doorway, then made his way up the stairs to the next biology level.

The door slid open and a woman, about ten feet from Roger, whirled around to face him. Something had ripped out her throat, leaving a few strands of tendon dangling from the wound. She made a sound that might have been a snarl but came through her destroyed windpipe as a wheeze.

The woman charged toward him, gnashing her teeth. She stopped a few feet from him and stared.

Roger smiled as the Reborn recognized her creator's blessings within him. After a moment, the woman walked past him into the stairwell and disappeared down them.

He approached the next biology lab but stopped and cursed himself. He turned and dismantled the door control switch, ensuring the stairway door wouldn't close, then resumed his walk to the lab.

When he'd freed the animals contained within the room, he stood in the corridor for a moment, listening to the sounds of the Reborn beasts filling the stairwell. He hadn't realized just how many animals had been on board DARC12. The labs had held enough creatures to fill a large zoo. They'd been trapped, pitiful creatures. Soon, however, all the doors would be open, and the entirety of the DARC would be their playground. The dead, both animal and human, could spread through the ship's corridors like blood through the veins of some great beast.

With all of their safe havens eliminated, the last of the living who hadn't found God would soon fall to His glory.

Stepping past a wondrous, slithering thing that looked much like a four-foot-long maggot with a simian face and tiny malformed limbs, Roger began the climb up the stairs toward the next door.

Chapter 4

The door to the captain's deck was still locked. The four of them stood in front of it, breathing heavily and staring at the cold steel, readying themselves for what was behind it.

Although she was trim and always considered herself in shape, the somewhat sedentary life of a DARC scientist had taken its toll on Lisa. Her legs and lungs burned from climbing the stairs, and her heart thudded in her ears. Still, she was surprised she was ready for the door to be opened and whatever horrors lay beyond it.

She'd pulled herself back from the precipice of panic, finding the forgotten strength that had gotten her through her youth. As an atheist, the thought of death scared the hell out of her. To return to nothingness, to the ether that held her before she was born, was terrifying. But she wasn't willing to go quietly, and waiting for death was worse than embracing it.

She would die fighting—not sniveling and sobbing like a weak little girl.

Wilson whispered. "Are we ready?"

Lisa looked around as the rest of the group nodded. She glanced down at the steel pipe in her hand. It was heavy, hard to wield. She'd gotten lucky with Roger, but the things they were facing now were far more of a threat than an insane engineer.

As if reading her thoughts, Rodney leaned toward her and held out his repeater pistol. "Here. I like my club better, anyways."

She hesitated, then took the weapon. It gave off a click and a beep as she gripped it and she looked at Rodney questioningly.

"I turned off the safety already," Rodney's voice was gentle, like the understanding father she had never had but often dreamed of. "Just point and pull the trigger. Shoot the bastards as many times as you can. You aren't biolinked to it so it's going to switch from the lethal setting to maximum stun, but it should still slow them down enough to give us a chance."

"Thanks."

Wilson had moved to the door and stood with his hand at the control switch, watching her and Rodney.

Lisa took a few more deep breaths and nodded to Wilson. "Let's get it over with, then."

"Remember—me and Rodney head in first. Collette and Lisa, you two try to slow them down with the guns."

Nobody responded. Lisa stood staring at the door, her pulse racing so hard she could feel the veins in her arms throb.

"On three. One…two…three."

Wilson pushed the button, and the door slid open.

Rodney charged into the room, the bloodied baton propped on his shoulder like a baseball bat. Wilson was right behind him, with Collette following close behind. Gritting her teeth, Lisa ran into the room with them.

She didn't see any of the reanimated dead at first, only a cold and empty flight deck. Ahead of her, Wilson drew back with his baton and swung it at some unseen nightmare. She moved to her left and watched as one of the monsters dropped underneath Wilson's attack, still trying to grab the security chief with undead hands. He slammed his weapon into the corpse's head repeatedly; a grimace spread over his face as thick, co-agulated blood burst out of the creature's broken skull.

Another of the things charged toward Wilson, and he turned to meet it. Beside him, Rodney stood like a statue. His head was tilted, and his arms hung limply at his sides.

"Rodney!" Lisa yelled, but the big man didn't respond. She glanced toward Collette, who was firing her repeater as quickly as she could at another of the things. The corpse was on its knees, trying to rise back up, but her shots restrained it.

Beyond Rodney and Wilson, near the door of the captain's room, the eyeless woman Wilson had told them about ran toward the sounds of the fray, straight toward Rodney, screaming like a hell-born banshee as she did.

Lisa raised the repeater pistol and squeezed the trigger three times. Only one of the shots found its target, and a spasm ran through the sightless corpse's body, slowing it by a step or two.

Lisa ran forward and fired again, watching as three of her nine shots struck home. The electrical charges had more effect this time, and the woman's legs gave out beneath her. She dropped to the floor and twitched as the shocks coursed through her. Lisa kept squeezing the trigger, hitting the woman with every third or fourth shot.

Beside Rodney, the other corpse had reached Wilson. Somehow evading the bludgeon, it was now locked in a struggle with the security chief for the baton. Wilson lost his footing and fell to his side, the corpse slamming into the floor alongside him.

Lisa turned toward him and raised her repeater. Before she could fire the weapon at Wilson's attacker, a hand grabbed her wrist. She whirled around, expecting an undead monster, but instead found Rodney holding her in a death grip, his face emotionless.

"Rodney!" she cried out, her gaze darting to her side as the blinded corpse continued its advance toward them. Rodney raised the pipe above his head, his focus locked on Lisa.

The horror of what he was about to do hit Lisa like a bullet, and she instinctively raised her other hand and fired the repeater pistol into Rodney's chest.

The pipe dropped from Rodney's hand as he collapsed to the floor, releasing Lisa's wrist as he fell. She staggered back as his body convulsed with the electrical charge.

Wilson's cries for help cut through her shock, and Lisa turned back to him. Picking up the metal pipe, she slammed it into the creature's skull, eliciting a sickening crack and freeing globs of thick blood.

The dead man fell forward onto Wilson, and Lisa started to help roll it off of him when screaming erupted behind her. She turned around, gun raised, and began screaming herself.

The blinded corpse had found Rodney somehow. She lay alongside him, gripping him tightly, face buried in his stomach. The security officer lay motionless beneath her, a dark pool of blood gathering around them, widening by the second.

"Rodney!" Collette ran to her fallen friend, leaving the corpse she'd been holding at bay twitching on the floor.

Lisa couldn't move. She knew she needed to. She needed to help Rodney, no matter what he'd just tried to do, but she couldn't will her body to do it.

Beside her, Wilson pulled himself to his feet and charged toward Rodney, hitting the undead in the back of the head with his riot baton. The undead woman turned her head to face her assailant and snarled, a gush of blood and chewed flesh seeping out of her mouth. Wilson took the opportunity to hit her again, his weapon slamming into her face and knocking her off Rodney.

Wilson followed the woman as she rolled, and he hit her a final time. Collette knelt beside Rodney, pressing her hands over his wounds to try and stop the blood flow. As she did, the corpse Collette had filled with re-peater rounds stood back up and charged toward them.

Lisa's body broke free from the paralysis, and she fired the repeater a dozen times, half of the shots connecting and sending the thing back to the floor. Wilson leaped past Rodney and Collette and attacked the fallen creature, messily splitting its skull open.

Collette's cries became the only sound in the room as she continued to apply pressure to the myriad injuries covering Rodney. There was little she could do. His stomach had been torn open in numerous places, the wounds seeping blood like a sieve. His breathing was slow, each breath marked by blood bubbling out of his mouth and nose.

Lisa fought back her tears. She had only just met the man, but he had seemed like a good person. She felt she was partially responsible for his impending death.

"Rodney," Collette said through her tears.

The dying man looked up at his friend, his lips working as if to speak. With a voice so strained it sounded as ancient as the stars, he gurgled, "It's all right, Collette."

She shook her head violently. "No."

"It is. Don't…worry."

"No."

A moment passed without words, and then Rodney's chest fell still.

"Collette," Wilson said softly, placing a hand on her shoulder. "I… don't know what to say right now."

"There's nothing to fucking say." Collette sobbed.

"I know you don't want to hear it, but we've still got problems. I don't see the captain here, which means he's still in his quarters."

She nodded.

"We need to get that card and get the hell out of here."

Another nod. "I know."

Wilson left her and Rodney and crossed the deck to the captain's quarters. Lisa followed him. They stood at the doorway, watching as Collette whispered something to Rodney's body. When her crying subsided and became less violent, she joined Lisa and Wilson at the door.

"All right," she said.

Wilson pressed the switch. Before the door had managed to open completely, Captain Carlson, clad in his bloody pajamas, charged out of it and tackled Wilson. The security chief tried to swing his weapon with one hand while gripping the captain around his throat with the other.

Lisa fired her repeater a half-dozen times, and Carlson's body jerked violently, then went prone for a brief time. Wilson took the opportunity and rolled to his side, pushing the captain off of him and leaping to his feet.

Carlson rolled to his stomach and planted his hands on the floor, pushing himself up to a squatting position in one swift movement and propelling himself at Wilson.

Wilson met the attack with a swing of his club. The left side of Carlson's face collapsed in on itself. The captain dropped to his knees, still snarling and reaching for his prey. The security chief swung again, and Carlson collapsed to the floor, still and silent.

Breathing heavily, Wilson walked back to the doorway that had loosed the rabid corpse.

He glanced over his shoulder at Lisa and Collette. "Wait here. I'll go find his keycard, and then we can get the hell out of here. If anyone comes through the door, scream."

Without waiting for a reply, he disappeared into Carlson's quarters. Collette walked back to Rodney's lifeless body and crouched beside it, visibly fighting back her emotions.

"He was like my brother," she whispered, her words trembling.

Wilson returned surprisingly fast. Lisa's mind hardly had time to process everything that had just happened to them when he rejoined them, keycard in hand. He walked to a console and picked up what looked like a larger version of the com-phones.

Lisa watched as Wilson pressed a few buttons, then pressed another series.

"Goddamn it," he said as he flung the phone back onto the console.

"We can't communicate with Earth, can we?"

Wilson shook his head. "Let's just get down there and get that fucking thing off the ship."

Collette looked up, tears in her eyes.

"I'm sorry," Wilson said. "I really am. But we need to go now. The longer that thing is on board, the worse things will get."

She nodded. "I know." She gave Rodney one last look, then stood up and joined Lisa and Wilson as they left the captain's deck. They entered the corridor, locking the door behind them.

Chapter 5

Sutter's blood boiled with jealousy.

The Chosen had spent hours kneeling before the Great One, each of them saying a silent prayer, praising God as he whispered his soothing promises of salvation in their minds.

And now, after calling Roger, that forgotten pariah, from out of the shadows and bestowing his blessings upon him, The Great One had chosen Lorenzo to be the first of the Chosen to receive his gift. Lorenzo stood and walked toward the containment room.

Sutter supposed it was because Lorenzo had ushered far more of the crew into death than he. It was Lorenzo who had led the assault on the sleeping quarters, opening the doors and bathing in the glory of the slaughter. But Sutter had been imprisoned and would have killed everyone on board for the Great One had he been free. He had sacrificed his wife, damn it!

When he reached the doorway to the containment room, Lorenzo dropped to his knees and lowered his head.

The room felt electric. The hairs on Sutter's arms and neck tingled. Air thickened and moved, as if God had taken a breath and then fell still. Lorenzo raised his head toward the ceiling and opened his mouth. Suddenly, the gray tube shot out from the Great One and found him, twisting and twitching its way down his throat. He fell backward and went limp, the tentacle holding him in a sitting position as it worked.

His body broke into spasms so violent that, over and over again, he flew upward, off the floor, and then crashed back down. As the tube darkened, Sutter realized the Great One's blessing would be different for Lorenzo than it had been for Roger. The darkening was moving in the opposite direction, flowing up and out of Lorenzo toward the Great One. The tube contracted and released, forcing the dark matter through it like the giant intestine it resembled.

Lorenzo's skin paled, turning stark-white in a matter of seconds. His eyes imploded, withering into their sockets. His body deflated like a balloon, the muscle mass beneath the white skin melting, then running up the tube.

Soon, he was reduced to a skeleton, with white skin dangling from the bones like grotesque sheets of paper draped over a wire frame. The tube snaked its way out of his mouth and retreated back to the Great One's body, dropping Lorenzo's empty husk to the floor.

There was a lull in the room, and then sound returned. Wet slurp-ing and sloshing, flesh stretching taut, quiet snaps and pops. Something pressed out of the Great One's body as if some other living thing were trapped within it and trying to escape. The creature's flesh tore. A thick, gray thing, like a massive worm, burst forth from the hole. It fell onto the floor with a loud, wet slap and began to flop around, growing in length. Larger than the other tube, it was as thick as Sutter's calf and ten feet long, stretching out of the containment room. The bottom of it was dotted with small, round suckers, like an octopus tentacle, and tiny teeth worked in the center of each circle. White viscous fluid dripped from the wound that had birthed the member.

The tentacle settled, turning onto its side so the tooth-filled mouths were visible.

Sutter's heart thudded with excitement. Lorenzo had been sacrificed for this new flesh. What would happen to the brittle, empty shell that had held Lorenzo's spirit? And what of the remaining Chosen? Was this their fate as well?

When the Great One had first spoken to Sutter, He had warned that to serve him would require sacrifice, but on the other side of their flesh was a new life. A perfect eternity.

To give up his body so the Great One could be whole was an honor. Sutter wasn't afraid, and he knew that none of his brethren were. This was their true purpose. The Great One needed their flesh, and they would give it willingly and be rewarded thereafter.

The voice coursed through his being again. All of the Chosen trembled from the sheer power of God's words. It whispered another name, asking for another sacrifice: Trevor Young.

Without hesitation, Trevor stood and walked to the front of the group, dropping to his knees just like Lorenzo before him.

Sutter watched as the process repeated. Trevor's body was sapped of all its life and nutrients; then, another tentacle ruptured from the Great One's body, this one on the opposite side.

The Great One called up two more of the Chosen and drained them, using them to spawn another pair of hellish appendages.

Two of the tentacles stretched out to the front of the containment room, the tips of them so close to the Chosen that Sutter could hear the teeth grinding against one another and scraping the metal floor.

Using the serpentine arms to pull itself, the Great One lurched out of the containment room, sliding across the floor and stopping a few feet from the Chosen.

Sutter stared in awe.

God was free.

Its body contracted, expanded, and then fell still, the only movement that of the red follicles quivering rapidly.

The two rear tentacles darted out like hellish pythons and wrapped around two of the remaining Chosen. They coiled until only the Chosen's heads and feet were visible. The men's eyes widened and their mouths worked as if trying to scream, but they couldn't force any air out of their lungs.

Beneath their cries, Sutter could hear the source of their agony. It sounded like a thousand ravenous lunatics feasting.

Blood seeped out around the tentacles, flowing down the append-ages in crimson streams as the tiny mouths devoured their prey. There were loud crunches and cracks as the teeth ripped through the bone, and a moment later, four feet dropped to the floor, reduced to chunks of gnawed flesh and splintered bone jutting up out of shoes.

The feeding went on for another few minutes before the crunching stopped; the only sounds were the wet drips of the blood pooling on the floor.

The two men's heads, some shards of bone, and a few pieces of flesh the hungry maws had missed fell to the floor. The tentacles wrapped around the heads and scooped them up. Another moment, and the arms unraveled and slid back to the Great One's sides.

A shudder coursed through its body, and it swelled, growing in size like a balloon being inflated. The whispers Sutter had heard for so many days now grew louder as the Great One grew in strength, shouting in his mind so loudly he could hear nothing else.

The tentacles lashed out again, wrapping around one of Sutter's re-maining two companions. He watched with envy as the woman was devoured, her flesh turned to sustenance for God.

His body was not to be given up to the Great One. Like Roger, he and William Jones were favored above the others, and they would receive the blessings of their god.

The orange hue of the Great One's body darkened, more shudders passing through it.

Sutter opened his mouth wide, silently praying for his turn to be touched by God. He had little time to wait. The segmented tube shot out and squirmed its way into his mouth, wriggling down his throat like a massive worm. His gag reflex forced up vomit, which the appendage forced back down into his stomach. The Great One filled his guts with its blessings. There was no pain—only a warmth filling his belly, spreading throughout his body. From the corner of his eye, he could see William receiving the same blessing.

The tube slid out of him, and he collapsed to the floor, out of breath but filled with elation. He felt no worry, no sorrow or pain or stress.

He had never felt more alive in all of his life.

Sutter watched as the Great One's arms stretched out and pulled it nearer to the door. One of the tentacles pounded the control button, and the door slid open. The tentacles reached through the door and flexed, pulling the Great One to the opening. It could barely fit through the doorway, and Sutter watched as it narrowed its body, sliding out of the biology lab into the hallway beyond.

He rose to his feet, euphoria sweeping over him like a drug, and followed God into the corridor. The Great One slid down the hallway in long, swift motions, still speaking its desires to him as it did.

William joined him in the hallway, and they watched as the Great One vanished around a corner. William kept step with him in silence. Sutter began to walk toward the stairwell. He didn't know where the Great One was going, and he hated to leave its presence, but he had been commanded, and he dared not disobey. There was a purpose far greater than his own desires that he had to fulfill.

The DARC12 was too small to contain such a glorious being as the Great One. And now, with the Great One's blessings, Sutter could move freely on the ship. And soon, he and William would guide it to a place far more worthy of God's presence.

Chapter 6

The blessing was changing him. Roger could feel it growing more profound with every minute. His vision had changed. Everything was brighter, clearer, and more defined. He could feel the slight electrical charge emanating from the lights and coursing through the very air. Anything was possible now.

He'd shorted out the doors leading into the stairwells on three more levels and had encountered seven more of the Reborn in the process. The more he saw them, the more his awe of them grew. He'd watched as they stalked through the hallways, hunting any of the nonbelievers left alive.

There were differences between them, at least in intelligence. He'd seen some of them open doors to the various labs and residences, while others mindlessly paced the hallways. One had been standing in front of a pair of elevators, pounding ceaselessly on the control button, until it had caught sight of Roger and charged him. The Great One's blessing had kept him safe, and the corpse had snarled past him, vanishing around a corner.

He returned to the stairwell and glanced up and down it. He could see a dozen or so of the reanimated animals, as well as a couple of humans, climbing and descending the stairs. Undoubtedly, the stairs on the opposite end of the corridor were equally filled with the glorious creations, if not more so.

A tremor passed through his stomach and ran up his chest, tickling and burning his innards. A flash of pain shot through his head, like the worst migraine of his life, and then a ringing filled his ears. He gripped the stair railing with white knuckles and fought to maintain consciousness as his vision blurred.

As suddenly as it began, the strange seizure ceased. His senses returned to him with a vengeance. His vision was now so immaculate that he could see the particles floating in the air, the minuscule pores on the steel handrails and walls. Above him, he could hear muffled voices. A woman trying not to cry, a man consoling her. Footsteps echoing through the ship.

Roger smiled.

The blessing intensified.

Chapter 7

Collette's entire body trembled. It was slight, and she hoped to God that Wilson hadn't noticed it. It was taking all of her willpower to keep from sobbing hysterically as they returned to the stairwell. Her tears weren't just from the sadness of losing Rodney; she was also fighting back a fear so dark and profound that she could feel herself about to plunge into a panic attack. Rodney was gone. What if Wilson soon followed him into death? She'd be left with Lisa and Jack on a ship filled with nothing but death.

With every step she took, she reminded herself of her lifelong wishes for excitement and adventure, and that she had to be strong now to face what was happening on board the ship. She'd been doing well, she thought. Even losing her fingers to a cannibalistic corpse hadn't crushed her will to survive.

But watching Rodney die right in front of her… It had nearly pushed her beyond her breaking point, and it was a struggle to keep from passing it.

Wilson glanced over his shoulder at her and stopped. He turned and walked to her, then pulled her close to him, hugging her tight. The act surprised her. He'd never before physically displayed any kind of affection toward her, aside from a pat on the shoulder or a handshake.

The hug brought her emotions out in full force. She cried uncontrollably, barely able to breathe, she was sobbing so hard.

They stood for a moment, locked in that sorrowful embrace, until her cries calmed into quiet tears. Wilson pulled back from her and looked into her eyes. "I'm sorry. I know it hurts. I know it's so fucking wrong. And I'm sorry I'm rushing us out of here, sorry we're leaving his body lying in there, and…I'm sorry this whole goddamn thing has happened."

"It isn't your fault."

"I know. But it feels like I could have stopped it when it started if I'd done more, and I'm sorry I didn't."

"Nothing you could have done would have stopped this."

He nodded. "At any rate, I'm sorry it's all happened. There's nothing I can say that'll help, I know. But Rodney would want us to stay alive, stay together, and get rid of that fucking thing. The more time we stay up here, the more time we waste."

"Let's just get to the lab and end this."

Wilson turned and made his way to the stairwell door, Lisa and Collette following behind him.

Collette felt better somehow. Wilson's small act of consolation had helped her pull herself back together, and she was thankful he'd done it. She glanced at Lisa, who seemed to be coping with everything just fine. At the moment, she looked more like a security officer on guard patrol than a scientist, clutching Rodney's repeater pistol, looking from the stairwell to the captain's deck and back again. It impressed Collette that such a shy, delicate, feminine scientist could handle the insanity and horror that had been unleashed on DARC12. That she wasn't a blubbering, useless shell of her former self was a testament to Lisa's strength.

Wilson pressed the control switch, and the stairwell door slid open. They stepped backward, Collette and Lisa raising their guns.

Hungry screams and growls, anguished cries and hellish howls crept out of the open doorway. Sounds unlike any Collette had ever heard chilled her blood. Hairy hands gripped the handrail on the landing, followed by a small chimpanzee. It wrapped its long toes around the top rail and squatted down, regarding them with milky eyes and an almost human, sinister grin.

Another animal shambled into view on the landing beneath the monkey, using short, malformed legs to carry its misshapen body. Its head, snout, and short, fat body suggested it was some form of pig, but its thick black hair and long tail betrayed its mixed genetic ancestry.

Without hesitating, Lisa fired three rounds into the chimp. Its body broke into spasms as it fell backward off the railing and disappeared down the stairwell, its receding screams echoing off the metal walls like the howl of a banshee.

The pig-thing darted forward. As Collette took another step back, Wilson ran toward the oncoming creature. Wilson drew back his foot and kicked, timing his attack perfectly, sending the thing tumbling back through the doorway. It slid to a stop on the landing, Wilson following it. Before the pig-thing regained its footing, he stomped its head with his boot. Three brutal slams and the animal's skull split open and the thing fell still.

Wilson peered over the railing. He turned quickly and ran back into the hallway, eyes wide with terror as he closed the door and slid his keycard through the lock.

"Get to the other stairwell," he said as he ran toward Lisa and Collette. "There's dozens of the fucking things!"

"What the hell are they?" Collette asked.

"Don't care right now!"

"What makes you think they aren't in the other stairwell, too?"

Wilson didn't answer her. The trio charged down the hallway in silence. After a few moments, they reached the stairwell.

Collette watched as Wilson opened the door. The landing was empty, but the inhuman shrieks still drifted out of the stairwell. He crept to the railing, glanced over it, and then returned to the two women.

"Sounds like there are only a couple of them. Let's go."

"What?" Collette said. "You want to run right into the middle of those things?"

"We don't have any other choice."

"We could go back to the captain's deck!"

"And do what? We'll be trapped in there, Collette."

"He's right," Lisa said.

"We can't waste time arguing about it. We need to go now."

Collette nodded.

He was right, of course. As much as her mind screamed for her to run and lock herself behind as many doors as possible, she knew it would only prolong the inevitable. She felt almost ashamed she was on the cusp of losing her cool while Lisa was rising up to meet the situation.

She reminded herself that only a few days ago she had been hoping for some form of excitement. Collette followed Wilson as he headed into the stairwell.

Chapter 8

The ship's elevators were no longer working. Sutter and William had waited for several minutes before giving up on them and making their way to the closest stairwell. This minor inconvenience frustrated Sutter. He didn't mind using the stairs, but the extra time it would take to reach the upper level annoyed him. They were on their way to the captain's deck so that William, one of the DARC's flight controllers, could set the ship on the path the Great One had chosen. He wanted to please his god as quickly as possible. If it took them too long, Sutter feared it might displease the Great One.

Already his mind was changing, his senses focusing. His life before finding God was forgotten.

They entered the stairwell and a cacophony of shrieks and wails—a choir of tortured cries birthed from unseen lips—met them. The sounds didn't slow their steps in the least. The blessing of the Great One would protect them from whatever miracles He had loosed on the ship.

After three flights of stairs, they encountered the sources of the cries. Sutter recognized all of the beasts they had freed before releasing the Great One; now that they were filled with the new life, they seemed so much more divine to him. Each of the creatures regarded them at first with malice, but quickly they sensed the blessings of God and ignored

William and Sutter, passing them by in search of more suitable prey.

The Great One's desires were being fulfilled: the Reborn were moving through the ship's corridors and rooms like antibodies spreading through the veins and organs of a diseased man. The impurities of mankind were being cleansed and replaced with God's wondrous, unspoiled aura.

He and William continued up the stairs toward their goal.

Chapter 9

"Don't stop running!" Wilson screamed as the trio darted down the stairs past the nightmare beasts.

They'd encountered half a dozen creatures thus far, but for the most part, their myriad deformities made the creatures slower and more clumsy than the reanimated corpses they'd been fighting. The only animals Wilson had seen thus far that didn't bear some grotesque sign of genetic manipulation were a handful of large rats with tiny, opaque eyes, and a good-sized potbelly pig. The rats he kicked or stomped his way past. They easily circumvented the pig and several slow and deformed creatures that were too close for comfort using Wilson's baton or rounds from Lisa's and Collette's repeater pistols.

Blessedly, there were none of the monkeys that had greeted them moments ago in the other stairwell. Those appeared as swift and nimble as their living counterparts.

He'd known these experiments were on board. Cloning and genetic manipulation were standard experiments on any DARC. The last thing he'd expected was for these failures to come back to life along with the slaughtered crew. And for them to escape from the tanks that had held them was unfathomable.

As if reading his mind, Lisa called out from behind him. "The apes were alive last time I checked. Whoever let the others loose must have killed the living ones first."

Wilson leaped over something that may have once been a pig, dog, or human infant but now looked like some combination of the three. He sailed over it, clearing a half-dozen steps and glancing over his shoulder as his feet found the landing.

Disgust was etched on Collette's face as the creature lurched in her direction. She kicked it squarely in its cherubic face and sent it tumbling down the stairs, where it rolled to a stop near Wilson. While it struggled to right itself on stubby limbs, Wilson instinctively raised his boot and crushed the child-like head beneath it.

He waited until both women reached the landing, then started down the next flight of stairs, his steps slick with the gore of the dead creature. They'd passed half a dozen monsters on the three floors they'd descended thus far, and although he could see none below them, their ungodly cries announced their presence.

As he reached the next turn in the stairs, a figure fell into view that stopped him in his tracks.

A huge ape shambled up the stairs. The animal was frightening enough, but its appearance was even more disconcerting. It had been shaved bald for some kind of scientific experiment. A thin five-o'clock shadow covered its pale pink body. A cluster of festering tumors, like a tiny malignant mountain range, spanned the side of its neck and spread across its chest.

"Oh my God," Collette gasped as she caught sight of the ape.

The animal locked eyes with Wilson and peeled its cracked, black lips back from its bloody teeth. The sneer was madness incarnate. It broke into a thunderous charge up the stairs.

"Shoot it!" Wilson shouted as he planted his feet and raised his club.

The two women fired their pistols, squeezing the triggers so rapidly that Wilson couldn't count the number of shots released.

The volley was a storm of blue sparks. The charges danced across the metal railing and lit the stairwell wall like fireworks. Dozens of rounds connected with the ape, and its muscles spasmed with the electricity coursing through it.

The shots stunned the animal, and it pitched forward onto its stomach, pulling itself up the stairs with trembling arms, its howls of pain and rage filling the air as Lisa and Collette continued to fire shot after shot at its hairless body.

Wilson ran down the stairs to meet it, bringing his baton down on the creature's head. The bludgeon glanced off the skull, slid down the side of its face, and slammed into the ape's shoulder. The awkward blow sheared off the monkey's ear, leaving it dangling like some hellish piece of jewelry.

The ape grabbed Wilson's ankle as he raised his weapon for another swing. It knocked him off balance, and he collapsed in front of the ape, struggling to keep from falling into its arms. It lunged, sinking its teeth into Wilson's boot and gnawing on it feverishly.

With his free leg, Wilson began to kick the creature in its face repeatedly, raining down dozens of blows that did little to stop the attack. He drew back his baton and swung it again, connecting with the monster's face, sending teeth and bits of flesh flying from its mouth as it loosened its grip on his foot.

The ape's fingers relaxed as it fell still. Wilson crabwalked up the stairs to the landing, spewing curses at his fallen assailant.

"Is it dead?" Lisa asked, staring at the ape.

"I think so." Wilson panted. "Again."

Collette helped him to his feet, draping his arm over her shoulders to help steady him.

"Let's go," Wilson said. "I'm fine."

They hurried down the steps, but before reaching the next landing, a woman clad in blood-soaked pajamas charged around the corner and up the steps.

Both Collette and Lisa raised their weapons and fired at the oncoming nightmare. Wilson was equally swift. Before the woman had even dropped to her knees from the shots, he was upon her with his bludgeon. His first swing sent the woman careening back down the stairs, her head slamming into the railing. She lay motionless, but Wilson quickly delivered two more blows to ensure she was no longer a threat. He stepped past her body without a word and continued down the stairs.

They rushed down the stairs and reached the door of the security office just as a small chimpanzee bounded up the stairs into view. It bared its teeth and screeched at them, then charged.

Collette and Lisa fired their guns, but the chimp's speed was tremendous. Their first volley missed it entirely. As it closed the gap between them, it jumped onto the stair railing, then leaped off it, its dead hands outstretched to grab one of them when it was close enough.

It slammed into Lisa, and she stumbled under the impact falling against the door. Gripping her shoulders, the chimp went for her throat. Lisa managed to get her hands between her and the chimp. She pressed back against its chest, just keeping its teeth from sinking into her neck.

Careful not to hit Lisa, Wilson quickly jabbed the butt of his baton into the side of the chimp's head. It turned and screamed at him, then dove off Lisa, coming after him.

Wilson spun to his side to dodge the attack, but as the chimp flew past him, its flailing hand found his head. Its claws sent trails of searing pain across his face as it tried to stop itself.

The chimp landed in the middle of the stairs, rolling down them a few feet until it regained its footing.

The chimp raced up the stairs and leaped for Wilson again, but he swung the baton and connected with the creature while it was in midair. A loud crack echoed off the walls as the animal flew over the railing and plummeted down the stairwell.

His entire face throbbed, and Wilson felt the warm flow of blood seeping from his wounds as he fumbled to get his keycard out of his pocket.

"Who the fuck is that?" Collette yelled out.

Wilson peered over the railing and looked down the stairwell.

A few floors beneath them, another chimpanzee, hairless and covered in scabs, was racing up the stairs. Four or five stories below it was a thin man, dried blood flaking from his face and clothes. The sight of him chilled Wilson. His maniacal grin was identical to the one he'd seen on the child murderer years ago.

"I think that's Roger Han," Lisa said as she aimed her gun over the railing and fired at the chimp.

Collette raised her gun and fired as well, but the creature's movements were so quick that their shots couldn't connect. The man yelled up at them, "Surrender to God! Give in to his will!"

"Hurry, Wilson," Collette shouted.

As he withdrew the keycard from his pocket and raced to slide it through the door control, the chimp charged onto the landing just below them. The door opened as the chimp leaped toward them, Collette and Lisa aiming their guns at it.

"Get in here!" Wilson shouted at the women. One of their rounds struck the chimp, and it dropped onto its hands, stumbling as the charge took hold. Lisa and Collette both ran through the metal door. As soon as they crossed the threshold, Wilson followed them, pressing the door control as he passed through.

The screech of the chimp pierced the air, and a heavy weight slammed into Wilson's back, knocking him face-first onto the floor, sending his baton clattering out of his hand and down the hallway.

The chimp grabbed a fistful of his hair and pulled his face off the cold floor. Before he could resist, the chimp bit into the top of his head. The sound of teeth scraping against his skull rampaged through his brain as it tried to gnaw through the bone.

As quickly as it had appeared, the weight of the creature vanished from his back, followed by a yelp that reminded him of a wounded dog. He rolled to his back to find Collette standing over him, firing her repeater pistol at the chimp as it tumbled into the nearby wall.

The electrical charges sent the animal into spasms. Within an instant, Lisa was upon it, wielding Wilson's dropped baton. She hit the chimp squarely in the face, crushing its head between her weapon and the metal wall. A second and third swing of the baton and the creature's skull split open.

"Lock the door," Wilson grunted as he sat up. "Quick."

Collette hurried to the door and slid her card through the control panel, then pressed the lock button.

Wilson watched until the red "locked" light came on, and then he struggled to his feet. The pain burning through his face and head was dizzying; his vision was blurry, and a low hum in his ears. He knew that the bite wounds on his scalp were bad. He felt the blood streaming down the back of his neck.

As Lisa handed him his baton, he glanced at Collette and feigned a smile. It did little to erase the concern from her face.

Before anyone could speak, footsteps echoed like gunshots through the corridor. The three of them exchanged glances before bracing themselves for another attack. Wilson held his baton at the ready while Collette and Lisa aimed their guns down the long, cold hallway.

Jack limped around the corner of the nearest intersection with his repeater pointed at the trio of bloodied survivors. He surveyed them each in turn, and then his focus fell on the corpse of the chimpanzee.

"What the fuck happened to you guys, and what the fuck is that thing?"

Chapter 10

Of all the crew on board the DARC, the only one Roger truly wished The Great One would have spoken to was Lisa. They'd shared something special, she and Roger. Before he'd sworn himself to God, he could only remember bits and pieces of their relationship—dream like flashes of them sharing meals and conversation. He didn't remember exactly why, but he knew he'd been fond of her. That they'd had common interests.

But she was nothing now, of course. God spoke to those He deemed worthy, and Lisa had obviously never heard His call.

Those vague memories of attraction to her caused Roger to feel a small measure of pity for the woman, but the pity was eclipsed by his anger and disgust at her decision to side with the last few living crew members on board.

There were others, he knew—survivors who had thus far managed to hide from the Reborn and the Chosen. And Lisa had managed to find survivors who were plotting against the Great One—true enemies of the Lord.

He had many more doors to open to ensure God's children had free passage throughout the ship, but now that he knew where these insurgents against God's will were, Roger had a far greater purpose.

He hadn't been a part of The Cleansing, hadn't helped the others kill the crew. But Lisa and her group were within his reach now, and killing them would no doubt please The Great One. The blessing bestowed on him already had heightened his senses tenfold. His heart raced with anticipation of the rewards he might glean from their deaths.

In a rush to reach Lisa and her newfound allies, Roger dismantled the door control switches as he made his way up the stairwell but didn't bother to cross through each floor and open the opposite doors.

A scream tore through the corridor beyond as he opened the door leading into one of the leisure levels. He stood staring down the hallway as a man in a maintenance uniform ran into view from a distant intersection. Soon after, another man appeared behind him, this one in a lab coat.

The two men caught sight of Roger and began screaming out pleas for help as they ran toward him, a blood-coated woman rounding the corner and chasing after them, screeching the call of the dead.

They'd made it halfway toward Roger when the woman reached the man in the lab coat, snatching his shoulder with one hand and his scalp with the other. She pulled him down, ripping into his throat with her teeth before he'd even hit the ground.

Roger smiled as the woman feasted on her prey.

"Help me!" the maintenance worker begged. "For the love of God, help me!"

An orangutan, hairless and covered in festering tumors, raced past Roger and charged at the oncoming man.

"This *is* for God," Roger called out down the corridor as the man skidded to a stop, his eyes wide with horror as the beast rushed after him. He turned and ran back the way he came, disappearing down an intersecting hallway.

Roger watched until the orangutan vanished down the corridor as well. He glanced back to the Reborn and her meal, then walked into the stairwell, dreaming of the rewards The Great One would bestow upon him once he had dealt with Lisa and her co-conspirators.

His stomach ached; a deep throbbing rippled through his entire abdomen, coupled with an intense burning in his chest. He pushed the pain from his mind and focused on his newfound task.

Death. It was the least the nonbelievers deserved.

Chapter 11

"Fucking monkeys?" Jack said as the group rushed down the hall-way. Wilson had given Jack a condensed version of what had happened to them, leaving out most of the details of Rodney's death.

Hearing Roger's taunts in the stairwell had chilled Lisa's blood, and she couldn't get his maniacal voice out of her mind. The difference in him was startling, horrifying.

"Monkeys and a whole lot more," Collette said.

"What the hell were you doing with the monkeys?" Jack asked Lisa.

"Spare me a lecture. Those experiments were close to helping lots of people. The hairless ones? Biology Team Two was close to using them to grow replacement organs for people. *Any* organ—sometimes two or three hearts to each animal. Some had goddamn kidneys hanging all over them, enough to give a dozen people a new pair. The pigs were part of the same study."

"What about the other things? The ones that looked like more than one animal combined?" Collette said.

"A lot of experiments were being done. Most of the animals you saw were failed splices with humans—a program for species-specific immunities. Certain animals aren't affected by lots of diseases that kill humans. We were trying to use their resistances to create vaccines."

"And those things are what you came up with?" Jack asked.

Lisa's tone became more defensive now. She had argued the validity of their research for years now and had become used to it. "You have to suffer through setbacks and failures to make progress. How do you think the HIV vaccine and Alzheimer's cures came about? Tests done on a DARC, performed on hundreds of animals over the years."

"Whoa," Jack said. "I'm not judging. I just want to know what the hell we're dealing with. But why the hell did you guys keep them alive?"

"We didn't. They died on their own. We kept the bodies in case we needed samples."

Jack didn't respond; nobody did.

They filed into the security office, and Lisa hurried to the open medical kit still on the table and rifled through it. As Wilson spoke, he leaned against the wall, probing the wound on his head with his fingers. "What do you think Roger's doing, and why the fuck are those things not slaughtering him like they have everyone else?"

Lisa collected the alcohol, the Wound Seal, and the PPA shot, then crossed the room to Wilson.

"Sit down."

He did as she said. She stood behind him, swabbing his scalp with the cleanser.

"He's right, somehow," Lisa said as she worked.

"Who?" Collette asked.

"Roger."

Jack chuckled. "He's been blessed by God? That thing?"

"I don't necessarily mean that it's God or that he's blessed." She tossed the container of alcohol onto the table and prepared the shot. "But if that thing is causing everything to go wrong—if it's somehow bringing the dead back to life—then maybe it *is* protecting Roger."

"Protecting him how?" Wilson asked.

"It might have marked him somehow—with a scent, or pheromone of some kind, that keeps them from attacking him."

"How could it do that from inside the containment room?" Collette asked.

"Hold still, Wilson."

Lisa lowered the needle to his head. Without hesitation, she stuck the needle into his scalp and depressed the plunger. He grunted beneath the pain, and she felt his body tighten, then relax as the drugs went to work. She opened the Wound Seal and slathered it onto his scalp.

"The only thing I can figure is, assuming I'm right and it's somehow manipulating the electrical impulses in the brains of the dead to reanimate them, it's using the same method to mark him. Maybe it stimulated Roger's brain and caused his body to manufacture something the dead can sense. A smell or energy aura—something like that."

"And now Roger can just wade through all those monsters?" Collette said.

"It damn sure seemed that way to me," Lisa said as she backed away from Wilson, unsure of whether or not to tell them the rest of her hypothesis. They were in this together, however, and she decided that they deserved to know. "I hope the brain impulse is how it marked Roger. Otherwise…"

Wilson turned and looked at her with questioning eyes. "Otherwise, what?"

"Otherwise, somebody let that thing out of the containment room."

"You said they needed Carlson's card," Jack said, anger lacing his voice. "That's why you guys went to the fucking captain's deck!"

She shook her head. "I said we needed his card to eject it back into space. Launching cargo isn't a minor thing. Even the captain would have to have clearance from Earth before he did it.

"But opening the containment room doors isn't as big of a deal. Even without the password, any security officer could have done it with their card."

"So all somebody would have to do is snag a keycard," Wilson said as he rose to his feet. "And they could have set the fucking thing free."

Lisa nodded.

"Goddamn it," Jack whispered.

"So," Collette said. "What now, then?"

"We go to the lab, same as we'd been planning," Wilson said as he headed for the door out of the office.

"What? Didn't you hear her? We don't know if that thing is even still in the lab."

"We don't know if it isn't, either. The last time I saw that thing, it didn't look like it had any way to move around. Unless it's sprouted legs, even if the door is open, I doubt it's out of the containment room.

"Besides, this is the only chance we've got right now. If it's still in the room—and I hope to God it is—then we launch the goddamn thing back into space. If it's not there… We'll figure something out then."

"That's a shit plan if I ever heard one," Jack whispered.

"Got a better one?" Lisa snapped before Wilson had a chance to respond.

Jack lowered his head without a response.

Wilson glanced at her, then at Jack. "As much as I didn't want to, we'll have to use the elevators. There's no fucking way I'm going back in that stairwell. Hopefully, those things won't notice the lifts are moving."

"And if they do?" Collette asked.

"We'll fight the goddamn things. It's that or sit here and wait to die. And I'm damn sure not going to sit and wait."

"He's right," Lisa said. "Whether it's in the containment room or not, we aren't going to accomplish anything just standing in this room staring at blank security monitors and listening to Jack bitch."

Jack gave her an icy glance. It looked like he was about to respond, but instead, he lowered his gaze back to the floor and said nothing.

"I know all of that," Collette said. "And I'll help any way I can. I just wish there was something else we could do."

"There isn't, right now," Wilson said. "Nobody was trained for anything like this. The ship isn't set up to deal with this situation. But we've got to manage."

He waited a moment, then added, "Are you ready?"

Collette nodded and joined Wilson and Lisa at the door.

Wilson glanced at Jack. "I assume you aren't going with us."

Jack shook his head, keeping his attention on the floor. "Sorry, Boss. I'll take my chances locked up here. I'm still moving at half-speed. I'd be monkey food out there."

Wilson pressed the door control switch and exited into the hallway without saying another word to Jack. Lisa and Collette followed him.

They hurried down the corridor, turning the corner that led to the elevators, and stopped dead in their tracks. At the opposite end of the hallway, walking toward them with a grin plastered on his face, was Roger.

Fifteen or twenty feet ahead of him was a chimpanzee, far smaller than the others they'd encountered thus far. It was legless. Its torso tapered off in size just below its chest, eventually ending in a tiny, pink, malformed stump that trailed behind it like a tail. The chimp dragged itself up the hallway on its hands, making good time despite its handicap.

"There you are!" Roger shouted.

"Wilson," Collette whispered.

"Wait until it's closer, then shoot the fucking chimp."

Lisa watched the chimp advance, baring its teeth and screeching maniacally. As it came, Roger screamed along with it.

"You should have bowed before the Great One! Accepted His love, His desires! You could have been Chosen! Now, you'll die in His name and be reborn in His glory."

"You've lost your fucking mind," Lisa shouted over the chimp's screams.

"You stupid bitch! I haven't lost anything. I've given my mind and my body to God. My rewards will be endless, especially when He sees I've given you all to His cause!"

The chimp was twenty feet from them now, and Collette aimed her repeater pistol and fired. It collapsed onto its face, its body wracked with spasms.

Lisa ignored the chimpanzee. She was too focused on Roger and his madness. She watched his advance as Wilson hurried forward and smashed in the chimp's skull. Roger's pace didn't change, and the emotionless expression on his face did not falter.

"You can't stop them all," he called out. "They're spreading through the ship, finishing off the few people who survived the Cleansing. And every person that dies joins them. It's God's work, Lisa! Who are you to stand in its way?"

As he neared them, Lisa could see more than Roger's personality had changed. His broken jaw had healed somehow, but dried, flaking blood caked most of his face and chest. It was his skin that horrified her. His arms, neck, and face were moving, writhing as if millions of tiny creatures lived beneath his flesh. Here and there, his face bulged outward and then receded—small clusters of tumors rising and falling, which gave his head a misshapen appearance.

"Goddamn it," Collette whispered, "what's wrong with him?"

"I have no idea." Lisa said as Wilson backed away from the chimp's corpse and rejoined Collette and her.

"Shoot the son of a bitch," Wilson said.

"You can't stop the will of God." Roger's voice rose in timbre to that of the preachers Lisa used to see on television in her youth.

Lisa and Collette raised their guns in unison, firing simultaneously. The rounds struck Roger and dropped him to his knees. He groaned, either in agony or anger. It sounded like the growl of a feral animal, and he locked gazes with Lisa as the charges coursed through his body. She could see no sign of the man she knew. His eyes were black, colorless things, as dark and devoid of emotion as the black hole they'd been orbiting. She kept firing, each shot finding its target.

The squirming beneath his skin quickened. The quivering knots pulsated violently, growing larger. The stench of rotten meat and vomit filled the corridor as Roger's growl turned to a scream.

The tumors sparked and exploded in a spray of blood and black bile, sending hundreds of dark, squirming chunks flying through the hallway. Roger's skin split like the flesh of a grape, and the same black liquid oozed from these tears. Small creatures, black and the size of Lisa's thumb, crawled out of the open wounds, twitching violently as they tried to escape the electrical charges. Roger fell forward onto the floor and lay motionless.

Lisa pulled her focus from Roger and scanned the corridor. The chunks that had burst from the tumors were the same creatures now pouring out of Roger's body. They glistened in the light, wiggling and flopping about like tiny fish cast out of the water. More than anything, they reminded Lisa of leeches.

The smell was horrendous. Beside her, Collette gagged and used her wounded hand to cover her mouth and nose.

A moment passed, and the movement of the small leech-like creatures slowed. A few fell still, and then more, until at last none of the disgusting worms moved.

"What the fuck just happened?" Wilson whispered, his voice filled with either awe, shock, or disgust. Lisa couldn't tell which.

Lisa was surprised at her emotional response to Roger's death. A small part of her was sad he was dead. She knew she would miss him. But more than anything, she was relieved. No matter how good of a friend he had been or where their relationship had been heading, he had been a danger. His only desire had been to kill her in the name of some imagined god; as such, he had become a threat to the one thing she valued above anything else: her life. She told herself that if she lived through this ordeal, there would be time for grief. Now, she had to focus on survival. Anything else would be a detrimental distraction.

"Do you have any idea what those things are?" Wilson asked, gesturing to the dead slugs dotting the corridor.

She thought for a moment. "My guess would be they're parasites."

"Parasites."

Lisa nodded and walked to the nearest slug, poking it with her shoe. "Beneficial ones. They're probably why those walking corpses wouldn't attack him."

"They could sense the…slugs?"

"They seem more like leeches, I think, but yea. They were probably feeding on him and keeping him safe from those other things. Somehow, the undead could sense the parasites inside of him."

"He didn't seem to notice they were there," Collette said.

"He might not have. Maybe they blinded him from their presence somehow. Or he may have known they were there and just didn't give a shit. I don't know."

"Are they dead?" Collette's voice quivered.

Lisa squatted down and examined a slug. A layer of black bile coated its smooth body, and beneath the fluid, its flesh shimmered in the light. She could see no eyes or mouth on the creature. It was a featureless black shape.

"They seem to be. If they are parasites, they probably can't live without the host. But there's a problem."

"Which is?" Wilson said.

"Unless those monsters filling the ship did it, the only way for these slugs to have gotten into Roger is for him to have been in contact with the thing in the containment room."

"Shit," Collette whispered.

"So," Wilson said. "He's probably opened the door. That doesn't mean that thing isn't still there. Like I said—it didn't seem capable of moving itself, so unless it's been loaded onto a transport cart, we've still got a good chance of getting it off the ship."

"I hope so," Collette said.

They navigated through the carnage and continued down the hallway to the elevators, leaving slick footsteps of blood and black bile behind them.

When they reached the lifts, Wilson slid his card through the lock and waited while Collette and Lisa entered the elevator. The door closed, and Lisa pressed the button for her lab level.

As the elevator lurched into motion, her stomach tightened with anxiety.

Beside her, she could sense Wilson and Collette tense up as well. Dread filled the lift and hung heavy in the air.

The descent passed in silence.

Chapter 12

Sutter and William's trip up through the stairwell to the captain's deck had been one of joy and wonder. Sutter spent the bulk of the journey staring in awe at the beasts that had been loosed on the ship.

The animals were more majestic now than when he had last seen them. There were Reborn crew members as well, stalking through their more animalistic brethren with little regard for anything save their ravenous hunger, itself an extension of God's desire.

Now, filled with the power of God, they were no longer mere animals or humans. Their deaths had ushered them into the Great One's bosom. Their deformities were scarcely a handicap now, merely the last vestige of their former existence.

Sutter envied them. They were one with God now and, as such, were in their eternal paradise. Soon, he told himself. When he completed his task, he would join the Great One, and he'd be in far greater favor than these creatures.

When they reached the door to the captain's deck, Sutter set about bypassing the electronic lock. Within a couple of minutes, the task was finished and the door slid open.

Heavy footsteps thundered toward the doorway, so quick that Sutter barely had time to register them before a giant of a man charged through it, skidding to a stop in the hallway.

The man studied Sutter and William, his dead eyes looking them up and down. A hole had been gnawed into his stomach, his intestines barely contained within the wound.

Sutter recognized the man. It was the security officer who had led him to his cell after he'd sacrificed his wife and her friend to the Great One. Sutter smiled and nodded. Enemies before, now they were united by the glory of God. Reborn and Blessed, with a singular purpose.

The dead security officer swayed from side to side, staring at William and Sutter as if trying to decide what to do next. Sutter knew that the man's hunger was insatiable, but the blessings of the Great One would protect the Chosen.

He stepped around the massive man and entered the captain's deck. Bodies were scattered across the room, and blood had been spilled here and there. The corpses all had head trauma.

"Someone was here before us," William said as he crossed the room to the ship's control board.

"Yes."

"What do you think they were doing?"

Sutter shook his head. "It doesn't matter."

"But they're infidels. They've slaughtered the Reborn. They could be plotting against God."

"They probably are. But the Great One is too powerful for them to fight. Do what we came here to do, and soon they'll be lost forever in the darkness, their petty struggle reduced to nothingness."

William smiled and went to the computer console, keying in commands with the skill of a professional. After a few moments, he stepped away from the controls, beaming with pride.

"Is it done?" Sutter asked.

"Yes. The ship has already broken from its orbit and is navigating for the new coordinates."

"Safety protocols?"

"By the time the ship registers the anomaly, we'll be too close for it to adjust its trajectory. Within an hour, we should be past the event horizon."

"Event horizon." Sutter chewed on the words.

"It's the point of no return. Theoretically, we won't even feel it when we cross over it. We'll be trapped in the gravitational pull of the black hole then. Even if they turned the ship around, the engines aren't powerful enough to escape that kind of force. Nothing in existence is. Nothing will stop us from passing through it."

"And the Great One will keep His followers safe as we journey through the void," Sutter said with a smile.

"We'll be one with Him on the other side," William finished.

"Come on," Sutter said as he crossed the room for the door. "We can still do God's work until that time comes."

The Reborn security guard was still at the doorway, watching them with amazement. Sutter stepped by the miracle and walked down the hallway. His mind filled with excitement. The mere anticipation of what was to come was enough to make him giddy.

A shudder of pain coursed through his body, dropping him to his knees. His vision blurred as another wave of agony came. Somewhere behind him, he heard William cry out as well.

His body trembled, and his vision returned. It was far more than it had once been, and he quickly realized that his hearing had improved.

The Blessing, he told himself.

He was seeing and hearing with the eyes and ears of God now. All of the Great One's promises were coming true.

He pulled himself to his feet and looked for William. The other man was already standing, and they shared a look, shared the glory of what was happening to them.

William's flesh came alive; it pulsated and squirmed like a separate living entity.

With the love of his god burning in his veins, Sutter turned and walked down the hallway. He thought of the distant black hole waiting out there in the vastness of space, not so unlike a god itself.

PART 5

Chapter 1

The elevator slowed and stopped. Wilson steeled his nerves and readied his riot baton.

"Be ready," he said to the two women, who already had their guns leveled at the door.

It opened, revealing the long central corridor that sliced through the center of the level, side hallways intersecting it at regular intervals.

The passageway was empty, as dead as everything else on the ship. Wilson waited, listening for the undead. He thought there were sounds, muffled and indistinguishable, drifting through the metal corridors, but they were so quiet, he hoped his adrenaline-soaked mind was imagining them.

He exited the lift and waited beside the door until Lisa and Collette were in the hallway. Then he locked the lift again to ensure it couldn't leave them stranded.

Leading the way, Wilson moved at a steady pace. He knew speed was important, but running blindly down the hallway could lead them to death. Each intersection could be hiding any number of nightmares. Any of the lab doors could open and unleash hell upon them. Better to take their time and stay alive, he figured.

Halfway down the main hallway, the trio turned left down a side passageway. Heavy thuds and loud hisses, like sandpaper grating against metal, were punctuated by lulls of quiet, broken only by the distant gurgles and growls of the dead. The hallways funneled the noises, amplifying them, making them sound more hellish than they already were. It was impossible to guess where the noises came from.

A few minutes later, the group reached Lab Five. Wilson glanced at his companions to ensure they were ready. The women both nodded.

He pressed the door control and entered the room, stopping a few steps past the doorway, staring in disbelief at the scene.

The containment room was empty. Panic swept over him as he tried to understand how it could be possible. The creature had—with someone's help or of its own volition—gotten out of the lab.

The lab itself was utter carnage. A large section of the floor was washed in blood, the crimson pool dotted with shards of white bone. Shoes with bits of flesh and bone poking out of them were scattered about. A severed head lay near the center of the lab, face twisted into a terrifying grimace. Two more heads lay a few feet from it, their faces pointed away from the doorway. A pair of corpses lay in front of the empty containment room, withered husks that looked like bodies exhumed from their graves after years of decomposition. White skin hung from the like tissue paper draped over a skeleton.

"Oh no," Collette said as she surveyed the lab. "It's gone."

"What the fuck happened here?" Lisa wondered aloud.

"I don't have the slightest clue."

Wilson was horrified. Despite all that had happened on board the DARC, he had never stopped believing that somehow, some way, he would survive the ordeal. And when he'd partnered with the last remnants of his security team, that faith in their survival had only grown.

Now, with the creature gone, their one chance for launching it off the ship had been stolen away, like the lives of most of the crew members. There was nothing left they could do. The dead had control of DARC12, their numbers too great for the three of them to combat.

"We have to kill that thing."

Lisa's words pulled him back from the brink of hopelessness.

"Kill it," he repeated.

Kill it? Why not? They'd planned to blast it back into space, but wouldn't destroying it serve the same purpose? It wasn't much of a plan, but it was something. Of course, it left one small problem.

"How the hell can we kill it?" Collette asked. "We don't even know where it is."

"If someone took it out on a transport cart, it's easy," Wilson said. "We kill them and use the cart to put the goddamn thing back in a containment room, or an airlock, or anything else that we can use to dump it back into space."

"And if it's changed again and moving on its own?"

"We'll figure it out then. The repeaters have given us a fighting chance," Lisa said. "They really fucked up those things in Roger. If that thing is anything like those parasites, maybe the electrical charges will hurt it, too."

Wilson scanned the slaughter again. If the creature from the containment room was responsible for the scene, he doubted they would have a chance. He didn't dare speak his fear out loud, though. Collette had only just now pulled herself together.

Hunting down the beast was the only course of action left. But the prospect of finding it made Wilson sick with dread. Not having a concrete plan didn't sit well with him. The sheer amount of variables they could encounter filled him with doubt. Lisa, however, appeared confident of their chances.

"However it left the lab," Lisa said, "it couldn't have gotten too far. Let's go."

Wilson frowned as she approached the door. He choked back his fear and joined her as she opened it, leaving the bloodied biology lab.

The strange noise still whispered through the corridors. As it moved farther away, all he could make out was a dull, distant *thud*. The DARC12 had spawned a metallic heart, beating in time with the slow, agonizing death threatening them.

"Let's find out what that is," Wilson said.

Unlike the thundering slams, the sounds of the dead were much louder, closer. They were undoubtedly on the move.

"This way," Wilson whispered, hurrying back the same way they had come. No matter where they went to search for the alien thing, getting away from the dead was their first priority. One or two undead they might be able to handle easily enough. If there was a pack of the things, they didn't stand a chance. If they were careful and lucky, they might be able to navigate the maze of corridors and avoid the monstrosities altogether.

Wilson glanced over his shoulder to ensure they weren't being chased. A step behind him, Collette and Lisa walked side by side with their pistols ready. He slowed as they reached an intersection. Looking from one passageway to the other, he approached the corridors carefully until he was satisfied that neither of them held any of the living dead.

"Which way?" Lisa whispered.

Without a word, he headed down the left corridor. The thudding came from that direction, and it was growing louder with every step.

The hallway ended in a T-shaped intersection, and Wilson tried to decide which path to take when Collette cried out in fear.

Wilson looked behind them, knowing what he would see. Sure enough, at the other end of the corridor, just turning around the intersection they'd been at a few minutes before, were a group of the reanimated corpses.

He counted four of them before he broke into a run. "Come on," he yelled as he charged the last few feet to the end of the hallway.

He took a left turn again, the corridors thundering as the chase began.

Chapter 2

It took Sutter and William little time to reach the security level of the ship. They'd bypassed all the floors between it and the captain's deck, only pausing to open the doors leading out of the stairwell.

There weren't as many of God's creatures on the stairs now. Many had poured through the now-open doors, filling the ship with their hunger.

The security floor was the most logical place for any survivors to flee to; therefore, it was the best place for them to search for any crew who had denied God and His divine will. The more they could deliver unto the Great One before passing into the darkness, the better. With every body He breathed His new life into, He would become stronger. And every life Sutter brought to God earned him increasing favor in the Great One's eyes.

The door control box had already been disabled, and the door stood open.

"Our brother?" William asked.

Sutter nodded. "Roger."

They moved swiftly down the hallway until they saw a man lying face down in a puddle of blood and black bile. Scattered along the corridor were thousands of slugs, and a few feet from the corpse lay a dead chimp. A trail of bloodied footprints led around the corner.

Sutter used his foot to turn the head so he could see the face. It was Roger.

"They've killed one of the Chosen," William said, his face tightening with anger.

Sutter stepped back from the body. "Calm down, Brother."
William nodded.

Sutter fished through Roger's pockets until he found the stolen key-card.

He stood and turned to William. "Now, let's see if anyone is left on this floor."

"But the footprints…"

"We'll follow them later. There may yet be work here for us to do."

They continued on, opening the doors they passed and checking the residence rooms for survivors. None of the security officers were in their rooms. Sutter had begun to give up hope of finding life to give unto God when he and William rounded a corner and caught sight of one of the Reborn passing through a doorway.

They quickened their pace, moving briskly until they reached the doorway. Sutter recognized their location.

It was the main security office for the DARC. Beyond was the security control office and the holding cells in which he'd recently been incarcerated.

The door slid open, revealing a pair of God's miracles. A dead chimpanzee squatted on a table in the center of the room, its teeth bared as it growled at the door leading to the cells. One of the Reborn stood in the open doorway, swaying back and forth as it peered into the room beyond.

Sutter crossed the office and peered over the dead man's shoulder. Another four of the Reborn lined the corridor beyond, joined by a pair of miraculous animals that had been filled with The Great One's new life.

Past the dead, Sutter could see the doors of the holding cells. Through the small glass window of the center door, he could make out a face looking at them. Even from down the hallway, the terror on the man's face was evident. He almost stunk of it. Sutter could have sworn he heard the man's racing heart before it was drowned out again by the wails of the hungry dead.

He stepped around the corpse in the doorway, weaving his way through the crowded corridor until he was standing in front of the locked cell. The man on the other side of the glass stared at him like a caged animal—eyes wide, mouth agape, sweat streaming.

"If you come out, it will be far quicker. You won't have to endure the fear you're feeling now or the agony you'll feel later." Sutter doubted the man could hear him. His time in the holding cells had proved to be most isolating, and the rooms were soundproof. Nevertheless, he hoped the man read his lips and realized the hopelessness of his situation.

"Help yourself," Sutter continued. "Help me. How long do you think you can survive in there? I can give you to God so quickly, you won't even realize it's happened until you're in his loving embrace."

The man seemed to comprehend what Sutter was saying. He shook his head slowly and backed away from the window, crossing the tiny room, sitting on the cot with his head cradled in his hands. Sutter could see he wore a security uniform, and one of his legs was bandaged heavily. He was surprised the wounded man had even managed to reach his new-found tomb.

Disappointed, Sutter shook his head. He turned his attention to the lock on the door. Somehow, the security officer had locked himself in the room.

Smiling, he left the officer to his own private hell.

The Reborn wouldn't find a way into the cell—that was certain. But they wouldn't abandon the hallway, either, not as long as there was a living being in such close proximity. The man would be trapped until the ship crossed the void and the darkness took him.

A fine end for a cowardly heretic, Sutter thought to himself as he rejoined William at the entrance to the corridor.

"Come on, then. We still have time to do God's work."

Chapter 3

Collette couldn't muster the courage to look behind her again.

Instead, she focused on Wilson's back and hoped he had a plan. They couldn't outrun the monstrosities forever. Her lungs were already screaming for respite.

Wilson darted left down an intersection so quickly that Collette barely had time to adjust her steps to make her own turn. Beside her, Lisa grunted out barely audible curses between her deep breaths.

Wilson looked over his shoulder, his gaze connecting with Collette's before surveying the nightmare behind them. She could see all of his emotions written in his eyes.

Fear, first and foremost. But beyond that, a sadness—an apologetic look that shouldered the blame for this and begged for forgiveness.

She'd never wanted to hold him as much as she did at that moment—had never wanted to touch him and share her thoughts, dreams, hopes, and desires more than she did right now. Panic tugged at her mind as she realized there was a strong chance she would never have the opportunity to do so.

"Try to shoot them!" Wilson yelled.

Lisa pointed her pistol behind her and fired it blindly down the hallway, squeezing off a dozen rounds before pausing to survey the damage. Correcting her aim somewhat, she fired again.

Collette did the same, her arm outstretched behind her and firing the gun a dozen times as she ran. She glanced back, only to see that none of her shots had found their target.

"Got you, you motherfucker!" Lisa screamed out over her shoulder.

Collette forced herself to look at their pursuers once more. Sure enough, one of the creatures had collapsed onto the ground. Its body still twitched as it struggled to pull itself up.

"Again!" Wilson shouted. "Keep trying!"

She fired off another volley behind her. The screams grew louder, angrier.

Either some of her shots had connected, or some of Lisa's had. Either way, one of the dead had dropped to the floor. Through some insane stroke of luck, one of its companions failed to maneuver around it, and it pitched forward clumsily, slamming into the cold metal walkway face first.

The third corpse sidestepped the others and continued its charge toward them as its comrades struggled to right themselves. Behind it, the one Lisa had shot had managed to stand back up to pursue.

"Right turn!" Wilson called out, and Collette returned her attention to the front.

A few feet in front of them, another intersection connected with their corridor, and Wilson darted down it without slowing down, Lisa a mere step behind him.

Collette reached the junction a second after Lisa and nearly slammed into Wilson as she made the turn. He had his back against the wall, barely hidden around the corner. He jerked his head quickly, signaling Collette to continue her retreat. She hesitated, then carried on down the hallway behind Lisa.

Thirty feet down the corridor, she stopped and turned back.

Wilson stood statuesque—a haggard, blood-soaked effigy of his former self. His attention was locked on the corner that was about to birth forth their pursuers. He looked, she thought, like an ancient warrior—a Viking, or Roman gladiator, despite his security uniform announcing otherwise.

His head wound was bleeding again. The bandage seeped blood. Dark, dried gore caked his body, and his face was tight with concentration, focused on only one thing.

Death. And the defiance of it.

She knew he blamed himself. That he somehow felt he could have stopped all the violence on board DARC12 before it started. But despite his self-blame, he stood now, gripping his baton as if it were salvation itself, prepared to defend the last few lives left on the ship no matter what.

A warrior born in blood and doubt.

Chapter 4

The sounds of hell filled the ship: the angry screams of the dead, the thunderous booms from somewhere nearby, Wilson's heart thumping a breakneck rhythm of fear through his head.

He told himself that he'd fight until his last breath left him, as if repeating it over and over would give him the strength to win this war.

And no matter what horrors came, he *would* fight, goddamn it, until the dark rushed up and greeted him with its cold embrace.

The corpse rounded the corner in a frenzy. As soon as it fell into view, he swung his weapon. The creature's head snapped to one side as the baton slammed into its face, and the sound of breaking bone echoed along the corridor. It stumbled backward a few steps and fell in the middle of the hallway, sliding a few feet before trying to stand again.

Wilson started to run toward it for the finishing blow, but another of the creatures charged into view and lunged for him.

He swung again, this time in defense. His clumsy attack hit the monster on the side of its head but didn't have much power behind it.

Nevertheless, the creature staggered to the side from the impact, its head striking the nearby wall as it fell. A small black spot greased the metal.

A gurgling growl drew Wilson's attention away from the dead man.

The first attacker pulled itself to its feet, its bottom jaw hanging limp from its face, giving it a strange, deformed appearance. It tried to snarl again, a thick ribbon of bile and teeth spilling from its mangled mouth. As Wilson braced for the impending attack, the sounds of the remaining two corpses grew nearer, so he backpedaled down the corridor to join Collette and Lisa. The wounded monstrosity dashed for Wilson. A few steps into its advance, its two comrades ran into view from behind it and joined the charge.

The corpse dove forward. Wilson swung his baton at the thing, but he missed the creature's head, his attack connecting instead with its shoulder.

It ignored the blow and crashed into him. He stumbled backward, trying to fling the creature off him while keeping his balance and failing on both counts. He fell to the floor, the corpse landing on top of him and burying its deformed maw into his chest.

He could feel the beast working its mouth, trying to bite into his breast. It couldn't, however, because its jaw was too shattered to bite with any force, but Wilson could feel a slight pinch and the thing's cold, dry, probing tongue.

He slid his left hand underneath the corpse's face until he felt its eye beneath his fingertips, and then he plunged his fingers into the socket. The eye gave way under the pressure, squishing like a rotting grape. Wilson pushed upward, raising the monster's head off his chest.

With his right hand, he struck the thing in the temple with the point of the baton. Its head snapped to one side, and it stopped trying to attack; instead, it wrestled to get away from Wilson.

He slammed the weapon against its head twice more, and the thing went limp on top of him. He rolled the dead man off him and sat up.

Collette and Lisa were pinning down the other two corpses with their repeaters, standing a few feet behind him and firing round after round into the creatures.

Wilson hurried to his feet and ran to the monsters. Their bodies twitched and writhed with the electrical charges, but they were still attempting to stand, to attack. They reached out, trying to grab his legs, staring at him with pure, black hatred in their eyes.

He planted his feet and raised the bludgeon above his head with both hands, bringing it down into one of the beasts' skulls. It split with the first blow, its face dropping to the floor while its body continued to jerk until the last of the repeater rounds ran their course.

He stepped over the lifeless body and did the same to the final corpse, cracking its head with ease and standing over it, watching until the electricity died out and the body fell still.

"Fucking hell," Lisa whispered.

"Fucking lucky," Wilson added as he returned to Collette and Lisa.

Collette wrapped her arms around him, hugging him tightly. Emotions rushed over him—love and fear mingled together with growing desperation.

"Are you all right?" she whispered into his chest.

"I'm fine. My head hurts like a motherfucker, but other than that, I'm fine. Thanks to you guys."

"So what now?" Lisa asked. "Do you still want to find out what the hell that thumping is or what?"

Wilson nodded. "I think so, yeah."

Collette released him, and he had to force himself not to pull her back near him. Staying focused was all that would keep them alive now. Allowing emotions to interfere with his thoughts and plans would be too dangerous.

Collette looked at him, her dark brown eyes failing to hide her fear. "Let's get it over with."

Chapter 5

Sutter and William left the security office and quickly retraced their steps back to Roger's corpse. Sutter studied the dead man and then passed by him, following the bloody footprints as they meandered through the passages.

They grew fainter with each step until they disappeared. Sutter carried on blindly down the corridor for another fifty feet until he reached the double bank of elevator doors. He stopped and stared at them, a smile spreading across his face. One pair of doors stood open, the "locked" lights on the control box lit.

"Back down to the labs." He pulled the keycard from his pocket.

"The labs?"

Sutter pointed to the illuminated numbers above the lift, each one corresponding to a floor on DARC12. "That one has moved," he explained, pointing to the lights above the closed set of doors. "It's back down at the biology labs. Somebody's still alive, and that's where they are."

William grinned broadly, his face mirroring Sutter's joy.

Sutter slid the keycard through the box and waited for the red light to disappear. When it had, the two men stepped into the elevator. Bristling with anticipation, Sutter closed the door and sent the lift on its descent to find the survivors.

Chapter 6

The strange, threatening sound had changed. There was still a concussion, to be sure, but it was no longer as steady and rhythmic. Instead, it sounded angry.

Lisa walked behind Collette and Wilson, watching the pair with envy. She could tell they had feelings for one another. Neither of them seemed inclined to act on them for whatever reason, but the attraction was obvious. She hoped to God they would at least take a moment to express their emotions before it was too late.

As for herself, suffice it to say, her relationship with Roger hadn't gone quite as she'd expected. She knew that love, or even simple companionship, had found its way out of her future. She envied Collette and Wilson, despite her frustration at their lack of acting on their feelings. They shared a connection, whether physical or not. And that, at the moment, was more than Lisa had.

But that didn't mean she'd lost the will to live. Quite the opposite, she thought as the trio stalked through the passageways in search of the alien beast. More than anything, she wanted to survive, to return to Earth and have another chance at living her life the way she wanted. She'd been on the verge of a breakdown just a short while ago, but that would not happen again.

She'd called up all the strength and fortitude from her youth, all the courage and resolve that could only be learned as a poor kid in the slums. It had gotten her through high school alive. It had fought off drunken perverts and thieving crackheads. It had taken her to her position as a lead biologist on board a DARC. And goddamn it, it would see her through this as well.

The banging was growing louder now, the force reverberating through Lisa's body.

Ahead of her, Wilson and Collette froze as they reached an intersection and started to turn right. She quickened her pace until she was alongside them, peering down the hallway. The thing they'd pulled from outer space sat a hundred-and-fifty feet from them. It was much like when she'd last seen it, only twice as large. And now it had grown tentacles. Four of them, each nearly as thick as a man, protruded from its urchin-like body.

The front two arms were pounding against one of the ship's doors. Dents slowly appeared as the steel gave way beneath the attack.

"It's trying to get into the stairwell," Wilson whispered.

The creature stopped its assault on the door, and the tentacles reached out behind it, latching onto the wall on one side of the hallway. With one swift, almost graceful motion, the thing flexed a tentacle and spun its body around one hundred-and-eighty degrees. There was no sign of a head, nor eyes, nor even a mouth—nothing to indicate that it was facing them.

It stretched its tentacles outward again, one gripping each wall of the corridor, sending out the thunderous booms they'd been hearing since reaching the lab level. It pulled itself forward, the grotesque body sliding effortlessly across the metal floor. It covered twenty-five feet or more with that single motion, then shot out the tentacles for another hellish stride.

Lisa raised her gun and fired. They'd come here to try and kill it, and they had no time to waste. She squeezed off a dozen rounds, and nearly all hit the mark. The thing was too damn big to miss.

It barely registered the shots, though. The serpentine limbs quivered, and its advance stalled briefly before propelling itself forward again. It had cleared over half of the corridor now.

"Run!" Wilson screamed at the exact moment Collette turned to do just that.

Lisa fired as the two security officers ran past her, and then she followed their retreat. The loud concussions of the monster's arms latching onto the walls shot through the metal, reverberating up her legs as she ran.

They raced through the ship, shooting up the first intersection then down the next, darting from passageway to passageway, but the thing was relentless in its pursuit.

And worse than the chase, worse than the burning lungs or the aching legs or the fear and adrenaline coursing through her mind and clouding her thoughts, were the voices.

They'd started the instant she had turned to flee from the approaching monster—quiet whispers that felt as though they were originating inside her mind rather than being heard. At first, it had only been a pair of feminine voices promising love and peace, redemption and salvation for all eternity. They spoke of her desires, of fulfilling all her wants and slaking every thirst and hunger she had ever felt.

Lies, of course, Lisa knew. As empty as the blackness from which everyone was born.

Suddenly, an epiphany struck her. She knew why the whispers had taken so long to find her. Her fears. Her dread, her newfound *weakness.*

Wilson, Collette, Lisa. They'd stayed strong throughout all that had happened. But now, fleeing from the creature, the possibility of death so close she could feel it breathe on her shoulders, there was a crack in her willpower. And the beast was using it to break her.

By the time she'd rounded the first corner, the voices had changed. The loving, caring, maternal whispers were gone, swallowed by a swirling cacophony. They spoke in a multitude of tongues—some recognizable, others so alien they scarcely seemed like speech at all—all of them calling out, screaming, and wailing like an army of the damned.

Legion.

The whispers of salvation were gone, replaced with promises of suffering and terror—torture that would last for eons. Punishment for rejecting a god, for daring to fight against His will. Beneath the words, she could understand the hellish song the alien tongues chanted, like a drumbeat of agony and abject horror.

They passed back through the corpses they'd killed moments before, weaving through the fallen crew members. Despite their unfaltering pace and the constant turns at every intersection, the thing was gaining on them quickly. Lisa could feel it growing nearer. The explosive thuds of its tentacles striking the walls grew louder and more powerful with each passing moment. The inhuman choir increased in fervor, nearing an almost indecipherable crescendo.

Lisa's mind raced. She tried to think of something—anything—that they could do to fight off this beast they'd salvaged from the cold darkness of space only days before. But to flee from it was the only course of action she could think to do. They had no way to kill such a thing. All they could do was run as if the devil himself were chasing them.

In that instant, something cold and wet enveloped her leg just below the knee. She pitched forward, throwing her hands out in front of her head as the metal floor rushed toward her.

Her face bounced off the backs of her hands, and the copper taste of blood filled her mouth. Before she could recover from the impact, a pain unlike any she'd ever felt before ripped through her leg.

She screamed and looked over her shoulder. One of the beast's tentacles had wrapped around her leg like an anaconda suffocating its prey. Blood oozed from above and below the serpentine appendage. It trembled as it chewed through her skin.

Lisa tried to fire her gun at the thing, but the shots went wild, ricocheting off the corridor walls, sending sparks of blue electricity flying through the air.

The pain intensified as the sound of cracking bones came from within the tentacles. She screamed out in agony and looked toward Collette and Wilson. Both security guards were running back to her, Collette trying to steady her gun to fire a shot at the thing. A second passed, feeling like an eternity, and Collette fired the repeater three quick times.

One of the rounds hit the thing, and Lisa could feel the tentacle spasm with the current, its grip on her not loosening in the least. A snapping sound echoed in the hallway, and suddenly Lisa was free of the thing. She tried to pull herself to her feet but collapsed when she tried to put weight on her throbbing leg. That's when she realized there was nothing there. The thing had gnawed it in two. Already the pain and blood loss were making her light-headed.

She crawled toward her comrades as they raced to help her, but before she could move even a foot, the beast grabbed her afresh. This time, around both of her thighs, a few inches above her knees.

The agony returned. Perhaps because she knew what was happening, it was no longer an unfathomable pain. She could feel the sharpness tear through her flesh. She cried out in pain, both physical and emotional, as she realized there was no longer any hope for her.

"Run!" she screamed at Collette and Wilson. They stood in place, staring at Lisa and the thing that had claimed her. Tears streaked Collette's face.

The edges of her vision went dim, and the sounds of the attack faded. The pain had all but vanished now. All that remained was a dull, burning sensation. She tried to fight back unconsciousness as her mind clouded.

"Run," she repeated. She realized the thing was pulling her away from Collette and Wilson. Another tentacle slid up her back, over her shoulder, and underneath her, forcing its way between her chest and the floor.

She felt it lifting her, then a flash of pain cutting into her chest, and then she felt nothing.

Chapter 7

"Run, Collette!" Wilson shouted and pushed her behind him, trying to urge her down the hallway.

He watched as the thing lifted Lisa and pulled her toward it. Her body went limp as Rodney's repeater dropped to the floor. The tentacle flexed, Lisa's blood spilling out from around it. The upper half of her body jerked downward, then fell free, crashing to the floor head first. The tentacle repositioned itself, sliding down and engulfing her legs. Another of the creature's arms shot out and scooped up her torso greedily.

Wilson had seen enough. Collette's face had gone pale; tears streamed down her cheeks.

"Come on, damn it!" he shouted as he pushed her again. "Get to the fucking lift!"

She obeyed, breaking into a mad dash down the corridor away from the thing, running so fast that Wilson could barely keep up.

He glanced over his shoulder before they turned down an intersection. The monster wasn't in pursuit yet; it was finishing its meal. One tentacle was still coiled around Lisa's remains like a giant, hellish snake. The tube-like protrusion that had once been its only appendage darted about the floor, writhing around in the spilled blood, drinking up the stuff.

Lisa's death came swiftly, but it replayed in Wilson's mind as he fled, stretching itself out into an eternity. He'd lead her down here, hoping to slaughter that beast, and it had torn her to pieces in seconds. Every plan he'd formulated, every course of action he'd taken, had only ended with more deaths.

He had no clue what he and Collette would do now. Return to the lifts, then return to the security office and regroup with Jack, who was probably the only other person left alive on the whole damn ship. But after that, his mind couldn't steer itself toward a plan. There didn't seem to be any point.

After a few minutes, the elevators fell into view, and Wilson forced his legs to speed up. The lifts were a temporary salvation, but salvation nonetheless.

Behind them, a concussion echoed through the ship.

"It's moving again," Collette said.

"Forget it. Just get to the fucking lift for now."

Halfway down the corridor, the elevator door on the right slid open, and two men strode out side by side. Wilson recognized one of them: Jim Sutter.

The sight of the man sent Wilson's mind reeling. Then suddenly, all the doubts he'd felt about his actions over the past few hours were gone. The blame he'd laid upon himself for all that had happened shifted immediately to Jim Sutter.

It had all started with Sutter, after all. He'd ushered in this pandemonium when he'd killed his wife and her friend. He'd even announced what was to come when Wilson questioned him, even if Wilson hadn't realized just what the madman had meant.

Fury welled up inside him, burning through his guts and erasing his fatigue, his pain, and his fear. He stopped trying to formulate a plan. There was only one thought raging through his mind, one single purpose: revenge.

Sutter had freed that beast. He'd deified it and killed for it, had somehow helped it in the slaughter of all the other crew members. He had created all the death and destruction on board DARC12, and Wilson knew it as sure as he knew they would all die on the ship.

Jim Sutter had to suffer for that.

"Shoot the fucker on the left," he whispered to Collette through clenched teeth. "Keep him down."

He charged forward, screaming like one of the dead they'd been fighting for so long.

His advance startled Sutter and his companion. Their steps faltered, and they glanced at one another before running forward to meet Wilson.

The man beside Sutter managed four steps before Collette's shots slammed into him and dropped him to his back. He writhed on the floor, screaming in what sounded not like pain but anger.

Wilson ignored the fallen man, his focus set firmly on Sutter. They charged toward one another as Collette's repeater rounds whizzed past Wilson, so close he could hear the crackle of the charges.

As they closed the distance between each other, Wilson could see that Sutter, too, had been infected by the same parasites that had filled Roger. The man's skin rippled and pulsated as the slugs squirmed about within his body.

Sutter squared his shoulders and lunged forward as if to tackle Wilson, but the security officer was too quick to be caught in the attack. He sidestepped Sutter and swung his baton hard, bringing it down solidly on the base of Sutter's neck, just above his shoulder blades.

Sutter dropped to the floor face down. He rolled himself over and looked up at Wilson, a mad grin stretched across his face.

Wilson tossed his baton to the floor. He wanted to feel Sutter's flesh split beneath his bare hands. He pounced on the man, punching at his face. Sutter threw up his hands, using one to try and deflect Wilson's blows and the other to mount an attack of his own. A couple of Sutter's punches connected with Wilson's jaw, but they barely registered. He was too focused on destroying the man beneath him to notice anything else.

He pounded his fists into Sutter's face, hammering away relentlessly. Muffled thuds gave way to wet cracks as Wilson beat his adversary, his rage and frustration channeling itself out of his psyche and into this one brutal assault. Sutter's pathetic punches ceased within seconds, and his arms fell prone beside his body.

Wilson continued until, at last, he had slaked his need for retribution. His punches slowed as his mind collected itself and his senses returned from the dark, blinding rage that had overtaken him.

Sutter's face was a mottled heap of red and blue and black, with a few broken teeth dotting it. Bloody bubbles formed near the center of the gory mess, accompanied by an almost inaudible wheezing and gurgling. A fat black slug slithered out of the mangled hole that was Sutter's mouth, and Wilson scrambled to stand. He backed up a few steps, staring as two more wormed their way out into the light and flopped to the floor, wriggling. Aside from those three, the slugs filling Sutter's body remained inside him. Wilson could still see them moving beneath the skin, only much weaker now.

He realized Collette's repeater had fallen silent, and he scanned the corridor.

Sutter's companion lay where he had fallen, a bloody mess. Dozens of the slugs that had infected Roger were scattered around him, their squirming already slowing.

Behind him, Collette approached slowly, her gaze flitting back and forth from Wilson to Sutter. The heavy slams of the creature moving through the hallways grew louder, and each impact caused Collette's body to jerk. Despite that, she wasn't sobbing anymore, nor did she seem to be on the verge of panic. Instead, her face was devoid of any sign of emotion.

"He died," she said flatly, jerking her pistol toward the corpse of the unknown man. "Same as Roger Han. As soon as the charges hit him, those things went crazy. He just…exploded."

Wilson stepped past Sutter's body, motioning for Collette to follow him. "Come on. We need to get the hell away from that thing."

They walked by the man, both of them watching as the slugs fell still, then they increased their pace until they were safely inside the lift.

"Where are we going now?" Collette asked, her hand hovering over the numbered buttons.

"I don't know. I would say the security level. It was the safest place on the ship. But Sutter and his friend had to have gotten in there somehow. Otherwise, they couldn't have used the lift."

She pressed the *close door* button. "I thought about that. Do you think Jack's dead?"

"No way to know for sure without going there. But it's probably swarming with those things. I guess we could either go back there, or to the captain's deck, or…I don't know."

"Why the captain's deck?"

"If the security level is fucked, the deck would be the easiest place to secure. Plus, we could try and call for help. Hell, we could even try to figure out how to change the ship's course and head back for Earth."

She didn't respond. Wilson watched her as she lowered her head and stared at the floor. Even after all she'd been through, she was still beautiful.

"Rodney," she finally whispered.

"I know. We'll deal with it if we have to. I'm sorry."

"It's not just that. I feel like we're running in fucking circles."

"I know. So do I. But at this point, what else can we do? Everything I've thought of has fallen to fucking pieces."

She shrugged. "So…where to?"

Wilson thought about it, listening to the approaching thuds outside the elevator. The voices that had filled his mind while fleeing from the monster were returning—tiny, near-imperceptible whispers growing louder by the second, murmuring threats and damnations directly into his soul. He tried to ignore them.

"The captain's deck." He pressed the corresponding button. "To hell with the security office. Odds are there's nothing there now but the dead."

"And Jack," Collette reminded him.

"If he's there, Jack's one of those fucking things by now. And even if he's somehow alive, he chose to stay there. There's nothing I can do now. I'm not going to risk losing you to try and save him."

The elevator lurched into motion, carrying them toward the top of the ship.

Chapter 8

The alien whispers prodding her mind had quieted as the elevator rose away from the beast, vanishing entirely mere seconds into their ascent.

Collette tried to will her pounding heart to slow itself, with no results. She was surprised, judging from its furious pace, that it hadn't given out yet.

Despite that, her mind was finally calm. She'd panicked, embarrassingly so, several times. Wilson, Rodney, even Lisa… They had all been rocks. Or at least, they'd hidden the fear Collette had let overwhelm her. Their strength had carried her through the Hell that had infested the DARC.

Watching the creature rip Lisa to pieces had nearly pushed her over the precipice of sanity, but, for some reason, when she and Wilson had met and dispatched Sutter and his companion, it had righted her mind. They'd taken back some sliver of control, conquering two of the architects who had designed the death of DARC12. And that victory, small as it was, had given her hope. That hope had saved her from the madness she'd been teetering above for so long. There was a chance, however infinitesimal, that they could somehow survive this ordeal.

Wilson sensed it as well. "You're all right."

Collette could hear the relief filling his voice. She nodded. "I'm still scared shitless. But yeah, I am. I don't know why, but I'm all right. I don't know how we're going to get out of this alive, but I guess I'm still holding out for a miracle. I know the odds of that are shit, but there's always a chance, right?" "

She looked at Wilson, almost expecting him to laugh at the statement. Instead, he smiled at her. It was half-hearted but still managed to help calm her more.

"I thought you'd lost it for a while there," Wilson said.

"So did I."

"And you're sure you're okay now?"

She smiled and nodded. "As okay as I can be. I don't want to die, but spending all my time dwelling on dying and being scared out of my fucking mind isn't doing anything for me except driving me crazy."

He didn't respond, and she turned the words over in her head.

"I'm sorry."

Wilson blinked. "For what?"

"For not doing more, I guess. For losing my shit—for wanting to just make some half-ass excuse and hide in the security office like Jack."

"But you *didn't* hide. That's the important thing. No matter how scared you were, you still followed me and Lisa every step of the way. You don't have to apologize for anything."

Tears welled up in her eyes—not from fear or panic or heartache, but relief that Wilson wasn't angry or disappointed in her. She choked them back and smiled at him. Their eyes locked in a gaze that, for only a split second, brought a wave of nostalgia washing over her.

It took her back to her youth, that look. Back to the moments leading up to her first kiss—that tingling anticipation mingled with doubt and hope and desire and excitement.

Wilson placed a hand on her shoulder and turned her body toward him. They embraced in the same instant he kissed her, and everything else in the universe melted away. For that all-too-brief moment, all of the horror she'd endured was forgotten. Even DARC12 was a distant memory. All that existed in that instant was her and Wilson, locked in the passion that had been building between them for so long.

She could have stayed like that for ages. Clutching Wilson close to her, their lips pressed together in the ecstasy that could only have been born from the years of longing they'd shared.

Instead of being granted the hours and days she dreamed of, the elevator doors interrupted them, opening with a familiar pneumatic hiss. The sound was menacing now, and Collette's survival instincts rushed back to her, washing away her desires. Instantly, she was back on the DARC, running for her life, trapped in Hell.

She assumed Wilson felt the same wave of fear, for he jerked away from her and raised his baton. The doors slid open to reveal the corridor beyond.

Wilson stuck his head through the doors and looked in each direction. "Let's go."

They exited the elevator and turned left, creeping down the hallway with their weapons drawn. Collette glanced over her shoulder every few steps, fearful the stairwell door behind them would slide open and unleash thousands of horrors.

They reached the corner of the hallway without incident and turned it without hesitation. Then they froze. Forty feet from them was the doorway to the captain's deck. Twenty feet past it was Rodney, walking toward them slowly.

His gaze was fixed on the floor in front of him. His mouth hung agape, and the corner of his upper lip twisted into a hateful sneer. A thick strand of intestine tried its best to escape from his wound. A loop of it dangled a few inches below his stomach, bouncing against his crotch as he walked.

Collette choked back a scream. She thought she'd prepared herself for this encounter, thought she'd steeled her nerves and made a solemn vow to put her friend out of his misery. Now, confronted with the reality of Rodney's fate, she could only stare in sorrow as the terrible remains approached her.

Rodney's gaze settled on Collette and Wilson. There was no hesitation or sign of recognition; he simply loosed a feral scream and charged toward them.

Wilson took a step forward and braced himself, readying his baton.

Collette forced her trembling hand up and fired off three quick shots. Two of the shots went wide, ricocheting off the corridor walls. The third connected with Rodney's chest, and the massive man stumbled, dropping to his knees.

Before Collette could fire again, Wilson darted toward the fallen giant, blocking Collette's shot. Wilson reached Rodney just as the repeater round had run its course, the dead man's body ending its violent spasms with a few twitches.

The big man lunged for Wilson, rising back to his feet as he did so. Wilson swung the baton, a scream erupting from him as he did. The sound of it chilled Collette. It was as wild and inhuman as any of the cries of the dead.

The club met Rodney's head and dropped the dead man face-first to the floor. Wilson squared himself above the fallen body, raining down blow after blow.

Collette watched in silence as Wilson finished his assault. His screams drifted off to a moaning, ragged breathing. Collette realized he was sobbing, his face red and covered with tears.

He stumbled back from Rodney and leaned against the wall, staring up at the ceiling until his breathing had calmed. Then he turned to Collette.

"I'm sorry."

She shook her head. "You didn't have a choice."

He said nothing for a moment, and then, "I locked the door to the deck when we left. Somebody let him out."

"Sutter?"

"Or Roger. Or someone else whose mind that thing managed to get into."

"Why the hell would they come all the way up here just to let Rodney out?"

"I didn't say they came up here just to let him out. But they definitely opened the door to the captain's deck for something."

"But for what?"

Wilson sighed. "Only one way to find out."

Chapter 9

The captain's deck looked just as they'd left it, aside from Rodney's body being gone, only a pool of congealed blood marking the spot where he had died.

Wilson scanned the room slowly, trying to spot something out of place. Some clue as to what the mystery visitor had done after freeing Rodney.

Collette stepped past him, looking around the room with her gun raised. She'd pulled herself together, and he was proud of her. She went from a woman on the verge of a mental break back to the strong, resilient security officer he'd been falling for over the past few years.

And that attraction had now been consummated, in a way. A mere kiss stolen between moments of horror, to be sure, but it had been a mutual display of affection and had been a bit of bliss tucked away amidst the hell infesting the ship.

He watched her now as she surveyed the captain's deck, beautiful despite her wounds. His sense of duty to her was different, thanks to that kiss. With their feelings for one another confirmed instead of hidden away, he felt an increased need to protect her.

Wilson pried his focus from her and walked to the closest control panel. Three screens displayed information. The first one was filled with dozens of groups of numbers and letters, all of which were meaning-less to him. The second appeared to be a status report. It listed the systems that operated the ship: REACTOR, DRIVE CORE, COOLANT, FUEL CELLS, and dozens more. All of them were accompanied by the word NORMAL.

The last screen was another series of numbers, but following them was a bright red message.

EMERGENCY AUTOPILOT ENGAGE__
THRUSTERS ACTIVATED__
TRAJECTORY CHANGE FAILURE__
TRAJECTORY HAZARDOUS__
ANOMALY IMMINENT__
EVENT HORIZON IN 3.93 MINUTES.

The numbers counted down, their rapid descent filling his gut with dread. He didn't understand physics in the least, but he'd heard the scientists on board the ship use all of the terms on the screen often enough to have a basic idea of what was happening.

"Motherfuckers," he whispered.

"Wilson." Collette moved to the front of the room and stood a few feet from the massive glass wall, staring out into space. "Something's wrong."

Wilson left the console. He didn't know how to operate the ship's controls, and judging from what he'd read on the screens, it wouldn't help them if he did.

He hurried to Collette's side and wrapped his arm around her, pulling her close.

Outside, directly in front of them, filling what was likely millions of miles, was a massive area devoid of anything. The universe, and all the things that filled it, bent and curved around this gigantic, unfathomable blackness.

The black hole they'd been orbiting. And now, it was growing larger by the second as DARC12 raced toward it. He let the blood-stained baton fall from his hand.

"Is that it?" Collette asked.

"Yes."

"Are we—"

"Yes."

He expected her to break down in hysterics.

Instead, she simply nodded her head. "Okay."

Wilson could see tears welling up in her eyes, and he held her tighter.

They passed a moment in silence, staring out at the approaching blackness.

"I feel...wrong," Collette said.

Wilson felt it, too—as if his entire body was being stretched. It didn't hurt. It was just a strange, uncomfortable tightness increasing steadily.

As the pressure built, so did his fear. He'd steeled himself for this moment, and now that it was upon him, his resolve was cracking. Panic welled up in him as the pulling sensation became painful.

Collette pulled away from him and dropped to the floor, screaming in agony. Wilson staggered a few steps forward and collapsed to his knees, his face pressed against the massive glass wall. His body felt like it was being turned inside out, every bone inside him on the verge of snapping. Every breath was a battle.

In the distance, the whispers of the thing from Containment Room Seven drifted into his mind. His pain somehow lessened, and he heard hushed promises of redemption and salvation. Of peace and unconditional love. An end to the agony. A way through the darkness.

But beneath it all, there was something sinister. Wilson sensed in the words a wanton desire for his life—for all life. For power, for control.

He pulled his mind from the voices, and the pain flooded back, a hundred times what it had been seconds before. Beside him, Collette's screams had fallen silent. He willed his eyes back into focus and stared through the glass, looking out one last time at the void before it claimed him.

ABOUT THE AUTHOR

Bryan Hall is an author living in a 100-year-old farmhouse nestled deep in the mountains of Western North Carolina with his dogs and kids. He's spent his life there, soaking up the history of the region, which sometimes finds its way into his work. In his free time, he plays guitar in local bands and does his best to sample the food and craft beers in the area regularly.

Now Travel Back into the Past and set sail on the Black Brig with…

Jeffrey Kosh's

Dead Men Tell No Tales

"Errol Flynn would be pleased, George Romero would be pleased, Howard Philip Lovecraft and Robert Louis would be pleased, and I think you'll be pleased, too."
–Trent Zelazny, award-winning author of *Tool Late to Call Texas.*

The Caribbean Sea, 1708 AD.

In Port Royal many have heard the legend of the *Black Brig*, a ship of the damned bringing a fate worse than death to the isolated colonies of the Caribbean Sea.
But few know the true story behind the tavern tales.
As the war between the Northern Alliance and the League of the Antilles looms on the horizon, an old captain is ready to embark on a venture to cease the blight of the Black Brig once for all and have his revenge.

Set in an alternate historical setting, where a supernatural plague caused the fall of the European powers and where what was left of humanity struggles to survive in the New World, DEAD MEN TELL NO TALES - THE FULL TALE narrates the ghastly voyage pirate captain Daniel Drake Davies underwent in 1676, and the events that will force him to confront those same horrors thirty years later. For the dead do not rest peacefully in the Devil's Sea.
Pirates, voodoo, and seagoing undead await you in this fantastic journey in a land that never was.

NOW
1708 AD

PROLOGUE

THE BLACK GULL

Scurvytown, Port Royal, Jamaica

Life on the *Account* was filled with danger, and those who made their living on the high seas were often hardened people with nothing to lose—except their life, and large cravings.

Sailors were paid at trip's end, so they often blew away the entire wage in their shore leave. Nevertheless, there was no way to spend it aboard ship, and one never knew whether their next journey could be their last. Better make good use of all that gold rather than having it weigh you down into *Davey Jones' Locker*—the bottom of the sea. Swabs, scurvy dogs, bilge rats, and true buccaneers had no hesitation when time came to squander their loots; the taverns and brothels of Port Royal became their haunts first and foremost.

The richest favored those dives lining the narrow thoroughfares of the docks, where food was the heartiest and whores the prettiest.

The desperate stuck with Scurvytown's wretched dens of scum, where food was barely edible and the whores…well, you couldn't tell if they were members of the opposite sex.

Scurvytown was officially labeled as the "Privateer Quarter," yet no one off the boat used that name. They reserved it for the whole dockside part of town, separating it from the "Toffs Quarter," meaning the genteel district, where "*landlubbers*" or respected merchants made their home. The unmapped borders of Scurvytown were generally located on the east end of the harbor. The place earned its nickname by the decrepit condition of its squalid tenements, the huge transient aggregation, poverty-stricken inhabitants, and the ample spread of diseases. Brawls and bobbing bodies in the harbor were common sights, as well as the loud carousing of drunken rogues of the vilest sort.

Scurvytown was the place for those that had given up, or had no other place to go, squashed together by the same fate—that of the losers. They spent their time wasting away, unwilling to crawl up from the pit of squalor they had fallen into, dreaming about their past, brooding on their present, and dread-ing the future. Most of these squatters survived by doing an odd job or another by day, and ending up spending the few coppers by night in taverns and inns. The vast majority of these dens were decaying wooden buildings that hadn't seen repairs or maintenance in decades, often dug out from old warehouses, and they showed it.

One of such places was the *Black Gull.*

It took its name from a huge raven the first owner, Willie Jameson, used to keep as a pet. One night, a sailor who was so drunk he didn't know where he was, looked up from his empty mug and said, "Avast! That's th' blackiest an' ugliest gull me deadlights have ever seen!"

Immediately, Jameson renamed the bar and replaced the sign out front with a painting of the bird. A fixture in Port Royal, the tradition of keeping a raven as companion by the *Black Gull*'s owners never died, and the actual one, Angus Mc-Ready, had a large specimen named *Bean.*

The *Black Gull* was the *punch house* young officer Robert J. Higgins was looking for. Not to quench his thirst, or to find warm company for the night. No, this young fellow was looking for his new captain. Come tomorrow, he would embark on a special mission for the League, acting as liaison officer for the *Revenge*, one of the sturdiest warships in the fleet. Still, even as an agent of the Council, he knew nothing of the mission's nature, something that had clearly upset him. How could he perform efficiently if he didn't know the goal? Being a dutiful and respectful officer, Higgins never questioned his superiors, even when they clearly showed lack of experience and common sense. Nonetheless, he had enough brains to know this time it was different. There was no actual secrecy in the mission, just laziness on the part of Commodore Brian Addams. That big pig was the shame of the League's fleet, having bought his rank and position with large sums of money. A notorious epicurean, Addams spent more time at orgies than at planning ship's rosters and assignments. Robert was almost sure his name had been picked randomly from a list. Not for skills or good conduct, but out of pure chance. Knowing this in his heart, Higgins had opted for an innocent investigation, and instead of wasting away his evening at futile pleasures, he had spent some coins on snitches to locate his captain-to-be. He wanted to know the man he was going to serve before feeling the *Revenge*'s decks under his feet.

He knew his standing and strived to stick by the rules. Rules were made to be followed, as doing different would lead to anarchy, and anarchy was just the threshold to chaos. And Robert Higgins hated chaos. So, his impact with Port Royal's wild nature had immediately been a negative one.

Even worse was the *Black Gull.*

The place was rowdy, smelly, and wet. Carousers were singing old mariners' chanteys by the fireplace, and a quartet of evil-looking…"*privateers*"…was playing cards surrounded by a small crowd of excited onlookers. Scarcely clad wenches rounded the tables, dodging some probing hands, yet welcoming others. Yes, if Port Royal was the wickedest city in the New World, the *Black Gull* was its main cathedral, from whose pulpit the verb of debauchery was spread.

Higgins scoured the place, looking for the man Peg-Paw Milton, a street informer in Scurvytown, had described to him. And found him seating in a darkened corner, his feet resting on the table while he seemed to be dozing away under the brim of his tricorn hat.

The young officer made his way with disgust amidst the crowd of smelly rogues, lifting a perfumed handkerchief to his sensible nose more than once.

"Excuse me, sir?" he hazarded almost in a whisper, fearful to cause a rude awakening to his future master. Yet, the large man didn't move. "Captain?" he insisted, this time a bit louder.

"Aye, me lad, have a seat next to me and listen to the true story of the *Banshee's Cry*," the older man said, addressing him without moving an inch. The chap wasn't sleeping.

Hesitantly, Higgins tried to introduce himself, but the burly, and rather unkempt, man shooed him instantly. "No need for presentations, lad. Just listen to me story and pay me some hearty company this night."

Peculiar. Quite peculiar, Higgins thought. Surely, the man was drunk, but he also was as alert as a weasel. Better to play by his rules.

"You know the *Banshee's Cry* legend, do you?" Higgins replied with a hint of disbelief as he rested his back on the nearby stool. In every tavern around the known world, there were dozens of people claiming to know details of what had happened at Cayman Brac. All of them were just calling for attention, or to gain confidence on greenhorns like him. Higgins was disappointed his soon-to-be captain could be another of those braggarts. He gave the oldster a dis-believing look.

"Aye. I know the legend 'cause I have seen it meself. I was there when the Plague ended once for all," the captain insisted.

****

The captain studied the intruder, evaluating his dress and manners.

All the same, these young landlubbers, coming on the account with star-crossed eyes, dreaming of adventure in this age of rebirth. They envisioned the growing war between the Northern Alliance and the League of the Antilles as a quick way to glory and wealth, yet they knew nothing of how this New World came to be, nor of those who had sacrificed their own lives to build it. And mostly, they ignored the Plague's truth. They curled their nose at the smell of Port Royal alleys and docks, forgetting about the pleasant fragrance the sea carried on westerly winds. Because they had not lived in a world perpetually immersed in rot and decay.

"Sir, go on. I'm curious. You say you were there," mouthed the young mariner eyeing the small wooden chest resting under the man's feet, "but where, exactly?"

The captain gazed at him intently, then gulped down a draft from his mug. "*Mabouya's Well*," he said, almost whispering, that simple word still sending a shock down his spine. Even after all these years, he couldn't shake off that ghastly sensation.

"*Mabouya's Well?* Never heard about it, sir. What's this? A place in the *Devil's Sea*, a cay? Or..." Higgins hazarded, "...a tavern?"

The old mariner pierced the boy with steel-gray eyes. "Blimey! Ain't believing me, ain'tcha? Fine, keep listening to bilge scum the Roundheads pump every day into the Recovery Effort. Come the morrow, bucko, you'll be pumping water yourself from the *Revenge*'s belly. Avast! Listen to me story and I promise you'll see with your deadlights the proof of what me talking."

He rejoiced at the sight of shock on the lad's face. Yes, he knew who he was and why he was here. Time to give the greenhorn a lesson about old seadogs.

However, the foppish boy didn't flinch; he kept his countenance, then straightened his back. "With all due respect, sir, I do not trust the Puritans. That's why I left New Hampshire colony and joined the Southern Royalists. Before discovering the ruse behind false promises," exclaimed the boy, his usually fine skin turning red by rekindled memories.

A smirk formed on the captain's face. Yeah, the lad was bold, maybe a bit stiff, but he could see he was the right one for the job at hand. He would fight valiantly. "Belay it, lad. Go to the bar and have this jug filled again. Then, I'll tell you a tale so grisly and scary you ain't going to sleep for months. And you be wary, 'cause the ghosts of those times still haunt us today, no matter what the Northerners say. The *Marauders* aren't a bunch of crazies, and the *Black Brig* still plies these waters."

"The *Black Brig*? A fairy tale?" Higgins exploded, clearly disappointed, then he recalled his position and quickly apologized to his commanding officer. Or at least his mouth did, for his eyes didn't. "At your command, sir. I'll fill your mug."

The boy was about to leave for the bar when the older sailor's hand reached out and grabbed his coat's cuff. "No need for that. Lissen." He invited the youngster to sit down. "Aye, this is a legend. Yet, this is also true. 'Cause that ship sailed under a different name once. Her name was *Banshee's Cry*, and she was a fine ship. She was…my ship."

THEN
1676 AD

CHAPTER ONE

<u>*THE SANTA ESMERALDA*</u>

25 Miles off the coast of Inagua

"Bring her about handsomely, now!" Captain Drake shouted to be heard above his boarding crew's cries. Smoke engulfed the prow of the Banshee's Cry, as the brig came closer to the wounded Spanish merchantman.

"Avast! Moor that pregnant sow before she goes adrift," echoed MacTavish below, snapping curses in Gaelic. Drake looked amused at his boatswain. MacTavish had been with him since the beginning. An almost gnomish creature, with ash colored hair crowning a childlike face, Mac—as everybody called him— had a direct and honest personality and everyone respected him for this. He was now manning the planks with Luther, the hulking German gun master.

The Spaniard merchantman—the *Santa Esmeralda*—was a large three-masted trade vessel. Although well armed, the ship had easily fallen prey to the smaller and maneuverable brig. Its crew however had refused to surrender even after the *Banshee's Cry* had released a full load of volleys to the transport, killing most of his crew belowdeck. They were now crowding the main deck ready to stand for a final defense. Their Captain, Marcelo Salazar, was among them, trying to keep a noble countenance, but clearly shivering in his foppish leggings.

"It makes no sense, Drake," shouted Mac. "Why are they fighting?"

"Ask 'em when we are in residence. Mac," he snapped, then rushed to the castle followed by the boatswain's laughs. "I just may, Cap'n."

Drake swung from a rope directly between the two vessels, and landed his boots on the deck, then ran his cutlass through a man, drew a pistol from the fresh-made corpse and shot another with the dead man's flintlock.

At that, a swarm of fierce fighters, seasoned by years of battles, flooded the larger vessel, and the ocean filled with the clangor of blades and the sharp sound of released shots.

Handsome, in a wild fashion, Daniel "Drake" Davies had clearly seen better days. His curly black hair, steel-gray eyes, olive-tanned skin, and robust nose revealed his Spanish blood; features he had inherited from his Andalusian mother. Daniel's father was an English fisherman from Jersey Island and this was reflected in the tall cheekbones framing his face. An unkempt and wiry beard covered most of his chin and jaw. On his neck dangled five different medallions, all coming from different parts of the world. A wooden bead necklace from Africa and a leather cord fastened to a tiny satchel from New England's natives. Another held a small metal cross from Spain, and piece of string tied to a shark tooth hailed from the Caribbean Sea. Last, a thin chain from which swung a Chinese coin. Circling his right bicep was an intricate armband made of crocodile hide, with two inlaid small teeth of the same beast. Drake had received it in his last trip to St. Lucia from a Carib, as a gift for helping him escape the clutches of a sadistic Frenchman who liked to skin natives alive.

A voice reached him. "Captain Drake. Face me."

He turned and smiled at the foppish figure wielding a well-crafted rapier. The Spaniard captain. It seemed courage had returned to him at once. "*Capitan* Salazar, *por favor*, there ain't need for bloodbath. Call back your dogs and this will be—" Drake dodged a swing from a mariner's sword, then, quickly, plunged his own blade in the assailant's throat. "—over quickly," he concluded, then booted the body from his blade.

"No. *A la muerte*!" Salazar raised his rapier in the traditional salute of duelists.

"This is stupid, *hermano*. Just surrender and we'll bring you to Port Royal, where you'll be free to pick your destiny not your ..." Drake never finished, as the Spaniard released a battle cry and thrust his pointed blade straight to his heart, forcing the pirate to jump backward to avoid the lethal strike. He rolled his eyes, grinned, tossed away the spent pistol, and wiped his cutlass on the dead body. "Well, *hombre*, you looked for it."

Blades flashed so quickly the eye couldn't follow as the two swordsmen exchanged blows, feinted, and parried with such mastery that soon, both the pirates and the merchantman's sailors stopped fighting to watch the incredible show.

"I was trained by Alonzo Mendoza in person," Salazar said while spinning on himself and tracing a small cut on Drake's already scarred face. "My family spent a fortune."

Drake jumped sideways, grabbed the opponent's cloak, and then yanked it, causing the Spaniard to lose his balance while he kicked him hard in the butt. The cloak tore off suddenly and Salazar fell facedown, his rapier escaping his hand.

"Really? A rum-sponge named Pete taught me. It cost me one doubloon and a night with the prettiest whore in Toffs Quarter." Drake kicked Salazar's rapier away while he pointed the cutlass at the man's nape.

Yells filled the deck as Drake's men saluted his triumph, yet he cut it short.

"Ahoy, mateys! Follow the rules and nobody will be hurt. We're not here to kill the crew of this floating barrel; we just want your gold. So, please, line up and collaborate with me lads. Do not, and as sure as me name's Drake, I'll have you pay a visit down to Davey Jones' Locker. And I mean the bottom of the sea," he announced, then to underline it, raised his hand and released a shot from the Salazar's own pistol.

The sailors seemed to understand because they immediately formed a line and extended their hands forward. Drake's eyes ran to his loyal boatswain and a smirk formed at the corner of his mouth when he met the little man's eyes: he was glaring. They had made a bet, the day before, that Drake wouldn't be able to refrain using that line about Davey Jones' Locker, for he always did after capturing a chase. And Drake had clearly lost.

Meanwhile, the rest of the boarding party busied themselves getting down to the hold, eager to put their craving hands on the precious cargo. After so many days spent on the cramped *Banshee's Cry*, the merchantman seemed enormous, and its belowdecks like the dungeons of a Donnish prison. Yet, the *Santa Esmeralda* was nothing compared to the great galleons that used to ply these very waters before the Plague. The legendary prize-ships of the Spanish fleet used to cart gold and silver from the Spanish Main to the crown back in Spain. Those gargantuan cows could reach sixty yards in length and twenty yards on the beam, with a tonnage of more than two thousand. But they were a rarity nowadays as there was no more the need to carry cargo back to defunct Spain. Gold just traveled from the Main to *Nuevo Madrid*, in Cuba.

Nuevo Madrid. Just the thought of that infernal place sent shivers down Drake's spine. It was rumored the place was one of the strangest sights in the whole world. The Spaniards, far from being in decline, as the Northern Alliance's propaganda said, were busy building something more akin to ants than to Christians. Tall tales were spoken of a city built like a beehive, a truly immense many-layered structure, reaching high into the sky, whose tapering peak consisted of the King's palace, also doubling as the center of Catholic worship in the New World. For the King of Nueva España was also the Pope of the Holy Roman Church, and his innumerable lackeys, bootlickers, and…concubines shambled inside the dark corridors of *El Trono de Dios*—as the King's palace was known—like mindless drones. It was said the entire city was built like a hollow cone, and people from all over the world crowded it from level to level. Yet, there were also tales of engineering marvels, and incredible machineries, as whispers abounded that the artisans of *Nuevo Madrid* had harnessed the power of the steam. Nevertheless, all this industry had caused the area surrounding it to be reduced to ash wastes. So, like terrible *anthills*, swarms of thralls of the Crown streamed out of the gigantic mound to feed the endlessly hungry forges, making of *Nuevo Madrid* a reverse *Dante's Inferno*.

The sun colored the horizon in orange strokes as it set down when Geist the albino, manning the Banshee crow's nest, issued an unexpected shout, snapping Drake out of his cerebrations.

"Sail Ho!"

Drake bolted to the rails, releasing his hold on the Spaniard captain, his eyes squinted at the sea, yet seeing nothing. Mac put immediately the glass at his eye, scanning the distance. "Shiver me timbers," he muttered, handing the tool to Drake. "Risen!"

Drake looked through the spyglass, and what he saw chilled his blood.

Huge holes gaped on the approaching *Slaver* and rotten boards jutted randomly from the sides. The foremast's top was broken off, and lay on the warped deck, amid dangling and trailing bits of ropes. Yet, what scared him most was not the sailing derelict itself, but the crew manning it.

Dressed in filthy rags, they were horrible to behold. Rotting away, yet, somehow still holding whole, with strands of algae entangled in their hair or hanging from their gnashing mouths. Bony and thin limbed they were, belying their powerful nature. Rubbery, dead-cold flesh, crisscrossed by innumerable wounds, hung loose from visible bones. Some were missing an arm or leg, but many had replaced them with other instruments. There, he could spot a blade jutting out from the stump of a burned forearm. Another had three sickles protruding as wicked claws. And axes, cutlasses, pitchforks, knives. Even more ghastly seemed the unholy decorations dangling from their very putrid skin. Severed fingers, ears, and toes had been employed by the hellish horde like earrings and bracelets. Notable among them were the truly hideous mutations; the so-called *Hullghouls*. Their bodies stood twisted in the extreme, with hairless leathery skin and evil talon-like claws. Their oversized, slobbering mouths were filled with razor-sharp teeth, made to rend flesh from bone, and their sick bodies were covered by unnatural pustules and bulging veins.

"All aboard!" Drake shouted. "Leave ship now! Whoever lingers shall be left here, hurry up!" He meant it. As cruel as it could sound, there was no other way. You couldn't kill the living dead, because they were dead already. Yes, you could delay them by chopping off their limbs, but it was impermanent. The only way to put them down for good was to destroy their brains. And that wasn't an easy task.

In addition, they carried the Plague.

It had all started ten years before, in now fallen England. Survivors said the Plague was brought into Southampton by the *Sea Venture*, a Navy frigate captained by Robert H. Hackett. Nobody knew where the crew had caught that unholy disease. Besides, none cared; they were too busy evacuating the Old World when they had realized it was not possible to contain it. When the Risen crew had shambled out the docked vessel, causing horror among the inhabitants, they were dealt with by the city militia, at least it seemed so. Then, the fiend bodies had been piled and set to flame, which cremated their cursed flesh to cinders. But soon, the dead from cemeteries and lonely graves began to rise, and people showed symptoms of the Plague. By Christmastime, it had reached London. Not even the Great Fire had stopped it. In less than five months, the Plague had spread to mainland Europe, killing off thousands of people and reanimating as much to this evil mockery of life.

Some said it was not a disease, but God's wrath, unleashed on mankind for his sins. Christians had flocked to churches, locking inside, endlessly praying the Lord to save their souls in the upcoming Apocalypse. Others blamed the foreigners, or the women, or cats, or rats, or whatever came to their blurred minds.

And everything Drake knew was lost.

Somehow, the Plague had not fallen on the New World—nobody knew why. Still, no one cared. The exodus from the Old World had been a messy affair, in which anarchy had reigned more than civil manners. Bribes and weapons insured survival to a higher degree than royalty and clerical influence did, and the New Word became a place for the merchant, not for the noble.

For years, what was left of humanity was busy at eking out a new existence in a pristine, yet alien land. New dangers and challenges were paired to new marvels and experimental societies, as the Europeans had tried to adapt and thrive. The most powerful royalties had desperately fought to hold their status quo in the colonies, like England and Spain, but others had fallen to anarchy and civil war. New kingdoms were born, and unbelievable alliances were formed, such as The *Directorate of New England* and the *Kingdom of Nouvelle France* pact. Then, wars had started again. For human nature never changes.

Wars were fought over ideologies, resources, even women. And when it seemed the reign of the human race had reached an end in this world, out of the blue had emerged the *Northern Alliance*. With the might of combined armies and advanced firearms—mostly due to the expertise of Chinese engineers—it had quickly engulfed and subdued the surrounding barbaric warlords. Soon, the powers that be decided that all colonies should unite under their rule. And again, there was some disagreement on that point.

A War for Unification started, causing a literal exodus to the independent colonies of the Caribbean Sea. Well, they didn't find a promised land here, for it was already wracked by civil war and piracy. In the League, a ship could bring you a job as an independent. But only a gun could help you keep it.

Six months ago, the first Risen vessel had been spotted near Hispaniola. There had been questionable attacks on small settlements and tiny colonies previously, yet the League blamed rogues, royalists, and the dreaded Alliance Peacekeepers. However, these bloodthirsty attacks left no survivors, and carried away none of the booty from their nightly raids.

Except people.

Raided villages appeared desolate and silent to those unfortunate berthing their ship in these dead places.

Then, the smell of decay had settled in, forever lingering as an evil taint.

Now, the Risen were approaching quickly, driven by unnatural winds. God only knew how it was possible for that wreck to float, let alone to veer and sail. Yet, it changed tack with swiftness, as would a monstrous shark giving chase to a tasty morsel.

"Leave ship now!" Mac outcried, desperately trying to have his mates abandon the boarded freighter. Drake was already at the tiller, frantically shouting orders to the crew, his gaze frozen on the incoming monstrosity.

"In the name of God, do not leave us here!" Captain Salazar pleaded, all hostility forgotten, running to the planks and grabbing Luther's arm. The hulking German didn't flinch; he got loose of the hold and punched the Spaniard so hard he fell overboard. At that sight, chaos ensued and more than ninety men hurried toward the smaller brig, recklessly pushing everyone on their path, fighting to reach the intact vessel's safety.

"Come off it," Drake ordered, eyeing the tattered sails. "Make speed. Bring her about!"

The *Banshee's Cry* maneuvered away from the *Santa Esmeralda*, causing most of the boarding mariners to plunge down in the frothing waters, while others clung to the keel, yet these too were easily dealt with by the pirates.

"God forgive us," muttered Mac, taking hold of the helm.

Drake nodded, but he knew there was no other choice. The brig had place for seventy men and twenty passengers; there was no space for all those people. He allowed himself a last view of the doomed freighter, before taking his decision. "Make for the Caicos."

Mac nodded and shouted, "Ready about!" And all the hands hurried to their duties.

****

Later, they took advantage of strong wind to gain distance from the ship of the dead.

Seen from a distance, the *Banshee* was beautiful to behold. Her sails were drawn in the morning zephyr as she cut a swift whooshing trail through the sparkling waters.

On board the brig, however, the image was different. Fighting men, brooding and wounded, shoved for space in the cramped ship. Their moral floundered; arguments easily broke off at every opportunity. These men had fought for nothing. They had come so close to sinking their hands in Indian gold, only to be yanked back by the arrival of that monstrosity.

Geist scanned stern-side, figuring to spot the tattered canvases at any moment. But the dead were not giving chase, and he knew why; they were busy capturing the stranded Spaniard crew. Tavern tales said the Risen ate the living.

He knew better.

The fiends had no need for eating or drinking. Nay. They liked their victims alive, to abuse and torture 'em for days, feeding from the pain they caused. They only wished to spread the Plague, until only Death would reign. It was told they could only move in the dark, as sunlight made them drowsy, so their ship's interior was kept in pitch black darkness where they mulled about waiting for the hated sun to go down.

Geist, born Sven Haralson, was a new addiction to the *Banshee*'s crew. Tall and gangly, he looked like one of those wretched creatures, more similar to a dead than a living being, with his stark white straight, long hair and sunken eyes the color of polar ice. More than an experienced sailor gave him a wide berth, for they chilled just by looking at him. They said he was born of the Devil. Or that he was a vampire, for he loathed sunlight and was mostly active by night. He was rarely accepted aboard pirate ships, and everywhere he went, silence reigned.

But Captain Daniel Drake was different. He had noticed the man's keep vision and excellent marksmanship. Ignoring all protests from Mac, he had welcomed him on the *Banshee's Cry.* And he had never disappointed his captain. Geist could see better than anyone in the darkness. More than once, Drake had gotten his ship through shoal water and dangerous reefs with Geist on the forecastle. So, it was natural Drake trusted Geist's eyes to spot the fiend's sails in time.

In the morning, they tacked southward, entering the Windward Passage between Cuba and Hispaniola. The sea was rough and winds came and went, yet the *Banshee* performed well, and by the next dawn, they spotted Tortuga on the portside. They continued on, never stopping to founder ship in a safe harbor, too fearful of being ambushed by the undead.

Five days later, they arrived in Port Royal with a sundered mood, and an empty hold.

As the *Banshee* made her way to the docks, Drake knew that within moments there would be gunshots and celebrating yells from the population, as the arrival of a privateering ship always signaled prosperity and trade.

Yet none came for them.

CHAPTER TWO

RED LEG

Port Royal, Jamaica

It was the cackling sound of Nero's croaks that woke him up from the deep slumber he had fallen into. Otherwise, Drake would have slept the whole day, wily scoundrels allowing.

Nero was the pet raven of Willie Jameson, the owner of the *Black Gull*.

He opened an eye, and immediately regretted it. The sun was too bright for his dizzy head, the fumes of last night's carousing playing wickedly with his senses. He tried to sit up but realized that something heavy was blocking his movements. He panicked, then noticed the reddish ringlets of hair sheathing his neck and shoulders and smirked.

That had to be Justine, the whore he had spent the night with.

Pain pierced through his weary mind as he took in his surroundings. He was lying on one of the *Black Gull*'s mangy beds in the bunkrooms on the second floor.

He shoved the prostitute off his belly and stood slowly, going for the window, where that noisy black pest perched. The girl moaned something unintelligible under her breath—a French curse, probably—then continued her slumber. At his approach, the raven flew away, cackling again, elegantly swooping down to reenter the building by the main floor.

"Damn you, matey," Drake mumbled, then took a deep intake of the harbor's late morning air.

Travelers from gentler parts of the world could delight in the delicious smell of freshly cooked seafood, seasoned with countless spices. Yet, they would retch at the rank stench of port waters, rotting fish, rubbish, and offal, which permeated Scurvytown's shabby moorings.

For Drake, a seasoned seaman, it smelled like orchids and roses if equated to the ripe stink of a Royal Navy's brig.

That was the perfume of freedom, the smell of liberty.

Drake loved Port Royal. Where in the world could you find a place as individualistic and unbound to rules as the buccaneer's town?

He also liked the sounds of the place. The city was never quiet, humming with the commotion of arguments, the cacophonic chorus of rickshaws rolling over cobbled streets, the screeches of alley cats blending with the constant snap of the vessel's flags. And most of all, the crash of the surf against the dock's bulwarks.

Next, came the wind.

There was always a breeze in the city, whistling constantly as it journeyed through the narrow and twisted streets, carrying the smell of sugarcane fields north of town.

Watching filthy beggars struggle through abandoned stacks of crates, searching for anything valuable enough amidst the rotten remains of discarded vegetables, reminded Drake of his duties, lest he was going to suffer the same fate.

He closed the shutters, easing the tired wench's slumber. Then, he reached out for his discarded clothes that lay in a chaotic display on the floor, like jetsam carried by the morning's tide. The faded brown leather breeches, he already wore, having slept with them on, apparently. He single-handedly fastened the crotch's strings, at the same time employing his English smallsword to lift the dirty, white cotton shirt from the timbered floor, scaring a hiding mouse in the process. Passing the garment over his head, while still holding the blade with the right hand, he secured it at the waist with the bead-embellished, heavy-buckled belt he never parted with—a memento of his exploits in the Spanish Main.

Last, he slipped on the tall leather boots, fastening them at the back of the calf. They were poor affairs, ill-tended and cracked at the seams, a shadow of their past glory—just like Drake himself.

Someone knocked at the door.

"Damn you to hell and be gone," he said while struggling with the left boot.

"Captain Davies," a burly voice seeped through the door. "You're expected at Admiralty. At once."

He smirked. Partying had been wise, last night. For this was the day of apologies and sorrow.

And he had a bad feeling about it.

****

Admiral Red Leg was waiting for him.

"Drake! You old scoundrel, I was eager for your return," exclaimed Red

Leg at the sight of the young captain entering his office. "That's good news to me."

Morgan "Red Leg" O'Neill, nicknamed the "Admiral" because he was one of the most influential men in Port Royal, was the only survivor of Captain Henry Morgan's failed assault to Puerto Principe in Cuba. Henry Morgan was destined to become the greatest member of the Brethren of the Coast had they not been slain in that perfectly planned attack-turned-into-a-trap. When he showed up in Port Royal claiming the Dons were ready to attack Jamaica, Red Leg was hailed as a hero. Thanks to this information, the raid was successfully repealed and he was commissioned by Governor Thomas Modyford as Captain of the Colonial Militia. For an Irish slave, sent to the colonies by Cromwell, it had been a great personal victory to gain such position among the Englishmen. Born in Ireland, before the Plague, Morgan O'Neill was of noble heritage. Yet, he lost all his privileges when Oliver Cromwell subdued the Irish Revolt of 1649. Morgan became a footpad at first, just to survive, then joined a band of brigands to prey on Puritans and finance Royalists' coffers. An idealist, Morgan embraced his Catholic upbringing, preferring an Anglican king rather than a Puritan tyrant. For years, he fought against Parliamentarians as a highwayman, until Charles II was restored to the throne. Yet, things did not go as he'd expected. Most of the land that Royalist supporters had lost in England was returned to them. This didn't happen in Ireland, however, and the old aristocracy was outraged. They had fought Parliamentary forces for the king, so why shouldn't they get their lands back? They formed themselves into bands called *Rapparees* and began raiding Protestant settlements, robbing from the rich and giving to the poor, finally united with their lower-class Catholic neighbors. These brave rogues lived in the hills of Wicklow, Tipperary, and other remote areas, swooping down at night and staying hidden by day. Betrayed by his king, Morgan became infamous as the *Red Fox*, a *rapparee* operating near Tipperary, until he was apprehended and sent to Barbados as a slave. There, he became one of the colony's "*Red Legs*," so named because of their easily sunburned fair skin. Forced to work in a sugar plantation for the Speight Company of Bristol, he led a slave-revolt, captured a merchant ship, and turned to piracy. With his crew of former slaves, Captain Red Leg preyed on Spanish, French, and English ships alike, until he opted for pardon at Port Royal and became a privateer. After the Chaos Years, during which all support was lost from the homeland, Jamaica fell into turmoil and civil war, as different groups battled for supremacy in that tiny colony.

At last, the League of the Antilles won by might of arms, supported by merchant's gold and piratical interests, and Modyford's royalists were hung at every lamppost. Modyford himself was lynched by the hungry mobs.

They had behaved no different from the Risen.

"Look, Morgan, I had a problem with the straggler—" Drake started apologizing, but was immediately shushed by Red Leg.

"Belay it! I don't care if you returned so early and without a prize on the tail. It's fairly evident that you botched it. Anyway, me dear friend, I've got something higher into me mind, than gold."

Drake stared at him, and then glanced back at the two heavily armed, evil-looking men standing guard. Better to look for a quick way out just in case this "*higher thing*" had something to do with his neck and a rope.

Red Leg's office was large, and exquisitely fitted with a sturdy, but finely, carved table covered by charts. Behind the table stood a plush chair, on which Morgan sat clutching a glass filled with red wine. A rarity these days; clearly a show of his influence. Not even the King of *Nouvelle France* in America could afford a single sip.

Drake gazed into Morgan's glowering icy-blue eyes, which were set in an oval face with a strong nose and a snow-white long mane. "What's this? A raid at St. Augustine? Or do you want to twist the Lion's tail at Jamestown?

Red Leg's laughter boomed in the large room. "Nay. None of that. We aren't talking lowly coups or sabotage of the Alliance war effort." He rose from his seat and, with a long stride, came closer to the younger captain. "This is an errand of mercy."

What was he talking of? Mercy and Red Leg were as opposite as cats and dogs. This old man had sent to the Almighty more than one-hundred souls.

"A little bird told me you were planning to leave for Tortuga."

"Nay, Morgan. I won't be here enjoying your company and," he pointed to the lonely glass of wine on the desk, "your good manners, if me planned that."

Red Leg glanced back at the crystal glass, then returned his gaze to him, lifting an eyebrow. "Oh, you want that? I do sincerely apologize for my lack of courtesy, Captain." He bowed ceremoniously, then snapped his fingers. Immediately, the two goons were on Daniel, seizing his arms.

"Do you think you deserve that, old scoundrel?" Morgan wasn't really upset; he was playing with him. Drake spotted the light of amusement in his icy eyes. "Why did you moor your vessel at *Northdocks*, instead of the usual *Turtle Crawles*? I know you're fond of the *Crawles*, Drake. Unless…"

"I know what you're thinking, Morgan, but isn't like that. Told you, I wouldn't be here. I had my opportunity at Tortuga a couple days ago." He smiled at one of the goons. "Now tell this ape of yours to take his dirty hands off me, would you?"

"Tell me why you docked there first."

Drake grinned. "Had to show an old friend I was alive and kicking. You know about me rivalry with Le Boussier. He was sure I wasn't coming back from this raid in Donnish waters."

"Indeed." Red Leg returned to his desk and took the glass of wine. "Speaking of old friends. I met another friend of yours here last day. Master Silas Kater, the Dutch, said I should say, 'hello' should I run into you."

Drake didn't flinch. "He did? Very nice of him."

Morgan O'Neill motioned for the thugs to push the young captain forward. "Aye, very nice, considering the large sum of money I hear you owe him." He had him sniff the wine. Nothing else.

"Morgan, I see your men don't see a *chica* by ages, but please, tell this one on me left to stop holding me so tight."

Red Leg smirked. "That wit. That wit of yours is gonna cost your head, y'know?" Then he snapped his fingers again, and the two brutes let him go.

Immediately, and without turning, Drake kicked back like a wild stallion planting the heel of his right boot straight into the groin of one of goons. The large man yelped like a wounded dog, reached for his genitals, then fell down like a sack full of potatoes. The other swung a roundhouse at him, but Daniel easily dodged it and quickly jabbed him square into the jaw, then sunk his right fist into the large man's belly, causing air to escape off him like a blowpipe.

"Enough!" Red Leg shouted. Drake heard the click of the flintlock long before the cold metal touched the back of his neck. "We have business to discuss. Stop messing with the kids."

Both guards stared at him with eyes full of rage, but Drake knew they wouldn't disobey an order from their boss.

"Fine to me." Drake turned and defiantly removed the glass from the Admiral's fingers, "Thanks for offering." He gulped down the wine in one swig.

Red Leg smiled and shook his head. "You never change, don't you?" He turned to his men. "Learn from this man, boys. He is the contrary of everything I taught you."

"You taught 'em well," snapped Drake, cleaning the glass with his finger and licking the last drops out of it.

Morgan took off the glass from his hand and placed it back on the desk. "I want to introduce you to a special flower borne out these accursed islands. Follow me," he said, then signaled his enforcers to stand guard while he led Drake to a side door.

The pair entered a lavishly furnished bedroom, partly illuminated by bright candles, in which a comfortable bed, covered by a brocade bedspread lined in silver, dominated it as a dragon warding its hoard. In a darkened corner, a shadowy figure rose and came into view.

Drake's heart stopped for an instant at the sight, as she was the most beautiful creature he had ever seen.

Perfect features, highlighted by lovely cheeks, were encased into a chocolate-brown face, as smooth and healthy as to seem unreal. Her figure was wavy and dainty, clearly shown by her lace vest from which a full bosom caught the eye of the onlooker.

"Kaya, this is Captain Daniel Drake," said Red Leg, breaking the spell.

The girl lifted her hazelnut eyes to meet Daniel's, and he felt a shivering sensation run to his stomach. "So, dis da man who will bring we t' *Mabouyacay*?" She spoke with a typical Creole accent. One more point: Drake couldn't resist a lassie with a French lilt.

"Aye. He's the captain of the *Banshee's Cry*, the fastest vessel on these waves. The perfect ship to carry out your master's will," replied Red Leg.

"*Le Baron* is no me *maître*," she said abruptly, coming closer to Drake, never lifting her stare from his eyes. "Me serve da *Lod*'s will, yet none is me mastah."

He couldn't spill out a single word, too charmed by the girl's beauty, or something else. '*What's happening to me?*' he thought.

Kaya came face-to-face and stared deeply into his eyes, looking for something. Then, she returned her attention to Red Leg.

"*Oui*. Dis is da righ' man. We have a deal, O'Neill."